Also by Fox Benwell

The Last Leaves Falling

KALEIDOSCOPE
SONG

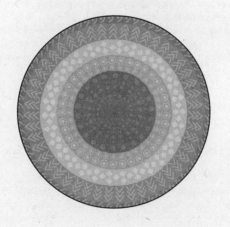

FOX BENWELL

SIMON & SCHUSTER BFYR

NEW YORK LONDON TORONTO SYDNEY NEW DELHI

SIMON & SCHUSTER BFYR

An imprint of Simon & Schuster Children's Publishing Division
1230 Avenue of the Americas, New York, New York 10020

For information about special discounts for bulk purchases, please contact
Simon & Schuster Special Sales at 1-866-506-1949 or business@simonandschuster.com.
The Simon & Schuster Speakers Bureau can bring authors to your live event.
For more information or to book an event, contact
the Simon & Schuster Speakers Bureau at 1-866-248-3049
or visit our website at www.simonspeakers.com.
Also available in a SIMON & SCHUSTER BFYR hardcover edition
Cover design by Krista Vossen
Interior design by Hilary Zarycky
The text for this book was set in Adobe Garamond Pro.
Manufactured in the United States of America
First SIMON & SCHUSTER BFYR paperback edition October 2018
2 4 6 8 10 9 7 5 3 1
Library of Congress Cataloging-in-Publication Data
Names: Benwell, Fox, author.
Title: Kaleidoscope song / Fox Benwell.
Description: First edition. | New York : Simon & Schuster, [2017] | Summary: In Khayelitsha, South Africa, Neo's passion for music leads her to her first love—Tale, the female lead singer of a local band—and an internship at the local radio station, and both experiences teach Neo about the risks and rewards of using her own voice to empower others. | Includes bibliographical references. | Includes discography.
Identifiers: LCCN 2017013065 | ISBN 9781481477673 (hardcover) |
ISBN 9781481477680 (pbk.) | ISBN 9781481477697 (eBook)
Subjects: | CYAC: Lesbians—Fiction. | Blacks—South Africa—Fiction. | Radio broadcasting—Fiction. | Music—Fiction. | Rape—Fiction. | Khayelitsha (Cape Town, South Africa)—Fiction. | South Africa—Fiction.
Classification: LCC PZ7.1.B4554 Kal 2017 | DDC [Fic]—dc23
LC record available at https://lccn.loc.gov/2017013065

For Marieke, Kayla, and Cinders,
who've loved this song from the first note,
and who gave me the courage to sing,
even when my voice wavered and
I did not know the words

KALEIDOSCOPE SONG

South Africa is *loud*. Listen. Footsteps, engines, radio. The lazy buzzing heat and the singing laughing joy. The slap of palms when business strikes. The dance of it. The movement and the bustle, the spring of young and creaking of the old. The bars. Street corners. Schools. It has an energy in everything, a song all of its own. And it's a song that only works with every part in place. Every discord pushing forward. Every rhythm. Every voice, including yours.

Every voice is different, its pitch and tone and intonation as distinct as the words we choose and how we wrap our mouths around them. But everybody has a voice, and everybody sings. Oh, we all do it differently. Some of us sing quietly, alone, only in the dead of night or in the shower. Some of us sing a cappella, and some stand on a stage beside a band and let the whole world share their song. Some of us, some of us don't sing at all, like that. We sing with other instruments: There's song in stories, and in art, and in getting up before the dawn and putting food onto the table. There are angry songs and sad songs and songs that make you want to dance. But everybody has a song to sing, their own personal story leaked into the world. And mine is one of love.

It starts in a bar. One of ours, in the heart of Khayelitsha. Nothing special on the outside, but inside, tonight, two hundred people cram together beneath the corrugated roof and wait, turned out in their Friday Bests, because everyone knows you have to look good for the radio.

Tonight is special.

Tonight the hosts of UmziRadio are here, in this little bar of ours, for us.

It's everything I've ever wanted. Worth the sneaking and the boom-boom-boom fear of my heart as I walked the streets at night, one hand curled into a fist and waiting, *just in case*. Worth the end-less all week talk from my best friend. Worth every moment that preceded it.

It started in a bar.

. . . Or perhaps it really started with the argument.

"Music isn't *realistic*, Neo. Isn't *useful*. You pick something else." Old words, tired. Hammered out so many times I feel their indenta-tions on my skin. And this—small and quiet as it is—is my rebellion. It's freedom.

And yes, I know *you shouldn't go into the dark alone*. I know it *isn't safe*. All the old words hammered out. But I didn't mean to be alone. My bestbest friend was meant to be here too. It was her idea.

"We'll show you what music is *really*," she said, all excited, "the being there and being seen. Being *part of something*."

"Being seen by who?" I smirked, but she stared right back at me, refused to be embarrassed.

"Yeah, well, all the better, hey?"

If you asked Janet, she would tell you how she's *made* for Maximillius, that their futures were entwined, that he just didn't know it yet. And tonight, Max was public property, right here on our ground.

It was going to be perfect. Max and music: Everybody's happy. But I waited by the BigTall tree, and Janet never came. So tonight, the night it all begins, I sit alone, my back against the bar. And I wonder where she is. Whether I should have waited or gone home. But I'm here, and slowly, as I sit, I let the safewarmfree of this place settle in my gut and the excitement build.

And there *is* excitement. Chatter. Bottles lifted, smiles and eyes and energy all shared and given free. And there's a hush beneath it, the black-shirts working to make sure the mics are working and the lighting's right. The *desk*, hidden in the shadows to the right side of the stage. All businesslike. So radio.

I should feel nervous. Terrified that somebody will see my schoolgirl aura and drag me homeward by the ear. I should feel *bad*. Rebellious. But all I feel is right.

Janet would be loving this.

"See?" she'd say. "Everyone is out tonight. It's a night to remember."

She's right. It's mostly bright young minds and music lovers. Umzi fans. But here and there the old guard stand among us. Shop-keepers and fixers, teachers and those men whose only job is to observe the world. We're here together: a community.

Max is just there. Close. The golden voice of radio, right there, and his bright-and-chipper cohost, Sammi, too. Somewhere in the shadows of that desk they're waiting to bring us the best of evenings.

Are they nervous?

No. Of course not. They're professionals.

Will we see them? Or will they hide back there all night and let the music have the light?

I wonder whether I should leave my seat, slip closer through the crowds so I can see? Get close enough to see them move the dials on the mixing desk, see Max's smile and give my best friend something to be jealous of. But here I get a wide view: stage and audience and ambience. Here, it's *music*, not just technicalities and fandom.

I settle in my seat, breathe in the hot stale happy air. And something shifts, like a movement just outside your vision or a silent hushing in your ear, and suddenly all eyes are on the stage.

You can see it, right? You can imagine? Staring out over the crowd, every single one of you together in the moment.

And then with one sharp crackle-buzz, it starts.

"Hellooooooooo, revelers—"

"Molweni!" Their voices sound strange, fill-you loud and not quite real, but close, inside you, none of the crackled distance of a radio.

"This is UmziRadio, and tonight in the very first of a new series, we are here to celebrate *community*. The same community that gave us our great leader, the community that birthed the Umzi legacy. We got *promise* in this place, and Umzi wants to share it. . . . Now across the series we'll be traveling through Khayelitsha and surrounding areas, bringing you the best of your neighborhood. And tonight, fittingly, we're starting with the music. We're *live* in Site B, and just *look at that crowd.*"

"Ahh, yes. Look at all those beautiful faces out there."

"So beautiful. And you know what *else* is beautiful?"

"Sunsets? Diamonds? Sunday-morning lie-ins?"

"Yes, yes, yes. More beautiful than that . . ."

He breathes a smile. "There's only one thing I can think of—"

"Local talent," Sammi cuts him off. "And let me tell you, I was listening to the sound checks earlier and some of these guys are ta-len-*ted.*"

"Right? Right. This is R-Talent with Sammi and Max, bringing talent *home.*"

"Ha-ha-ha, you know how many times we just said 'talent'?"

"Sho', and that's one more. Let's bring it, before we wreck this show. You all know how this goes, the musicians are out in force and—"

"Yeah . . . Please welcome our first and bravest: Tale and the Storytellers."

My bestbest friend was right. This night is perfect. Even before the first band steps into view, I am in love. With everything. The thick, wet air, heavy with anticipation. The richness of voices. The clink and hum and body crush of a live audience *so* different from school events or Sunday-morning church. With the *promise*, from Umzi's Mr. Sid to us: a handshake, a you-can-make-it. With the mine-ness of it all.

I'm in love with the night even before I'm in love with the girl.

And the band steps up and there she is, and it feels like that moment when the CD player loads your favorite track, and you wait an infinity for the song that makes you whole and breaks you and changes something every single time. All in one forever-second.

There she is. The girl.

She's not even opened her mouth yet, just stands there waiting, fingers toying with the mic lead, teasing as she looks away and mutters something to the band, but the whole room is there with her, waiting.

And she knows. Draws it out, longer and longer until you'd think we'd all drop dead from breathlessness.

But if you watch, you see it coming: swelling inside her, pulling at her muscles, drawing her onto her tiptoes until she's bouncing with anticipation.

Can you taste it in the air?

And then it comes. She turns, fluid, and her dreadlocks rattle out a brief applause against the mic. Her lips part in an easy smile.

And just as I think I'm going to topple right off of my stool into those arms, Tale opens her mouth wider and she *sings*.

There's a story that my mother likes to tell of a girl who married for security. "A home over happiness," she'd say. But she never stood beside a stage, looking up into eyes as deep and dark and dangerous as sticking mud. She never heard that *voice*.

Every note draws me closer. Every word pushes the world further away, until there's nothing left but her. Her and me. The singer and the schoolgirl. Us. I'd like that.

In an instant, I can picture it, the two of us poring over old CDs on Sunday mornings, her putting discs into my hands and urging me to listen, change my world. Walking along the shore, arms wrapped around each other, her singing quietly into my ear—a whispered love song—as she leads the way across the sand. In an instant I map out our relationship, and I am hers.

Hers? I catch myself. *She doesn't even know me.* And the world comes flooding back.

I glance at the crowd—all too close, too many—expecting torch and pitchforks. *That girl, she is not right in the head.* But the room is lit only by fairy lights and lanterns, and besides, all eyes are on the stage. Everyone is lost.

I breathe.

Tale winks as she picks up the pace, shimmying just ahead of the drummer, like water slipped right through his fingers.

Does he know? Is this how they rehearsed?

You can almost hear her taunting, *Want me? Come and claim me.* Pushing him to run.

Right? You hear it too?

Tell me you don't want it.

The drummer chases, grinning madly at the crowd, but Tale is too quick and drives him faster, faster and wilder with every bar. And before I know it, I'm swept up and chasing too, with all my heart, and there's laughter in Tale's voice. She knows.

Brighter and louder she climbs with the song, and everybody in the room is right behind her, backs stretched to the heavens and lungs filled with a weightless joy. On and on she soars, higher and higher, until the whole room looks as though we could fly, and then she's *there*, right at the top of the song, hovering, and the whole room holds its breath. And as she sings she smiles, and her voice warms, and she sweeps her gaze from left to right across the room and I know she's meeting every person's gaze. Every single one. Still singing that one note.

I can see her coming for me, and I want it so, so bad. I want to meet her eyes and smile back at her, tell her everything in that one wordless fraction of a second. But I'm not brave, not even a little, and right at the last moment, as I feel her eyes upon my face, I can't. I twist away.

And I look back up immediately, wishing I could drag her back to me, yell, *I'm sorry, Tale, I didn't mean it*, but she's gone, continued on her way, and three seconds later it's all over.

Silence.

And foot-stamping applause.

"Ladies and gentlemen, did I tell you we had talent?"

"Smokin' *hot*, guys, smokin' hot."

"Eish. Tale and the Storytellers. Wow."

"She's good, yah?" The bartender leans across the counter, close, so I can hear her.

I nod. *"Yah."* One word is all I've got.

She slams the top off of a Green and holds it out to me. Beer is another of those things my mother would not understand, but the iron roof traps the essence of the crowd, all the heat and sweat and used-old-breath of it, and that sweet, sweet, bitter brew has been sitting in ice for hours. I take it gratefully, and lick the condensation from the rim before pouring half the bottle down my throat.

I turn back toward the stage, watch as Tale disappears into the crowd and the next act—a young boy with a bright-painted *ramkiekie*—steps up. He looks nervous and the crowd fidgets, on edge.

I close my eyes and press rewind, replay Tale's last note in my head, over and over, wishing I could live right here wrapped up in it forever.

And it's only when the applause rises and Sammi's voice cuts through the air thanking the *ramkiekie* player that I realize I've completely missed his song.

The night closes out with wild applause, people waving empty bottles, less than steady, whoops and cheers and an impromptu chorus of our national anthem spreading out across the audience, proud-happy-infectious.

"That's it, folks. And what a night it's been."

"What a night indeed."

"Next week, we'll be leaving the Friday music scene and bringing you the best of Cape Town's township teachers, getting to the minds of children right when they are young."

"Yah, the next generation's where it's at."

"But for tonight, my beauties, we've been Max and Samantha—"

"Hey!"

"—with R-Talent on UmziRadio. *They*'ve been fantastic. And here's Wilma with the news."

"Good niiiight!"

We stand there, stunned, "God bless Africa" still ringing in our ears, and then the crackle-buzzing ends and behind me the bartenders shift gears, all business and no small talk.

And then there's stumbling and floating out into the night, arms around each other, full of love for everything that Khayelitsha holds.

Walking home felt like a dream. Music does that; I would often dawdle home to make it last, all calm and wide awake and bouncing-still, and music would be everywhere, in everything. I'd hear the rust gather in raindrops, bouncing hard-metallic off the earth; hear the way the wind played through the gaps in lean-to walls, slammed at shutters, whistled across every part of our discarded left-out-in-the-open lives and made it sing. I'd see marimbas and balafons in every sheet of corrugated iron. Every hollow tree or gutter pipe made up a world-sized organ waiting for a melody. Every washing line or power line: a string, taut and waiting for a bow. And I would wander through, imagining that I could reach out, play the landscape as I passed.

But this was different. I would never have admitted it back then, not even to myself, but my heart was lost; the night air felt like kisses on my skin and my thoughts were nothing but a mess of melodies and breathlessness.

I imagine walking through these streets with Tale by my side, slinking through the dark, our fingers interlaced. Or racing, chasing, reaching for each other like we're back inside that song.

I weave dazed through the maze of shacks and washing lines,

ducking under night-damp sheets and crossing over shadows, as the private late-night melodies seep through walls into the darkness: the blare of someone's television, music, laughter, anger, snoring, the clinking of bottles and groaning of beds.

Khayelitsha's night song has a rhythm of its own, frenetic-still, lyrics full of secrets laid bare in the dark.

My mother, in her lectures about never wandering, would say that our true natures appear in the dark. That, sure, some of us nested with our prayers and loved ones, but Khayelitsha's lost came out at night. And I would nod, remembering this night sound, but I never truly understood, not then. . . .

And so I stray, walking through the shadows, adding my own secret song into the chorus.

Does Tale hear the same sounds as she wanders home? Does she hear the movement of the people, of the trees, its own, old music? Does she linger in the quiet to sing along?

Does she hear the world at all? Perhaps the echoes of the stage ring in her ears: the closeness and the clamoring, or the buzz-quiet of the speakers as her last note left us stunned.

As I walk past crumbling homes of nailed-together dreams I imagine Tale, free and strong, climbing up into the branches of a tree and sleeping with the universe all at her feet.

And I stop just short of home, stand there wrapped up in the darkness, hold on to the evening for a moment more, and imagine Tale bidding me good night.

*P*utt.

Putputputputt.

A beat. A rattle against drum skin.

I don't open my eyes. I'm not awake. But my brain takes the sound and uses it, imagines Tale at the window, calling me outside to dance. It takes the sound and twists it into something deeper, solid. Dance beat. And we hip-sway off into the light.

And then it comes again, only this time it sounds different. Real. Drilling right through sleep with an urgency I can't ignore.

My phone. Janet.

Sent: 02.41 From: J
Sorry sorry sorri.
Next tym?

Sent: 02.51 From: J
Don't be mad. Sorry u wasted
snEking out.
He was gud isit. U Listn?

And I *so* want to answer, to tell her *Yes, he was,* tell her that she missed the night to end all nights, that she was right, to let the night spill out from my fingertips and share it with my bestbest friend. And I can see her face, equal parts mad-proud and just plain mad. But when I try to wrap the magic into words, it sounds all wrong, and the memory of Tale's eyes sweeping across the room feels fragile, as though sharing it might break the spell.

I tap out:

Send Message: J
Not mad. C u l8r.

And I shove the phone under my pillow, and with it I shove all thoughts of my best friend and of Max and Tale, and then I close my eyes.

I hear nothing else until my sisters stir and even then I do not rise.

I lie and lie and lie, hardly dare to breathe in case I breathe too hard, breathe her away. And finally I cannot take lying here alone. I reach for the radio. Max was there. He knows. He'll share the burden of it, isn't it?

"Gooood MORNING, Khayelitsha. *San'bonani.* This is Maximillius on the Breakfast Crunch at UmziRadio, and it's Saturday, land of impossible, improbable adventures."

The heat. The thrum. The *freedom.*

"Orrrr, if Friday nights are more your style, maybe it's the land of blankets and a bag of Lay's. Make sure you hydrate."

Music, lapping at my skin like water. Yes.

"Leeeet's talk about last night, folks. Oh. My. Goodness, what a night! This community is *wild*. How was it for you? Did you see? Were you listening at home? Or was your Friday something different?"

Tale.

"C'mon, we wanna hear it. All of it, the gross *and* the beautiful."

My night was *definitely* beautiful.

I lie here for a moment longer, limbs all iron weight and my eyes closed against the too-hot, too-late sunlight heralding another day.

And I would give my world to lose myself into the thick swirls of voice and music and exhilaration, but as free as I was last night, this morning I am bound.

"Neo Mahone! Get your ass out of that bed *right now*," my mother yells right on cue, hustling toward the door.

It'll have to wait. I haul myself up, and by the time my mother bursts into the room three seconds later, I am clothed, at the dresser, staring at the mirror and pinning back my hair.

"Did you hear me? We're going to be late!"

"One second, Mama. Promise."

She *tssks*, but she retreats, leaving me to contemplate my face alone.

I stare harder.

Is that me?

It *looks* like me. But I feel changed. Too clumsy for the room. Too big. Too small. All wrong.

"A Clement C. says midnight surf was *swell* and that the Monwabisi crowd is *sweeeet*. That . . . I dunno, man, that sounds dangerous. How d'you see the *sharks* by moonlight?"

And the voice of UmziRadio sounds just exactly like he always does, and I don't know whether I am comforted or I'm disturbed. Because it's *not*. Everything is different now, and he was *there*. Can't he feel it too?

Last night something cold and bright and desperate burrowed right into my skin and wrapped around my heart. And it can't just be me.

"Ahhh, Thanduxolo says—and I'm just going to read this out—she says, 'Maybe catching sharks is the whole point. I know I spent my night lookin' for a man wit teeth . . .

"Eeeeeeish, that's *hot*. I think. That might be hot. And p'raps a little TMI this early, but hey, maybe you and Clement C. could go shark baiting together?

"A'ight, San says she put on her heels and danced, danced, danced and it was *fine*. Sammi—not *our* Sammi, I don't think—says Friday nights are family time. Chicken dinner and karaoke with the kids. That's *nice*. And a whole bunch of you are in agreement that last night was rad. Sharpie says he wants to play if there's a next time, and Umi says she'd like to buy that last singer a drink."

And I long to simply crawl back underneath the blankets, to float on Max's voice until it takes me back into last night. But my mother believes in two things above all: hard work and good intention. Madame Serious is the cleanest salon in the area to prove it, and it does not get that way by magic.

So I grab my Walkman and leave Maximillius and the perfect evening memories behind.

All right. I suppose I should just make it clear before we carry on. It wasn't *only* Tale. It wasn't even only that night at the bar. There is more than a single refrain in any song. There are harmonies and instruments and repetition all seamlessly sewn together so the new is old and old is new.

Music wasn't new. It was the oldest, surest thread, faded so it almost looked like skin. It was a chorus, familiar and always, always there.

Music was my life.

Mama sang when I was young. Underneath her breath, all day. And I learned that song was safety. She still does, but my mother's song is one of regiment and marching to salvation. It is quiet and obedient and *always* follows rules.

My song is . . . well, you'll see.

Baba works for Mr. Sid. My hero. Mr. Sid is one of us, a Site C boy made good. He grew up wanting something *big* and when he couldn't find it in the rust and dust and dealings of our streets he left . . . and learned the big-man skills and made the big-man friends, and then came home and gave us UmziRadio. Gave back.

But somehow, working for this great, great man did nothing for my parents' understanding. Little Neo asked her father every day as he got dressed for work and downed his tea: "Take me, take me!"

He never did.

I used to ask Baba to get me an interview, for school. I tried to get them to listen to the shows I loved, the voices that knew my

16

life and sang it back to me. But my parents would just shake their heads and point to the laundry and potatoes and my schoolbooks.

"Focus," they would say. "You build your own life, not your Mr. Sid's." But music *was* my life. My one true weakness and my strength.

Mama and Baba hated it. Grades, they understood: education, opportunity, and hard, hard work. But music? Shame, not even when the music empire gives Baba his six-till-six. The feeling of a beat that dances just beneath your skin? What's the use in that?

It is a fantasy. And one which does not—without luck and prayer and luck again—put food upon the table.

Beauty? Sure, there's money there.

Accounting.

Tourist trade.

But music?

I wonder, if you asked them now, if they would say they saw it. Saw me before I did. Maybe they saw music as a symptom of the wider problem, or the cause. I wonder. . . .

They hated it. And so I tried to fight it. Honestly. I am a coward by true nature, and songs are easier to sing when it is more than one voice and a microphone.

I tried to get on with my schoolwork, to lose myself in other people's dreams. But everywhere I went music trailed behind, just waiting for me to look over my shoulder.

Oh, it was always there. That night, Tale simply . . . brought it forward. Made it shine.

Mama's salon is small, jammed between Colonel Mandela's and the ShopShop Laundry & Cell Phone Repair in the middle of a leaning, narrow alley, but it is well kept and well known, and when she's open there's a steady stream of customers who'd *only ever* trust my mother with their hair.

My mother has a talent, as much for people as for hair. She prides in it. Primps their egos with an at-ease concentration.

My eldest sister *loved* that business, always fawning over Mama, watching how she worked. Sometimes, now, she was allowed to spritz the hair or balance up the books. And no one doubted that one day she would inherit the shack. Weekends were her *jam*.

The rest of us—Cherry and Jeso and me—were not interested in coifs and colors and fishtail braids. If there were a song for this it would be a work song. *"Shosholoza."* Slowed to heavy, painful beats.

I longed for Tale to walk by and sing, push the tempo, race me to the finish line so I could leave. But she is only in my head and as Mama stands outside the door, fishing deep into her bra for the padlock key, I groan involuntarily.

"What, child?" She pulls open the door, painted on the inside with a smiling, hairless head, and the slogan WE CAN MAKE YOU ANYTHING YOU WANT TO BE. It creaks.

I breathe deep, suck in the damp and dusty air. It's always cooler—stiller—in here; the tangle of lean-tos crowds out so much of the sun, but that will not stop us baking later, and the air in

Mama's shop is always sticky with hair spray and oil and dryer heat. I'll take what I can get.

I'd hoped it would come off as a determined breath, readying for work, but Mama frowns and you can *see* the complaint sitting just behind her teeth.

"Nothing, Mama. Sorry."

"Hm." She nods, not entirely satisfied.

Behind me, there's a scuffle. We have not even started work and Jeso and Cherry are already at each other's throats:

"I want the broom!" my brother wails.

"You're too little. It's a *big* job."

"No it's not! I'm going to sweep and then I'm going to spit-polish the mirrors till they *shine*."

"Euurrrgh."

"What?"

"Spit-polish? Who wants to look at a spitty mirror? *Siff,* Jeso!" She pushes him away, hard into the salon wall. It shakes, and for a second we all hold our breath in case it falls and leaves us in the open, even though it hasn't fallen yet, in years of service.

It doesn't. Obviously.

Jeso barrels back and grabs my sister by the arms, leans in toward her, and won't let go as he lets a thick string of spit dangle from his bottom lip.

"Excuse me!" My mother's voice cuts through the street. "This is not a fight cage! Inside, *now*. I won't have this nonsense."

You do not want to see my mother vexed. When she sucks the air in through her teeth, like *tchhhhh*, and when her ample bosom heaves, you *move*.

We scuttle inside, sudden-silent, and take up our positions to scrub and sweep and air the place.

Shosholoza,

Kulezo ntaba . . .

Hear that song? Sometimes we sing it for grit and courage, but Saturdays it's nothing more than punctuation to a never-ending sentence.

Stimela siphume South Africa . . .

And I just want to be free.

Today is worse than usual. Slower, twisted like a well-worn cassette tape so that it plays at half the speed and sounds like something from a horror film.

We reach up high and get down on our knees, sweep out the floor, the step, the corridor outside: No dust nor earth shall dwell in Mama's place. And slowly around us the town wakes up, and still we work.

"You should take pride," Mama would say. "People see your work ethic right there. They see you are reliable. They'll remember, when you come to need them. Let them see." But today I don't want them to see: It feels as though I am on show.

With every passing nod, each, "How is it with you?" I wonder whether they can see inside my head, see exactly how it is. How there is music, and a girl, and—

"Good morning."

I look up to see Grandma Inkuleko laden up with three whole feet of cloths upon her head, leaning heavily against the door. I grin. I cannot help it. The old woman has been in my life forever— probably the whole of Khayelitsha's—but for all her wrinkles and her slowing bones, she's fierce mischief incarnate.

"Madam." Mama nods, full of respect. "You're well."

"Yes, child, yes. Although I could use your magic on this bonnet. P'raps today at noon. Over a good sweet tea."

Linda moves toward the desk and Mama's big appointments book, but my mother stops her with a look. You accommodate Grandma Inkuleko without fail. She earned it the way people earn their teeth: with time.

"Always for you."

"You're a good girl."

I smile, slight and inward, at the image of my mother as a girl. She's *never* been one.

"And *you, Neo*." The old woman grins and her entire face grins with it, creasing to the edges. "What's that look you wear today?"

I blush.

"You got yourself a hobby?"

Mama *tsk*s. "My daughter won't be getting any hobbies until she is thirty, thank you very much. She's not throwing all of this away."

"Ahhh. That way, is it? Fine, fine. You be careful not to look too interested now, then." She winks at me, and then with a promise to return after her business, she's gone, wide hips swaying wilder than the lightest easy-woman.

Somehow, after Grandma Inkuleko, last night sits more comfortably inside my skin. I imagine her there, set against the back wall of the bar, watching over her community, smiling so her whole face wrinkled. I imagine that she'd save a wink or two for Tale's drummer. And it's like she was there all along. Grandma Inkuleko and the spirit of this place go hand in hand.

Somehow, that thought gives my brain permission, and after

Grandma, Tale creeps into my work-song rhythm, shakes it up, infects it with a giddiness at odds with Mama's work ethic.

Twice, she *tchhhh*s at me for drifting, and the third, she whaps me round the head with a damp, cobwebby dishcloth.

"Neo Elisabeth Mary Mahone, get your head out of the rafters."

And I try. I do. But *dreadlocks rattling against the mic*. And *rhythm*. And that *smile* . . .

There's everybody rising, rising, rising with the song, and spilling out into the street so light that they could fly.

There's music, in its proper form, and not even a morning working for my Mama can take that away.

The hours pass and our neighbor vendors arrive one by one to open up, stack fruits and vegetables and cakes, and pull rails of cloth or bootleg jeans into the street until you'd have to dance the upright limbo to get by out there. Crowds begin to jostle, full of weekend freedom. The bright-happy-desperate noise of business fills the air, all compliments and haggling. And still we work, Mama *tchhh*ing every other minute, until finally, when our knees hurt from the kneeling and our fingers are nothing but bone, a lazy-gaited customer wanders up and knocks upon the door.

It's late. *Surely* we are done?

Jeso stops his polishing and pulls a face at himself in the mirror. "It looks *good*, Mama." He beams. "Very shiny."

"Are you in business, Madame Serious?" the gentleman asks, and Mama glances around the room. She nods, and he steps inside, sits in the swivel chair, and sighs contentedly.

Mama reaches into her purse and pulls out eight ten-rand

coins, two for each of us. She might act all cross, but deep inside she's warm and generous. "Go on, get. All of you. I have no place for all your dross today."

I pocket mine. Usually, I save every coin for music—old cassette tapes and downloads alike—but today I imagine sidling up to Tale's table with two green glass bottles, one for me, and one for her.

"Can we borrow these nails, Mama?" Linda grabs two sets of stick-ons from the counter, one faux-leather, the other sharp and neon pink.

"By 'borrow,' you mean . . ."

"Sorry, Mama. Can we *test* them? Good service for the customer. We'll make sure they stick on right. Test their durability."

Mama's eyes roll. "I'll remember that for tonight's chores." But she does not say no, and Linda and Cherry skip off arm in arm to *beautify* themselves.

Jeso spills outside and pushes through the alley out into the wider road and sunshine, a whirlwind of joy. "WHEEEEEEEEE!" he yells, spinning around and around with his arms outstretched. "THE DIRVISH SHOOTS! AND LOOK, IT SAILS ABOVE HIS OPPONENTS AND HE DOES IT! HE SCORES! LADUMAAAAA!"

I follow, slowly, pull the headphones from my pocket and slip a bud into one ear. Free from servitude, the day stretches out before me, and I want to savor it.

Sunshine, music, radio.

It's bliss.

But I've barely heard two bars before my brother stops up ahead. His arms fall, and he barrels back toward me.

"Neo, Neo, Neo!"

"Mm-hmm."

"Want to go get *Cokes*?"

"No thanks."

Sunshine, music, radio.

Jeso's eyes go wide, his bottom lip all fat and sad, and he leaps onto my feet, although he's been too big to really fit on them for years.

"What're you doing, fool?"

"Pleeeease?" He rests his head against my stomach and looks up at me.

And I try to walk away, but not even Janet and the promise of a shady tree and memories can win over that face.

As long as he's quick.

"Oh, all *right*. I'll come with you, at least."

He beams.

"But you have to walk yourself. Lump."

He leaps to my side—honestly, I've never known another kid with so much *bounciness* as Jeso—still beaming. "Okay! Let's go!" And he grabs my hand and half swings arms, half drags me along until we get to the MotoloCafe.

MotoloCafe is my mother's favorite place to rest her feet between her clients. Small—three tables in, two out—and decked in wine-pink everything: the pink-checked curtains, plastic tablecloths and painted counter, and dust-grayed pink silk roses on the tables. But it's clean and cool and Old Man George will leave you be.

"Coke, please!" Jeso chirrups.

George leans over and grins at Jeso. "Would Sir like anything else with that?"

Jeso looks questioningly at me and I shake my head.

"A straw and a table for two, please."

"Certainly." And he places a dewy-cold can and a straw upon the counter.

"Thank you!"

We sit at the white plastic table by the window and Jeso leans conspiratorially across the pink-white tablecloth.

"Soooooo?"

"What?"

"Soooooooooooo." His eyes dance.

I wrinkle my nose at him. "You're weird." And he shrugs.

We sit in silence—except for the *thud, thud, thud* of my brother's *takkies* against the chair leg.

Thudthudthudthud.

He raises an eyebrow at me, grinning over his straw.

Thudthudthudthud sluuuuuuurp thudthudthud.

"Bru! What?"

"What you thinking about?"

I shrug. "Nothing much."

"Is it that Max guy?"

"What?"

"You're different."

I *am* different. Sho'.

Suddenly I am not comfortable; too big for these plastic chairs, too open for this tiny space.

Does Old Man Sam's ear cock to hear us?

"*Wys*, you."

"Is it him?"

"No. Is *what* Max? Which Max?"

"The boy . . . You and Janet always whisper about him. Did you—"

My laugh is almost real. "Eh, *Max*, Max? That's . . . Janet likes him. From the radio."

"You too."

"No," I say, with as much *drop it* finality as I can muster.

Jeso cocks his head to one side, studying my face. "But you're definitely different."

"I'm not."

I *am*. And if he didn't know it before, the tiny blush across my cheeks gives it away. My brother never ever tells a lie, and he can spot one from a hundred miles away.

He's a *kid*: How did he know?

I glance around the room. George is busy with his till, and the big mama in the corner is—I swear—asleep. God, how is it so quiet?

Jeso keeps on talking. Talking with that loud *I'm right*ness that he always has. "Are. You've gone *gooey*. When Linda met Tsimo, she sighed and stared and was all quiet and not half as bossy as Linda is. And when Baba comes home from the hole at night, all sour, Mama looks at him with those big eyes and goes soft. Like you. Gooey."

I toss a napkin at him. "I am not."

"Yes you aaaare. Grandma saw it too."

"Jeso!"

"Neo and a booooy, sitting in a—"

Oh my gosh, shut *up*. "Jes, *no*. There's nothing between the biggest name in radio and me. Or *anyone*. I promise. There. Is. No. Boy." And it is not a lie. It's not. But still there's heat inside my cheeks, and . . . it's not true, exactly.

He sniffs. "Fine." And then, "I'm not a kid, you know?"

"I know, football head. You're the big brother to end all brothers."

Jeso beams over the last dregs of his Coke, but before he's done, his face turns serious. "He *plays*, right?"

"Huh?"

"This is-no-boy. He can kick a ball?"

I picture Tale bouncing a ball on her knees, keeping it high in the air, counting soft and low—*hundred and one, hundred and two, hundred and*—all that power concentrated into the even rise and fall of leather.

And I have to shake my head and look away.

"Right," I say, breathing out the *hot* feeling even as I scrape back my chair and stand. "That's it."

"What?"

"You're done here. I'm done. And there *is* no boy, but you've got me, and I am going to *kill you* on that field. Let's play."

I do not get back to Janet. After Jeso and I tire of one-on-one, we fetch Mama's lunch: fries and mix-veg and a large hot tea, an Old George staple—and it's *busy* in the salon, so she has us running errands for more coconut oil, drinks for customers, and a fresh receipt book, and by the time we're done it's well past three and I am peopled out.

What I *want* is music. Memory. So as Jeso curls himself in Mama's chair to watch her work on one more customer, I slip my headphones in and walk.

I try to escape into the rich old voices I love best, but I keep hearing Tale's voice above them. And then Jeso's, too: *You're different.*

Who wouldn't be, though? After a night so full of the thing you love that it literally spills into the street? Who wouldn't be in love?

And Tale . . .

It's too much to think about. Too big and good and wrong to turn it into proper worded thoughts. And I don't want to spoil it. So I hold the whole night close, and walk until the smooth-worn grooves of Miriam Makeba meld with Tale's voice and they are one.

Music is religion.

Sunday morning, and I wake with Tale on my tongue. A musical refrain. A prayer.

On the other side of our room, Cherry and Linda lay asleep, their limbs entwined. I love this time of day. I always have. Not dark, not light, just cozy. And I'm almost tempted to stay. But a quiet morning is too good to waste.

I pad into the kitchen, and my mother is already there. She does not turn, and for a moment I just watch her standing there, over a pot of sweet tea at the stove, lost in morning thoughts.

The radio is on, and I'm surprised to find it tuned to UmziRadio.

"Music is religion."

Yessss.

But Mama bristles, *tchhh*s. And when I cross the room to greet her, the softness of her morning face is already a memory.

"Good morning."

"Mm-hmm?"

"I mean, look at concert halls, man. All those people gathering beneath one roof. All that hope, all that belief. It's like a shared experience."

I lean over to kiss her cheek, and she stops for long enough to let me.

"Morning." But she is busy and concerned and there is no time for pleasantries. She pushes a bag of *mieliepap* into my arms.

"I see what you're saying," Sammi argues, "but it is *flawed*. We can listen to music and *never* share a thought or feeling with the person next to us."

"Nahhh."

"I'm serious. I can listen to—ahhh, Britney Spears, and I hear screeching, but somebody else, you might hear the angels fly out of her mouth and sing."

"Ha-ha-ha-ha-ha."

I fill a dented pot with the coarse yellow flour, add water and a dash of milk, and set it on the stove beside the tea, and Mama bustles about, filling jugs with water, heaping bright pink jam onto a serving plate.

It all makes music, of a kind; the shlucking of the grain and water against tin, the hissing bubbles of the tea just boiled, Mama's hard-edged sighs and the soft movement of her hips with every task.

Morning music, quiet and unsung. A shared experience.

"Okay, bad example. But it's true. We feel different things. We like different things. It's like they say with books, no two people ever read the same book. It's the same with music, yo."

"I hear you, I hear you. I do. But if you've ever stood in a big venue—I'm talking big—and felt that *hush*?"

"Mm-hmm."

I stir.

"And at the end, the applause, every man and woman rising to their feet and *screaming*? You can't tell me that's not *shared*. That changes people, man."

And Mama's had enough. I can see the bitter comments on her lips, the *You listen to this? Neo, it defiles your brain.* The *We tried to raise you better.* The *No more. We forbid it.* And I expect to hear it all over again, but Jeso wanders in, dreams still plastered on his face, and dissolves her words away.

"Morning, Ma'aaa." He yawns, reaching up to give Mama a hug. And then he skids over to me and *grins*. "Put the stick down."

Mama switches stations.

"No way." I brandish the porridge stick—coated in a thick grease film of maize—in front of me.

And on the radio, a choir sings of our salvation.

"No weapons in the kitchen! No weapons in the kitchen!" Jeso shrieks, leaping at me so that I step back and almost knock the pan right to the floor.

I catch my balance just in time, but Mama is *right there*.

"Oh for goodness' sake, get *out*, both of you." And she takes over, pulling the stick from my hand and herding Jes and me out of the way.

"Ohlezi kulona akanakwesaba, nokuba umhlaba uzanya zanyiswa.
Whoever abides in refuge, will not fear despite the storms of life."

He latches on to me and *climbs*, reaching for my scalp with his bony little fists. "Diiiiieeee!"

"Get off, get off!" I squeal, and grabbing at his waist I tickle him until he can't hold on, and flip him to the floor. He lands half under the table, trapped.

"Mamaaaa!"

In the corner of my vision, I see Cherry and Linda shuffle in, slow, like great, disoriented snakes waking after hibernation. My sisters don't appreciate the mornings.

Whatever.

Jeso wriggles out from under me, tries to get a grip around my waist. And we roll, giggling, as our sisters step right over us in careful horror and take the seats farthest away from danger.

As Jeso rolls, he pulls his arms in, uses them for leverage, and for a moment it seems he might win, with his bony elbows and spider hands, but no. I have a secret weapon: Jeso has a weak spot.

I grab at his ankles, run my finger in a tiny circle at the bottom of his foot.

He *howls*, kicks out with his other leg and knocks a chair across the room, and wood-on-concrete joins his voice.

I win!

"When you two have quite finished behaving like wild cubs . . ." There's an edge to Mama's voice that stops us in our tracks, and I drop

Jes and stand, straightening my blouse before I pull him from the floor.

"Come on, football-head, let's eat."

Linda looks up from her plate—and the compact mirror in her hands beneath the table—and rolls her eyes at us. "So immature."

"Hussy," I mutter, hoping it's just loud enough for her to hear.

"Mama," Jeso asks, "what's a h—"

I *glare*.

"H-ospital like? Benedict from school says that it's where the people go to die." He does not lie, but he is *fast*.

Mama's face goes thin and tight. "Yes, well. Not always. And this is not a conversation for the table."

Jeso nods, all serious, before he switches topics. There's a rule. Three paces. Three subjects away from any danger zone. My brother and I are a *team*. A *unit*. And we always stick together. "Mama . . . can I borrow those nail things? The really long ones? I want to show Emmanuel how they scratch out people's eyes, like that time that Linda nearly did it." He giggles, and I imagine his friends laughing till they fall as he recounts the tale.

I listen as he tells whoever pays attention about Emmanuel's father's leg, and how it's made of wood and comes right off, and how Emmanuel tried to take it to show everyone at school, and his father went right after him for three whole blocks.

Apparently a wooden leg is very good at walloping.

And I listened as he wondered whether it was any good for football. But eventually my mind drifts off and I'm imagining a show-and-tell all of my own. In private. In the dark. Just a show-ing, really; I didn't ever want to tell a soul.

Does Tale move like that when she is not onstage? Wound up

like a spring? Or is she different when the lights are off? I imagine us lying on soft Cape sand, the moon and the whispers of the sea our only company as Tale serenades the night.

Thankful and content.

And as the gospel voices on the radio weave in and out like tides and mingle with the breakfast noise, my skin bristles and my stomach churns and I'm waiting waiting waiting for another voice to save me.

Waiting like we waited Friday night.

Because if music is religion, then Tale is its god.

Baba was not happy that night.

He walked in from work and sat down at the table and he *brooded* until Mama fetched him cookies on a flowered plate, and not even the sugar sweetened him.

We moved quiet by instinct. Dulled the radio and buried our heads in our schoolbooks.

Later, I watched him as we ate, held a sigh back with my teeth. He looks tired. Worn and weary. And I *long* to reach across the table and to really share.

I long to ask him about business, because my Baba has an inroad; he's quite literally the gatekeeper of Umzi, working the door from six to six, and he sees *everything*. I long to tell him that I'm proud. To tell him all about that Friday night and how wonderful it was. And to take him from behind his desk at work and show him what he's part of. How it makes his people feel.

But Baba frowns into his rice and broods, and no one says a word.

Somehow it is Monday, the territory of unending uniforms and drudgery and learning everything we ought to know. A place where music rarely sits. School is a requirement, and today, more than others, I don't care for it. The clock hangs crooked, the eleven where the twelve should be, as though it's racing for the future. Still it ticks slow. And the teacher's voice stretches, scratches, is unwelcome. All I want is quiet. I want lips and softness and song-sound, not *Use the formula i = prt, where i is the interest earned, p is the principal (starting amount), r is the interest rate expressed as a decimal, and t is the time in years.* And I cannot wait for the bell to ring.

Across the classroom, Janet tries to catch my eye, practically bouncing in her seat with a whole weekend's worth of commentary underneath her skin. And suddenly the weight of everything I've felt since Friday night is *big* and I cannot wait to tell her all of it.

The teacher *drones.*

The clock ticks loud. *You. Will. Not. Leave,* it says, as though it's irritated that it has to move forward at all.

And in my head, there's Tale, and in the corner of my eye my best friend waiting.

I stare hard at the blackboard, affect a look of concentration as I reread the equations. Business. An investment for the future.

And it's not that I don't want to invest, really, but the only business I care for is song, that night replayed for my best friend, on loop, far away from books and the chalk dust and the expectations that settle on everything.

I imagine leaping up onto a creaky wooden desk in one swift ninja movement, opening my lungs, and singing wild, loud lyrics about music and how *I. Choose. Life.* Or taking Janet by the hand and running running running, leaving nothing but our footprints and one less layer of silence in the room.

Finally, some first year's sent to swing the bell—you can hear the manic pride-and-power in it, right? *Ring ringRing ring Ringringring RING:* uneven and loud. And we're so ready for release. Eager, fractious bodies rise and pour out of the classrooms all at once. An anthem of relief.

"Ehhh, did you *see* that freshman?"

"Eish, that's tough."

"He's looking at you."

"Hey, have you completed yesterday's assignment?"

All around me, people gather, pull themselves off into their groups. Huddle over books or hang from the yard tree. Circle, dancing, singing. All around me, I see people's song.

And Janet sidles up behind me, grabs my elbow. "Heyyy."

"Hey. Howzit?"

"How wild was Max, eh? Friday night?" She bounces, and I'm honestly surprised that she stopped to say hey before Max slipped out. My best friend is like a drummer without skins—all enthusiastic energy atop a strong and steady downbeat. Nothing stops her rhythm.

"Wild." I grin. "And the—"

"Shame. He was *brilliant.*"

—*Music.* I nod, and the Storytellers push against my teeth; *Yes, and the music. Did you hear her?*

But Janet does not leave them any room, babbling hard and fast as she shoulders her way through the throng and pulls me with her.

Behind the row of upper classrooms it is quieter. Nothing lies back here except four brick latrines: two boys', two girls', far enough away that we won't be disturbed.

It's the perfect place for sharing secrets and opening up hearts.

We lean against the wall, and Janet is still talking. "I could just listen to his voice all day."

"He *was* good," I agree. *"But—"*

"Eish, I know. I know. Better if we'd made it. I'm so sorry. My mother. *My mother*, with her promises to Pastor Simphiwe . . . Eighteen robes, can you believe it? All with the fancy collars, all by Saturday's choir practice. And of course she made me help." She holds up a hand pricked with needle marks, and pouts. "Are you mad?"

"No, I—"

"I'd be mad. I *am* mad. Boarish, overbearing spinster woma—"

Usually, I'd let her run her course. Sit quiet until my turn, until she fed me the words she needed me to speak. But this time I have something she does not: a story she has not invented, orchestrated. This time, I feel Tale rising, rising, rising up my throat, as sure and wonderful as when she sang, and—"Janet!"

Janet stops.

"I *went*."

Eyes like dinner plates. "You what?"

"I went. On Friday. When you didn't show."

"No!"

I shrug, run a finger over the rough brickwork, but I cannot keep the night from flooding out across my lips into a grin. "The *music*, Jan! It was—"

"Yeah, yeah, yeah, the music. Tell me . . . tell me *everything*."

Yeah, yeah, yeah? That hurts. But if I can just make her see. "It was *alive*! You could feel it move across the room."

My bestbest friend stares at me like I swallowed a live cow, and laughs. "You sound like Pastor Simphiwe: 'Let the Spirit move you!'"

"No, it's . . . There was *energy*. And this band. The first one. Did you hear them?" *Did you hear* her?

"Eh." She shrugs. And then she frowns all awe and serious. "You *went*?"

I nod. I went. "And it changed my life! She was . . . *It* was . . ."

She grabs my hands. Squeezes. "Wohhhhh," and she's bouncing on her toes, one move away from squealing like a child. "My Neo, all brave! Tell me *everything*. You don't get to go off on adventures—*my* adventures—and then keep the details to yourself. Spill it."

That *yeah yeah yeah* sits heavy where it landed, and I want *so* to hold out on her, to keep Tale and the bar all to myself. To laugh and tell her that I fooled her: a-ha-ha-ha-haaa, of course I didn't go. But Janet *bounces*, and bestbest friends share secrets and I *want* to share. I do.

"It was *terrifying* walking through that door without you. But I got there and, like, Umzi were in there, of course I went. So I'm sitting waiting and it's like I'm meant to be there. And there are microphones up on the stage made of black boxes and there's Max and Sammi in the corner like they're not even the stars and—"

"Wohhhh. You *went*?"

"Yes!"

"Oh my God, you didn't? You did! You . . . you were actually there."

"Yeah. And—"

"You *actually* saw them? In the flesh? Up close?"

I nodded.

"Wohhhh. Did you speak to him? Tell me you did. Tell me that after all the trouble of sneaking out and sneaking in, you spoke to him. That you *bought him a drink* and then rode off together into the moonlight—Wait. No. I want that. You can't have him."

And all of my excitement drains.

How do I explain my night of epiphany—the sound of parts of me all falling into place—if all she wants to hear is Max?

It's not her fault. It's always Max. He's wired into her or something.

But *Tale.*

What if she's my Max?

I sink to the ground and pull the headphones from my pocket, grateful for the familiarity of it: the feel of rubber at my fingertips, the grooves of friendship worn in every song we've shared. Maybe . . . I just want her to hear.

Janet follows, reaches for the left bud. We both know this move.

But today she grabs them both and holds them out of reach. "You didn't *get* with Max, right?"

Hah! I feel the truth of Tale sitting in my gut all spiky-hot, but as it rises all I hear is Janet's scorn, and it tastes bitter, dangerous. She'll take the night and ruin it. I swallow it down and force out a laugh instead. "No thanks; he's all yours. I just want the beats."

The *voice.*

She nudges my shoulder, gently. "Prude."

"Am not."

"Are so. You're in a bar at night with R-Talent and all you want is *beats*. What's wrong with you?"

I don't know how to answer that. I should defend myself. Protest. Just *tell her* about Tale, how I'm so confused and so in love. But Janet wasn't there. She did not see those eyes, or hear that voice. How could she understand? And I realize in more gut-drop surprise that it isn't only that she doesn't let me speak or that she did not come, keeping me from saying. It's more. It's fear, and guilt and too-goodness. It's two people on different paths, trying to hold a conversation over roofs and trees and villagers, too far away; an unpleasant bee sting that you do not want to look at closely, because looking makes it worse.

And anyway, there isn't room for it. "Oh, well. Start from the beginning; every little detail."

"Every—"

"Everything! His hair. How was his hair? Did you get close? Did you talk? Of course not; he was working. Does he sound *that good* in real life? Did you *smell* him? Is he tall? He's tall, right? Och, you were in the same room! Did his Max vibe rub off on you? *Please* tell me you haven't washed whatever you were wearing."

My best friend has that glazed look in her eye, the one that sparkles with imagined picket fences and three children with the same self-assured voices and same perfect, perfect hair as their golden-wonder father. There'll be no stopping her until she runs out of details to imagine answers to. And I could sit here telling her that Max was green and bug-eyed and she wouldn't hear a thing.

I nod. Grunt a few answers. And I hold Tale and the rest of that night close, where she can't see.

After lunch, there's chaos in the classroom. Residual freedom in the air, seventy teen egos puffed and fed and squeezed into the same size room they had this morning. Everyone competes. Over in the corner, someone drums upon the table. Someone else is singing, laughing. Joseph Mthandeni, whose father owns the ShopShop, tries to hold a headstand on the top of two stacked desks, and the band of populars are whispering, just loud enough that everybody knows. And beside me, Janet is still starry-eyed and mumbling. Everywhere there's *life*.

"Hey, can I borrow your phone?"

Janet's phone is not like mine—old and battered with a crack across the screen and room for only ten texts and a game of Snake. Hers has Internet, and suddenly my dreams of Tale alone aren't enough.

"Eh?"

"Your phone? Can I borrow it?"

She hands it over without even looking at me, and slumps dreamily across the desk.

I'm glad. It means I don't have to explain as I pull up UmziRadio's Web page, searching through the homepage for any trace of Friday's show: tweets or write-ups or a roll call.

UmziRadio's R-Talent
Friday: 10-1   Max and Sammi
Join your favorite radio hosts for the Sounds of
Khayelitsha, as we travel through the township and

meet the people who really make this place *move*.

There's a string of tweets in the sidebar too:

GETTIN READY FOR A HOTHOT NITE AT TAMS PLACE. PREPARE UR EARS.

Max & Sammi in da house. ARE YOU READY KHAYELITSHAAAAA?

There's a picture with that one, the radio hosts up against the bar wall, all moody bar light, chunky earphones, and big grins.

WOW. ARE U GUYZ LISTININ TO THIS?

That's a wrap guyz. Join us next week for the next adventure! Xx

I scroll through for something—anything—that mentions the musicians, *so* sure that it would be there. But there's nothing, and it hurts.

I need her.

More of her.

I think for a moment as my gut spirals disappointed to the floor.

I Google "Tale and the Storytellers" and get thousands of "folk tales for storytellers" pages.

Nope.

Facebook?

Much to my best friend's dismay I have never used the account she set up for me. It sits untouched with a picture from when I was twelve, my birthday, and "music" listed as an interest. I don't even know the password. But hers is permanently open, just in case there's something that she *cannot* miss, so I just search from there.

Tale and the Storytellers, I type, holding my breath and crossing my toes. Pleasepleasepleaseplease . . .

Yessss!

I shiver, happy at the sight of it.

The page is sparse: no pictures, no comments, and only contact-for-hire details and a short list of past appearances, but it still takes all my strength not to hug the phone right there.

It's her. Them. Right there. And for a moment I just stare at it, imagine crafting a request, hiring the whole band to sit beneath the stars and turn the night into a magic otherworld.

Mine.

A paper plane barrels kamikaze right between Janet and me and it yanks her from her daze. "Hey!" I snap, and Janet sits bolt upright as the room misses a half beat, then answers with the time-old leer of "eeeeey," ready for battle to erupt.

"Good afternoon!" The teacher's voice cuts through all possibility of war. "Everybody seated, please, and quiet."

And that is that. I push Tale away and close the app with one swipe of my thumb and pass the phone to Janet underneath the desk. Joseph tips himself upright and everybody scuffles for a seat, and just like that our lives are put back in their sleeves and filed away.

The whole week feels like that: as though somebody pressed pause upon my song mid-note. I *itch* in the silence, long for the next line, but the week *drags*, leave my muscles taut and tight and ready-waiting.

I try to make it play, to hear Tale in my head, but she feels out of place, warped by being squashed into the confines of my life, and with every passing second her notes fade until I strain to hear them underneath the algebra and chores and expectations.

Social Project.

The words sit double underlined upon the board, and the whole class *buzzes* with excitement.

Every year the school puts on a show day and invites our parents and the local businesses and everybody's uncle's dog. There'll be pamphlets, presentations, plays, and everyone will clap and nod and say how much they've learned, and then it's over for another year.

This year, our class gets to take the lead.

"We're doing sex, right?" Joseph Mthandeni grins.

Janet blushes and looks right back at him. "Be more specific, stud."

"Ohhh, you know."

"No, I don't."

"Come back behind the classrooms and I'll show you."

"Eisssshh!"

"See, this is why we need it: for the pressure."

Mthandeni holds up his hands, surrendering. "Hey, no pressure, just offering my services."

"Don't do it: He's a brute." Big Rudo laughs.

And Khwezi, the fifth member of our group, shuffles awkwardly. "Can we just get on with this?" *Thank you.* "*Sex,*" he continues, "orrrr . . . gangs and guns and—"

"How to shoot the fastest?"

"How to stay in school." He rolls his eyes. "Health problems? Water hygiene? Irrigation? We could build a sprinkler system."

"Uuuuugh," Janet huffs, "where's the drama in that?"

"It doesn't *have* to be a drama." He stares hard at the floor, pushing the glasses higher on his nose.

"But where's the fun in *school stuff*?"

He shrugs, and does not say another word.

"So!" Janet stomps her foot decisively. "What about *sexual health*, eh? If that works for everyone?"

"AIDS?"

"Or gonorrhea. Or all of them."

I swear Mthandeni pales.

"Or *size*. We could do a play on its importance."

My bestbest friend does not know when to stop.

"And how exactly is that going to benefit—No, don't answer that."

She and Rudo grin. "Too easy."

We settled on pressure—the pressure to say yes—and I did not point out that two of us, at least, squirmed. We settled on a play, and Janet automatically cast me as the girl who has no problem saying yes, who practically *drags* her boyfriend to the back streets.

"It'll do you good," she nudges playfully, and my stomach drops. But I don't say no. I can't.

And by the time we've decided who's who, and what our end scene is, we barely have time left to divvy up the work before the day is done.

"Want to come over and study?" Janet shoulders her school bag, and sags under the weight of it.

I *never* want to study, but homework does not do itself, and her mother likes to feed us while we work, where mine will *tssk* and bustle and Jeso will be hanging from our necks all afternoon.

"Yah, I guess."

So we turn right instead of left, past the surgery and the big market.

Janet grins, and when I ignore her she sighs the loud-wistful sigh of someone who's in love and sure.

I shove my hands into my pockets and walk faster, wishing I could increase the distance between us to escape the same.

It's been like this before. Janet and me, for all of our history, all of our laughter, sometimes it's like we live in worlds so different that they do not even trade with one another.

There are some things that will always be the same.

Once, when we were five, Janet pulled the purple daisy crown right off my head.

"I'm sorry. You can't be queen anymore."

My lip wobbled. "Why?"

"I want to marry Mothusi. We're in love. We're running away."

I shrugged. Mothusi was tall and sour and spoiled.

"So? Have him."

"Ehh, 're you *dof*?"

Was I?

"You can't be queen without a king. And he's mine. Sorry. Maybe you can be a secretary or something."

I . . .

Secretary?

I cried, then. Loud and hot and ugly, as Janet flounced off with my daisy crown and months of friendship.

The next day, I watched surly as they whooped and danced a celebration right along the street, and married with rings of grass beneath the midday sun:

"I promise to cook and clean and wash the babies' diapers, if you fetch the water because the spiders are big and you're a boy."

"I promise to smash the spiders. And you'll make me supper every night and make me babies in the morning."

"C'mon. Mama will be making sugar cookies."

I was not invited to the after party. Sugar cookies on the porch is a five-year-old's honeymoon *dream*. So I went home, baffled and hurt and knowing that my world had changed but not really sure *why*.

"I'm sorry, hey." Janet grabs me by the wrist, pulls me up out of the memory. We stop, and she looks me in the eyes. "I'm *sorry*."

"What?"

"I'm sorry. For teasing."

I shrug. "It's all right."

"Really?"

"Yes."

But it isn't.

It is not her fault, but it is not all right. There are some rivers—deep and fast and strong—that you cannot build a bridge across. And *There is this girl* is one of them.

Her mother lays the table with sweet guava juice and sandwiches of thick white bread and bright pink jam.

"There." She nods, satisfied that we'll have fuel for our tired, growing brains; that she's played host. "What are you working on today?"

Janet shuffles through her books. "All these."

"More English?" Janet's mother frowns. "I thought you did that yesterday."

"Just some revision: Neo needs the practice."

"Oh, good." She smiles a smile which does not leave her mouth and then, straightening the plate between us one last time, she retreats to her office.

"Deadline?" I ask.

"Grading."

Janet's mother is a teacher at the university, and she's always busy with a paper or with students. "Ah. So we'll have a while before she tries to chase me home, then."

"Yahhh."

I stretch my legs out underneath the table, rest them against Janet's, and lean back in the wooden chair.

The house is big and airy. Sturdier than ours, with its brick walls. And on the white, white wall beside the fridge, there hang two frames, one with a picture of Janet and her parents, the other proudly holding Janet's last-term grades. Her mother has an *office*. I like it here. It is a house of learning, where there's room to grow.

Janet says she likes the noise at my house. But she does not live with it.

When I'm at Janet's, I can *breathe*.

We settle at her big, clean table with our stack of homework books, and everything feels *right* between us. Normal. Exactly as it always is: my best friend and I.

Even now, with this *thing* between us. Janet is my best friend. We're okay. We're here, as always; at the same table we used to learn our alphabet, studying just like we always do.

Janet *giggles*, breaking through the silence.

"What?"

"Jonas . . ."

I turn the textbook page, and there is Jonas, crudely cartoon-naked.

". . . Look at his *thing*. Are they all that big?"

"I hope not."

"Can you imagine?"

No.

"Is *Khwezi* that big, do you think?"

I squirm. I do *not* need that image—all-arms-and-legs Khwezi naked and hung like an elephant. But Janet is still laughing and I force myself to join her. "He's tiny. He's a *mouse*."

She snorts. "You're right. How would he *walk*? Maybe Humbe, though? Or John-Michael?" And then without missing a beat, "What about *Max*? Is he that big? Did he look that big to you?"

"*Radio* Max?"

"Uh-huh."

"I don't know. I wasn't looking. Come on, we have work. What's the *questions*?"

Janet grins, big, mischievous. "Circle three risks of sexual activity . . . pregnancy, contracting HIV/AIDS, dropping out of school, love . . . impaling yourself on something that *huge*. It must be a risk of internal injury."

"Janet!" My skin *burns*.

"Okay, okay, so . . . Max?"

"No! We're studying!"

"Neoooooo. You haven't really said a *word* about the other night!"

I shrug.

"What is it? Was there a boy? There was. Tell me! Did your eyes lock across the crowd? Did he fight his way to you and woo you with an illicit beer and the promise to see what he keeps in his, er, region?"

"No! No, no, no, no, no! Nothing happened. *Nothing*."

I wish that I could tell her. Really. But *It'll do you good* still echoes in my ears, and there's a textbook open at a giant schlong and nowhere, *nowhere* in there does a cartoon Neo ask another girl to prom.

"Okay, *fine*." She mock-huffs. "You are hopeless . . . but I want gossip, and if you're not going to give *me yours*, at *least* dish up on Max."

Somehow, in these so-few words, my best friend's sucked the magic from my night and made it nothing more than scandal. Just gossip. Just another boy-fest.

But she's my best friend. My headstrong, always-there best friend. And so I let her have the usual grin, and I give in. "Maximillius is every bit the god you imagined. He looks *good* in bar light. You should marry him and have a dozen babies."

"Yessssss!" She grabs a sandwich and bites into it with relish. "Yes, yes, yes. Neo! I. Am going. To marry. Max."

"Yep. Undoubtedly." And I'll be the spinster bridesmaid.

All week I fantasized about sneaking out and finding Tale. I borrowed Janet's phone again and again, memorized their details, the contact number, and every bar and area they'd played in, until Janet eyed me with suspicion and I had to triple-check that I had deleted all traces of my search.

At night, I tapped that number out into my phone. Deleted it. Tapped it again. Dreamed of hearing Tale's voice right in my ear.

Hello?

Howzit? This is Tale. What can I do for you?

What can't *you?*

Wednesday, when Cherry and Linda had been snoring dead for hours, I hit dial, let it ring just long enough that Tale would know I was there.

And then I panicked. She'd know I was there. And the prank is not only for cowards, it's the mark of *I have no credit; please call me.* What if . . .

I lay there, panic thudding in my ears.

What would I *say?*

What if my sisters heard?

If—

I switch the phone to silent, stuff it back under my pillow. But it's there, right under my head. It's not enough. I grab a pair of socks. My school jumper. And I wrap my phone inside them and push it underneath the bed, and close my eyes and wait until the earth swallows me whole.

• • •

The sun rose, and the day passed and nobody called back. And despite it all, the next night I tapped out the number once again, stared at it until the numbers swam before my eyes.

I dreamed of running out into the night, to every place I knew she'd been until I found her. Every night I'd leave my jeans uncrumpled by the bed, easy to slip into without fumbling and noise.

By Friday I was *desperate*. Short with Jeso, snapping at my bestbest friend. All I wanted was to feel that safewarmfree. And halfway to school, I know. I'm going back to Tale's bar tonight. Maybe, *maybe* she'll be there. I could get lucky, right?

It's the music, I told myself. *All of it. I just want to relive everything about last week.* And it was true.

But not the whole of it.

"Can we, can we, can we?" Jeso skips along beside me, keeping his ball just in front of us.

"Sure," I say, but I don't know what I agreed to: my head is filled with the clanking chatter of that place before the song.

Tonight.

School *drags*. I do not hear a single word the teacher says. And as the evening edges closer, it gets worse. Time slows, and all through dinner I can feel the seconds, sitting between me and Tale like a wall.

We're all there, at the table, around Mama's waterflower stew and a side dish of the dumplings that I like. But tonight I am not hungry. I don't want togetherness. I don't want dumplings. All I want is Tale.

Jeso swings the seconds with his legs as we join hands for grace—

"Heavenly father, we thank you—"

Kick.

It lands on my shin.

"—for your guidance and protection—"

Kick.

Harder this time.

"—for our good health and a will—"

I open one eye just a little bit to glare at him, and he stares back at me, of course. And grins. But he doesn't kick again.

"—ingness to grow and learn, and for this food, which sustains us as we live to serve in your name, always. Thank you, Lord. Amen."

"Start that again and I will *hurt you*." I growl at Jeso, brandishing a roll with malice the second grace is over.

"Neo!"

I don't *care*. I just want to be out of here.

Jeso stares across the table, a picture of innocence.

"Hard day, Nee?" my father asks, all stern-eyebrow as he heaps a spoon of stew onto his plate.

"Sorry, Papa. *Sorry*, Jes."

Papa grunts. "So. How *was* your day? What have they been teaching you?"

Tale. All I saw and heard all day was Tale.

"Eh, you know."

The spoon went down, the disapproving eyebrow up. "No, I don't know."

He waited.

I scramble for anything, anything that would let me off the hook.

I can see my teacher standing at the board, hear her barking questions, hear the singsong voices of my classmates. But the details are not there; there's nothing but the faint-fierce voice of Tale and the promise of a future I have yet to meet.

"I don't know." I tense, waiting for the explosion of rage. Quiet, out of respect for Mama and her cooking, but definitely there: the promise of dire consequence.

But: "Me me me me me! I learned LOTS. We did farming. Chickens. When they die and how to look after their feet and all about the cycle."

I could have kissed my baby brother then.

"The cycle?" Father's eyes danced.

"Yes. There's a girl and a boy chicken—a cock and a hen—and an egg, and a fluffy yellow chick. And when it gets big enough you kill it like this"—he mimes twisting its neck—"and you pluck it and eat it, or you put it with the other girl and boy chickens and the cycle starts again. But if they're sick you don't do that unless your chickens will be scrawny."

"Is that right?"

"Yes! And when they get sick you give them powder and it makes them alllll better."

Father reached across and laid a hand upon my brother's head. "See, Nee, *somebody* in this family is going to grow up to be president. Because he *pays attention.*"

But Jeso was babbling on about the number of eggs a single chicken can produce per year, and our father was pleased enough that he would let my inattentive laziness go by tonight.

I let them talk, and pushed the food around my plate—delicate green petals in tight buds. And I imagined one unfolding and a tiny Tale stepping out to serenade us.

"And tomorrow, we're going to . . ." Still babbling. And beside that, my sisters flit from dresses to Hollywood diets and settle on the contestants from *South Africa's Got Talent*.

Baba tells us that he worked and worked and he expects some order, then quizzes Linda on her English vocab.

Eh, I swear, sitting at that table, my mother and father and siblings and me, we had the slowest meal there ever was. If anyone had seen us, we'd be in the *Guinness World Records*.

My mother sits atop the table and surveys her work. She *preens*.

And I sit willing time to pass. Willing everyone to chew faster so that I can check off "dinner" from the list of things between me and the girl.

It *dragged*.

I listened to the clink of forks on plates and the dull thudding of a football in the street outside.

A fly, whining, landing on the water jug, then whining as it's swatted off again.

It was almost rhythm. Almost music. But none of it was Tale's, and it made me itch to get away.

It still dragged after dinner: Chores stretched out and homework swam beneath my eyes, and the silent concentration in the room was tortuous, time proclaiming that it had the upper hand.

I longed to break it, but the inane conversation that would bring about is worse.

When it was finally bedtime I crept under the blankets without a single word, *daring* my sisters to ruin the peace as I stared at the ceiling and waited for their breath to slow.

Finally, finally, finally, a stillness fell upon the house, and I pulled on my *takkies* and slipped through the door.

Excitement tore across my skin and danced to Tale's beat.

I was *free*. I'd beaten time, and had not fallen famished at the wayside.

And she'd be out tonight. And I'd be there.

Even before I pushed into the bar I heard her; her voice grabbed me by the chest and pulled me right inside. And it occurred to me as I slunk through the doors that if she asked, in Janet's stage-play dialogue, I would not be saying no.

And there she was, rising above the applause, and I was hers.

She was beautiful. The way the husky bar light made her skin glow, and the green of the bottle in her hand reflected in her deep black eyes. The way she moved, all muscle, like a big cat slinking through the grass.

A hunter, even when she wasn't looking for a meal.

And as I slip along the back wall, settle in the shadows, Tale *sings* and the whole world melts away and there's just sound, rich and beautiful and strong.

My stomach churned, hot and warm and heavy, as though I'd swallowed a whole mug of hot honeyed milk in one big gulp.

And there was me and that sound and that *one thought*.

Over and over. Not even in words, just recognition: *Tale is my honey-milk.*

Warm and sweet and deadly.

Warm. Safe. Mine.

It may not have been so crowded without UmziRadio and all the hype, but it *was* full enough. Intimate. Somehow the extra space around the room just makes you breathe the sound in differently, as though you're sharing air, and all that sound goes straight between you; great gulps of a common song.

So I sat, with no crowds between us, and I watched, and

listened as she sang. And I swear she aimed her voice right at me, hurled every note right at my chest.

Song after song, she sang: with no Umzi, there was time, no sense of urgency, and the Storytellers stayed onstage, singing first mournful and long, then bright like polished bronze. And I was stuck, suspended by her presence, as light as air and heavy as the earth.

And then she looked right at me.

She couldn't have seen me, tucked away in the darkness at the furthest point from the stage. She couldn't. But she did. She looked right at me, and she smiled.

I would have sat there watching her forever. But her set came to an end, and she was gone, and finally I could stagger from my spot and into the half-light, to the bar.

Tale.

Honey.

Mine.

And even though she's finished playing, I'm so lost that she just *keeps going* in my head so when the bartender looms before me and asks what it'll be I blurt out: "Honey," before I even really hear her. ". . . Oh."

She stares. The man beside me snickers.

"I mean . . . beer, please."

Neo. What? *Who does that? Nobody* does that.

Run.

The bartender grins, slides the bottles at me one after the other. "You sure you can handle that?"

I nod. Turn. *Run.* Except I turn straight into someone heading for the bar and that cliché moment where there's beer down someone's Friday outfit and glass clatters to the floor? That's *real*. I watch the amber liquid froth across the concrete, and two strong hands at my shoulders are all that stop me from crumbling in embarrassment.

"I'm sorry! I'm so sorry!"

And I look up and it's *her*.

Suddenly, this bar seems vast and tiny all at once. I'm standing on an open plain and Tale is the lightning rod.

Did this whole place just *stop and spin*?

"Eeeeasy." Tale laughs. "It's okay, no harm. Are you 'right?" Then, as the beer froth disappears, leaving nothing but a slick damp stain, "Gee, what'd you *do to her*, Tam?"

The bartender holds up her hands in protest, laughing easy. "Nothin'. Watch this one, hey? I don't think she's used to the *intoxication*."

"Huh?"

"Oh, nothing. D'you want another?" She nods at my empty hands, then turns to Tale. "And what can I get you?"

"Four. That lot are melting."

"Heh. That was some set, girl."

Tale releases me and steps back to take a bow.

My shoulders feel suddenly lost, as though they're less solid without her. And as she moves away I catch her scent. From a distance I'd imagined fizzy aftershave and coconut-oil hair, but up close Tale is all sweat and rubber and excitement. And it's *good*.

The bartender reaches underneath the bar. "Eh, crap. We're out. Let me change the buckets. One sec. Sorry." She flashes an apologetic smile and hurries off.

And I should go. I should stop staring. I should tell her—

"Ahhh, shit. You're *soaked*. I'm *so, so* sorry."

"'s all right."

"No. It's not. I'm clumsy. I'm an idiot. . . . D'you at least have a spare shirt?"

She shrugs.

"Uuugh. *Sorry.* Listen, it's *cold* out there. At least take my jacket?"

I'm already shrugging off my I ♥ BEATS letter jacket, a birthday gift from Jeso and my sisters. I *love* that jacket, but suddenly, as Tale looks from it to me and back again, it seems inadequate. "Please?"

She hesitates. And then, "Okay. But only coz I get to give it back to you."

Does that mean what I think? Could it? I warm right deep down in my chest, and my stomach leaps for joy.

"What'd I miss?" The bartender returns, pushing five dripping-fresh bottles toward us.

Tale grins. "Thanks, doll." And she shrugs the jacket on and grabs the lion's share of bottles.

The striped cuff of the jacket catches excess moisture from the glass. It *itches* when it's wet, and I imagine pushing the sleeves up off my wrists as though I'm still the one wearing it.

Or pushing them back for her, gently rolling up the cuffs so they don't touch her skin.

And that's weird and I'm embarrassed all over again.

And I know I should *say* something, or just leave, or *anything* except just standing there staring at her wrists, but what?

"Tale . . ."

"Yes?"

"Your voice is amazing!"

"Thanks." She smiles that easy smile, and that should be that, but I don't think she believes me, and suddenly I need nothing more than for her to know how much I mean it. I'm blushing, I can feel it, but she's here, looking at me, and I've started something. I have to keep going.

"No. really. It's . . ." It's what? How do you sum up that much raw *everything*? "Intoxicating."

I wait for the ridicule. The *That's a big word for a little girl.*

Her eyebrow quirks, and then she laughs, and it sounds like rain on bright green grass. "You know, you blush a beautiful shade of pink."

And that only makes it worse. I am on *fire.*

Tale shifts her grip and lifts a bottle to her lips. And I see her singing, mouth close to the microphone, making sounds so beautiful they hurt. Those lips are strong.

"Ahh." She smiles. "I'm Tale, by the way."

I nod again. I *know.*

"And what do I call the blushing princess?"

I . . .

I manage to force out a sound that's almost "Neo."

She bows. "Well, Neo, I have to get these to the crew, but I'll see you around, yah? For the jacket."

I . . .

And she takes my hand, still holding that beer so that the tips of my fingers graze against wet glass. "As the French say, *enchantée.*"

She speaks *French*?

But I don't have time to ask her. Because there's my fingers against hers, and she bows her head, and those lips brush across my skin.

And time stopped for a second, like the whole room held its breath, and then she's gone.

Enchantée.

There's so much music in one word.

Rhythm and enchantment.

Enchantée.

And I can't help it, I replay that moment. Washing dishes, copying the teacher's notes, lifting, carrying, all *normal things*, feel different now; they're tempered by a tingling, buzzing *enchantée* permanently tattooed onto my skin.

W hat's *with you?*" Janet frowns over the Walkman.

"Nothing."

"Nee, you *can't fool me*. What's up?"

"Nothing. I just . . ."

Enchantée.

"You coming down with something?"

"No." Nothing she would understand.

"Mm-hmm." Janet stretches like a puppy in the sun. "Because we're listening to *pop*. For fifteen minutes, four whole tracks, and you haven't even tried to skip to something else."

I shrug. "Maybe your appalling taste is finally beginning to rub off on me."

"As *if*."

"Yahhh, right. As if. I don't know, I'm just *tired*. You get a free pass today."

She laughs, falls back into the music. And beside her, so do I, but the soundtrack in our ears is dulled by lyrics of a blushing princess and her big strong singer-knight.

Music is obsession.

Like jumping in a river and getting swept away, too fast, too hard, hoping that you find an eddy somewhere that will let you gasp for air.

I replay those moments on a loop: the bottle-green glow, the honey-milk, those lips upon my skin.

Oh, I am in *love*.

With everything.

With Tale and with music and the *scene*: the way the right voice can make even corrugated-iron walls feel like a palace fit for queens. A palace just for us.

I worry. I replay those moments—the *enchantée* and solid hands, and her lips against my skin—until they shine. They happened. And they meant something; you can see it right there. But—

Girls don't—

You don't—

It's not done.

Perhaps it's only in my head.

But I am in love, and there's that voice, and *enchantée* and *only coz I get to give it back to you*. And I'm floating on a cloud of desperation and of joy until I cannot wait a second more. I cannot wait for Friday, even.

Wednesday nights the band's been playing at a place called All the Rage, on the boundaries of the township, out by the big road. And I'm going. This is torture, and I have to know.

I imagine a much bigger place with solid walls and a tidy clientele, and I make sure to pick out my best shirt—black, with BLUES, BROTHER embroidered right across the chest. It's clean and pressed and I really, really hope she likes it.

Surely . . .

I imagine nodding to the doorman—this place has a doorman—all calm and sophisticated, and sipping from a glass until I can catch Tale's eye. Imagine her gliding from the stage and folding my hand into hers. Imagine *enchantée*.

I slip out into the night, and everything feels fresh and light like the first hushed a cappella beats from Ladysmith, the whole choir leaning in toward each other and bouncing on their toes.

Khayelitsha stretches out before me, crisscrossed streets and alleyways full of hidden song, and as I walk I imagine Tale's voice wrapping around every building, warming it, adding something, brightening the night.

Somewhere along the way, that excitement slips. The roads widen and the space between the buildings grows, and suddenly I'm scared.

All Mama's warnings flash into my mind, and I wonder whether all the wheeling, dealing men and smart-mouthed boys are bigger out here too.

There is no cover. And I do not know the back ways to escape through, should I need them. I do not belong here.

I pick up a stone and hide it in my fist, sharpest point between my knuckles. Better. But it's not enough. I pick up the pace, imagine myself there already, up close, flesh to flesh with Tale.

Except . . . in my mind the whole place smells like flowers and open air instead of hot-close crowds. That throws me, and I stop dead in the shadowed, lonely street, hit with longing for the closeness of our first encounter. I do not belong in fancy flower bars.

What if Tale sees me, in my unfancy skin, and realizes that I'm just a nothing child?

The cold dark of this unfamiliar road presses in on me from all sides. Leers.

What if Tale hates me?

Did I read her wrong?

She's nice. *She was being friendly. She probably didn't even want my stupid jacket.*

I imagine her offstage, rolling her eyes, cursing at her ruined shirt, telling everyone about the stupid drunken schoolgirl.

I stop dead, turn around. But as I step toward home, I hear Tale's voice, feel her tugging at me from afar, and I remember *enchantée* again, and see her her up onstage wearing my beats jacket as though it were her own.

I'm doing this.

It's real.

She's mine.

I t isn't what I imagined at all.

Well, okay, the building is big and brick, but Khayelitsha street grime still clings to the walls, perhaps more so with its once-white paint and grandiose appearance.

It does not smell of flowers, just warmth, brick dust, and beer, but the roof does not press down on you and the bigness of this place does not sit right. I feel watched. Judged. And the crowd does not feel *one*.

There are couples everywhere. Young men wearing too much aftershave pulling their dates into the corners of the room, hemming them against the bar. Groups, too: wild women tugging shirts to reveal just a little more as they dance dance to the synth-y keyboards and clunking heavy beat, and men laughing loud, pulling away every now and then to press up against the other dancers or pull loose-limbed shapes before sliding back into their niches.

No one's really *listening*, it's just bodies for bodies, fast and feral.

I shrink back against the wall and try not to be seen, and wait for Tale and the band to rise up on the stage and save me.

Slam.

A man with roving, rolling eyes and hair that would have Mama sprawled dead on the floor misses the wide door and slams into the wall beside me. Sees me.

"Ehhh, want something, beautiful?" He grins, all blackened teeth and glee, leans in close, and reaches for his pocket, and I don't know whether he is offering his body or whatever makes him *bounce* like that.

"No thanks." I look over his shoulder, not at him. Try not to breathe any of him in, to acknowledge he's there.

Don't make eye contact. Do not give him permission.

I reach into my pocket for that stone, still there. But he's already pushing off the wall and stumbling toward the night.

And when my heart begins again, I slide farther back into the shadows, just in case.

This. Isn't. Music.

Not the real kind, the kind that you can feel beyond your sternum.

And I hate myself for thinking it, because *everything* is music, but everybody stares at everybody else with as much connection as you'd find looking for the fattest chicken in the market, and I just can't feel it.

I should go. I do not belong here. But Tale and the Storytellers are billed third, and the promise of her keeps me glued fast to the wall.

I pull my arms around my chest, hug tightly, and wish that I were smaller; made of shadows.

I watch the men in sharp white shirts behind the bar, nodding deference as they hand bottle after bottle, glass after glass, to the clientele.

I watch the groups pull apart and cluster, watch the way they move, with the beat, all slick and confident, and I can't help but flash back to the awkward fivesome in the classroom: Janet, Fat Rudo and Khwezi, Joseph Mthandeni, me, testing out the lines between rightgoodsafe and wanting to be wanted, wanting to be first. Seeing how they sound.

Pressure.

C'mon, baby, c'mon.

No.

"No" is not a bad word.

No.

But everybody here is here by choice. It's what you do.

Everybody wants to feel they're wanted.

"Aaaand, now for something slightly different. We're changing the pace with this next act. Vocals, and a little soul, and it's time to grab your partners, pick your honey, make that move," a voice booms out across the speakers, and she's there.

The Storytellers do not pause to settle on the stage tonight. This is not that kind of crowd. Tonight, they trip right into a syncopated, quick-footed beat, all dancing drums and Tale's voice sliding smooth above it.

There she is.

And "no" and "pressure" disappear right from my thoughts and I just want to sink into her voice, slide next to her, up close like these other bodies, close and wanting. Wanted.

Oh, I want it. I've pictured this, me striding across the room, leaning cool beside the stage until I catch her eye. But in this too-big, too-sure room, I freeze. All I can do is stare and hope she senses me across the hundreds of close, rising-falling heads.

And somehow, in this too-big, too-sure room, the crowds are between us in a way they weren't before—so obvious. I try to focus just on her, to lose myself like that first night, but I see people all over each other, wrapped up in themselves instead of music, and it gets into my head.

There she is. So beautiful. So strong. Singing out across this space as loud as any woman could. But somehow I can't reach her, or she can't reach me. It's different.

As time passes, the leaning in gets more pronounced, the whisper-shouted conversation slower and exaggerated. And even though there's Tale's voice bright as copper in my ears, I hear every word:

Ehhh, girl. Wanna have some fun?

Nice moves.

Let me show you something.

You know your boyfriend should be threatened.

And the rest of it, the words their bodies scream:

You want it.

You want it.

I *want it.*

Look at me.

. . . Back off.

Give up.

This one's mine.

You're mine.

And I wonder, as I stand here so uncomfortable, is that what I'm doing too? Am I just like them? What would it mean to reach Tale like this, here, in this marketplace of bodies?

I cannot stay after that thought. This isn't me and isn't us. And I slink away, past broken bottles that weren't there before, past the rolling-eyes-and-wild-hair man—with a woman now, kissing something off his fingers, laughing, dancing underneath the moon—down the big wide looming streets and back across the crisscross narrow roads.

Home.

I'm so intent on walking, one foot then another, marching off the crawling feeling that my world is wrong or that I am wrong for it, that when I reach my door I do not even notice the blue television light seeping out into the night. I walk straight in.

And as I click the latch behind me, my breath fraught and heavy, the stillness of the house drops on me like stone. Too quiet. Full of anger, full of disappointment.

And I turn to Mama looming in the doorway.

Time *stops*, hangs on to her expression: looming fury. Hangs on and enlarges it and traps me there forever. Shadow time. The breath before the beat.

"Well?"

"I—"

And it comes crashing down, all dissonance and cymbals.

"Don't you *I* me, child. I want an explanation."

"I was—"

"What? Running out with some crew? Boys with jeans about their ankles?"

"No!"

The bar flashes through my brain, the leaning and the wanting and the distance. And Mama's voice above it all: *You shall walk the path of right and true.* "Nothing. I was . . . nowhere."

Mama *tchhhhh*s, and sucks all the oxygen in the entire room in through her teeth, and *moves*. I duck, but she's *fast*, and she has the collar of my shirt before I can take even half a step.

"Nowhere *where*?" she hisses. "And with whom?"

And I can't look at her. I let my gaze fall over her shoulder, because I *can't* tell her any more than I can tell her about music and the deep dark eyes and wanting more.

"Ehh. Well, you needn't answer *where*. I can smell it on you."

Silence.

"Beer? Really?" And she's really angry now. "Do I have to tell you about what it's like out there?"

"No, ma'am."

"Whsshht. You *quiet*. Clearly, you forgot your *privilege*. Clearly, you forgot that we have worked worked worked to get you kids in school, off the streets, and out of harm. We fought the oppression and the poverty and *this* is how you think to climb? Sneaking off for drunken fumbling behind the liquor store?"

I shudder, seeing *You are mine* whispered close. "No, I—"

"No? What then? *Music?*" She spits out the words as though they're sour, and it burns more than the sting of palm on flesh, hits me with the strength of every argument we've ever had:

Music is no life.

The only future you'll find with those musicians is a one with babies in your belly and sucking at your tits.

What is this noise? The devil's tongue?

Somehow, to my mother, music is the biggest risk of all.

I bristle, all protective of my one true love, of Tale and the band and the bare truth of song shared. The lie slurs thick across my lips: "No, Mama. Not music. There's a boy." And I know I should feel sorry, guilty, wrong, but there's *enchantée* and everybody rising to the roof and endless days and nights of finding comfort in the melodies of others, and nothing, nothing is going to take that away from me.

. . .

The lecture is *long*. Full of heavy, sagging disappointment.

"I will not have a girl of mine running loose and free. It isn't safe. It's dark. Who knows what lurks in shadows? And men . . . they are not to be trusted. Not even the young and pretty ones. Especially those . . . All it takes is one wrong glance, one too-dark street."

And finally she stills, with one steeled word and an imperceptible sigh. "Bed." And it is over. Matter closed.

And I know she only worries because she doesn't *know*, but there is so much more to life than school and work and dirty laundry. And I want it all.

I slip into the bedroom ready to fall to the mattress but Cherry and Linda sit up in their bed with moon-white eyes.

Not *now*.

"Ehhhhh." Linda shakes her head, all slow. "You got *busted*."

I ignore her. Sit. Swing my legs up off the floor, and start to shuffle myself down to sleep, but my elder sister grabs my arm. "Where were you?"

"Get off."

"*Hayi.* Spill."

"Yeah, where did you go?"

I can't explain. I won't. A million emotions run beneath my skin, and all I want is quiet.

I yank my arm free and turn away from them. "Good night."

I exhale slowly, try to force the shakiness right out of me. And behind me, they just sit and wait and stare.

"Nee," Linda says again, clearly bored of waiting.

"You heard, anyway," I mutter.

"Yeah, but . . . really?"

"Who is it? Anyone we know?" My younger sister cannot contain her excitement even in the wake of Mama's wrath. Sometimes, when she shucks off her schoolbook exterior, she reminds me so much of my bestbest friend. "Is he cute and does he have good brains?"

"And are you being *safe*?"

"It's *late*," I growl. "I'm tired, and if Mama has her way I am going to die a spinster. Can we go to sleep, please?"

They fall quiet at that, but you can hear the questions crowding in the dark.

I worry. The night clings sticky to my skin, burrows under it, and each new wave of feelings pulls up something anew.

The *wrong* of everything. The clamoring and whispering and lust.

And Mama and her bitter disappointment.

Guilt.

Guilt.

Guilt and not belonging.

I feel sick with it, and feverish, and I dare not lie beneath the blankets, dare not get the night upon my sheets, so I lie on top and listen to my heart beat hard and fast.

And I remember Mama's accusation: *Music?*

But she's wrong.

From lullabies to songs of praise to protests, music wraps itself around our hearts and keeps them safe.

It's everything. I cannot let her have it.

That first Friday night with Tale, it was every moment right from *man finds fire* until today. Every instinct. Every beat of every song.

I curl in on myself; a ball of flesh and bone around that one true thing, and I will myself back to that night, where everything was right.

I focus on the memory of it: the rattle of dreadlocks and sweeping eyes, jubilant anthems and arms around each other, and that *voice*, filling everything.

And breath by breath my heartbeat slows and I feel good instead of every kind of bad.

I expect penance. I expect Baba to take all of my tapes and CDs and burn them. To condemn me to a life of psalms and quiet prayer and no more radio. I expect shackles.

At breakfast, there is silence. The *You will think about what you have done and worry*. But there's nothing more.

At dinner, Mama passes the rice dish without commentary.

And then it's Friday. And I know deep down that Mama only worries because there is reason to. You see it in the swagger of young men, the cocky sway and backward glances from the girls. . . . There was a girl in my class last year, good as anything until she noticed the butcher's son, the way he looked at her and how she liked it. And I know now what Mama means about the sin of it; I've *seen it*. But I need to prove that it's not all like that, that I will not be led astray.

Now my classmate's desk is empty, and the last I heard she's shut away at home, with another on the way.

But I need to prove that it's not all like that. It's not.

We had a connection. Music. Future.

I need to go to prove that it's not all bodies and coercion in my future, to know that some parts of this world are safe and good.

I need Tale, and I have to go.

I'm careful. Really careful. I leave my shoes off, hold them in one hand as I escape. And I slide along the wall where the shadows gather thickest, and I do not dare to breathe as I slide the bolt back with both hands, lifting it a little so it does not scrape.

It's risky. But my parents think I listened, and they work hard and sleep soundly knowing we are in our beds; I make it out into the night.

I stand there for a moment, gulping the night air, fizzing with nerves, imagining Mama leaping out of bed and pounding after me. But nothing stirs. And I know I shouldn't, but I have to go. I have to see that it's okay.

Every time I think I'm going to falter she creeps back into my mind, a soothing lullaby of sorts. Singing. Whispering, *Okay. But only coz I get to give it back to you.*

And anyway, she has my letter jacket.

So I go, and then I'm standing by the bar and *waiting waiting waiting*, clutching a bottle so hard my knuckles pale.

Tonight, the smell of beer is as sour as my nerves, and it shrivels my stomach. But at least the bottle gives me something to hold on to; to occupy my hands and make it look like I belong.

I turn to the stage: a comfortable disguise, the music lover, nothing more.

Tale isn't there, and no one really watches the keyboard player and his smooth cover of "Cape Town Flower" so easy. He's just gently filling in the gaps between a dozen conversations as though he couldn't care. He doesn't need us; he has Abdullah Ibrahim.

I want to watch him. To prove that this thing that I feel is all about the music, but we all know that it's not, and instead I'm watching for wild dreads gliding through the crowd.

Nothing.

Perhaps she didn't come.

Perhaps she spotted me the other night and thinks me one of that crowd and now she's hiding in the shadows, disappointed.

No. She's *there*, three short forever paces away; no time at all

for me to ride the shock of her in front of me, all smiles and eager-
ness and power.

"Hey, Princess!"

"Uh, hi."

"Howzit?"

I nod. Grip the bottle tighter, hope that she can't see me shaking in the bar light.

She's here.

Say something, Neo.

Tale raps upon the bar. "Can I get a round, Tam? We've got a
philosophical debate goin' on over there and I can't take it without
juice."

"Sure."

Four bottles slide across the bar.

"And one for the princess."

"No, no, it's okay." I swallow hard and lift the bottle in my
hand. "I still have this."

"What, you can't have another?"

I *shouldn't*. Not tonight.

"C'mon. You can hang with us. I could use an ally."

The bartender laughs. "What is it this time? The mathematical
equation for getting a girl to *spill*?"

Tale recoils. "What*ever* do you mean?"

"Oh, I think you know."

"I'm *shocked*."

"You are ridiculous. Get on with you."

And I should have asked her what she meant. I should have
seen, but Tale stood before me, leaning in so that I'm breathing
in her deep-sharp scent, and there's the *clink* of glass and hum of

people who don't care and *God*, she's beautiful. And as she wraps an arm around me, leads me through the crowd, I find the voice to ask, "So what *are* you debating, then?"

And Tale adjusts her grip so that she can look at me and almost-wink. "Desire."

We stop at the farthest corner of the bar. High-backed couches form an almost booth, draped in fairy lights and better lit than much of the bar, close to the stage but quiet, private. There's a RESERVED sign in the middle of the table, nestled between rim-wet coasters.

Tale peels herself from me and dumps the bottles on the table, stopping conversation.

"Who's this?" The band stares.

"Oooh, fresh blood?"

"This, my friends, is *Neo*."

She remembered.

"Ahhh, the jacket girl."

They talked? Of course they talked. What did she—Is that a flicker of a grin?

"Oh, yah. It's with our gear. Get it before you go?" I nod, but she's already moving on. "This is Cap, Jed, and Zebra." She points at each of them in turn.

Jed and Zebra smile above their matching shiny purple shirts, mirror images except that Jed's a full head taller. Cap peers out from underneath a baseball cap, and nods.

"*Neo*'s come to rescue me from all your asinine and futile arguments."

"Sure. That's what she's doing."

And suddenly I feel small, and scrutinized, and utterly unworthy. Who am I to hang out with these *music makers*? But the band shuffles up, makes room, and I somehow find myself sitting with them, Tale at my side.

"So, Neo," Tale says, so close that I can feel her hip, her thigh—her flesh, my flesh, barely kept apart. I lift the beer up to my lips, ignore the bitter stomach-churning, swig. *Numb it.* "These two oafs here think desire is a sin, that it *damages* us."

The backing-and-guitar guys grin.

"Not that we're *arguing* with that. We want it—"

"But we're *human*. Wanting doesn't mean it's not a fault."

"As faults go, it is a pretty good one."

"Wait, so—" I start, but Tale reaches out to touch my arm, stops me.

"Slow down . . ." And her gaze flicks to Cap. Mine follows, and I wonder how it is that somebody can look at you so completely intently while giving off the impression that he's not looking at all.

"It's kind of dark in here," Tale continues. "And Cap needs the light to read your lips. Speak a little clearer, okay?"

"Oh. I—"

"It's okay. It's cool. Just, slower."

"Uh-huh." I nod, burning with embarrassment. I feel so *rude*. And then I—"Wait."

"Hmm?"

"How?"

"I lost my hearing when I was three years old." He speaks, soft and shy, and it sounds . . . different, somehow, although I couldn't tell you what was wrong with it.

"No, I—Oh."

I want to say *I'm sorry*. I want to say *I didn't mean that* and *How do you play if you can't hear? You can't. It isn't possible.* I want to ask how he can *speak* and does he sign and how has he not walked into oncoming traffic by now if he cannot hear.

But I don't know what's right or wrong to say. I look away.

"It's okay," he says. "You can ask."

"Cap will give you one free night for stupid. Just not *reeeeally* stupid."

"Yah. You treat our drummer like a monkey and the rest of us will kick your ass." Jed grins to let me know he's mostly joking.

I weigh this up for a moment, testing questions in my mind, and they just sit and wait for me to catch them up.

Something safe. But interesting. Interested.

Something that shows them you're not a complete doff.

Finally, I settle on "The drums?"

And the drummer lifts his head and *beams*, and he's so handsome when he smiles. "I feel them. I can't hear. A little, if it's really really blow-your-brains-out loud, but not really. But . . . look. Put your hands flat on the table."

I oblige. Zebra puts one of his out flat too.

"Feet on the floor."

I lower my heels. "Okay."

And the drummer taps a beat out with his fingers and the bottom of a green glass bottle. Louder, faster. Less again, still there. And I feel it in my palm, my fingertips. The louder parts, my feet feel too.

And then he stops and my hands thrum with memory.

"I feel the others, too. Unless we're playing something really quiet. Then we practice, practice, practice."

Tale laughs. "Love-lost songs are just the *worst.*"

I nod. "I . . . Wow. You'd never know!" And then, "I'm sorry. I don't mean—I just—"

And he closes off, sinks beneath his cap again, and when he answers, he sounds sad. "I know. But what, you think we can't have jobs? And lives? We can't appreciate the arts?"

"No!" *Oh God, Neo, shut up!* "I'm sorry. I didn't mean . . ." I break off, swig from the fast-warming beer before I say something worse.

Jed and Zebra stare at me like I'm a sideshow. A train wreck, and they cannot look away.

I squirm.

And Zebra *snorts*. Actually snorts. And the snort turns quickly into laughter. And beside him Jed is shaking his head slow, but his lips twitch into a grin. And Cap just sits there, staring at the floor. And I'm going to apologize again, right after another courage swig.

"Might as well just throw her in," Jed says, around his laughter, and he leans in to Zebra and they *kiss*.

I choke, knock glass against my teeth.

Beside me, Tale smirks, stares pointedly into her drink. But I can't look away. They're all tongue and teeth and hands and *can they do that?* What if someone *sees?*

"Ahem." They stop with one last tug of teeth on lips, and *grin*.

"Aw, Tale, you picked up a *baby one* tonight."

"Nahhh . . ." She peers at me and suddenly *everyone* is staring and I'm trapped between them all on show. "Oh, shit. Guys, you *assholes*, don't just flaunt like that. Shit. Shit. I'm sorry, I thought you knew—I thought you were—"

"What?"

". . . That bothered you, didn't it?"

She looks taller, suddenly. Straighter-spined, uncomfortable.

And she's going to cut ties, let loose the disappointing find, I *know* it. Why shouldn't Cap be deaf? What made me think he would be hearing? And my eyes flicker toward the other two. I can't help it. And they sit there, leaning in together, holding hands beneath the table. And why shouldn't they do . . . that?

I just never knew you could.

I mean, I knew. But I didn't *know*.

I swallow, drag my eyes away. "No, of course not. Sorry. What were you saying before?"

There's silence for an endless moment as the judgment's passed. I stare hard at the table, at the rings of beer where bottles stood, drying-sticky but still wet enough to catch the light.

I wish that I could drown in it. Dive deep to where they cannot stare like that.

I'm sorry. *Like me. Please.*

And Tale breathes, and the tableau of judgment breaks.

"I think *you* were offending the best drummer in the township."

I squirm. "Before that?"

And Tale smiles beside me, and I feel her close, and all the awkwardness just melts away. "Oh, that. Desire. These passionate idiots think it's a sin, although they *clearly* have no issue with it. But . . . I'd argue it's imperative anticipation. Key to everything. Apathy and listlessness would let the species die. But possibility? Anticipation? It's what motivates us all to move. And surely the ability to move—to grow—is gift, not sin."

Desire.

"Yeah." I nod, thinking, *Sing for me.* Thinking, *I can't believe*

I'm here. Thinking—underneath the surface—*Would I do that? Could I?*

"So, which is it?"

"I . . ."

All I want in the entire world is to agree with Tale, to agree so she agrees with me, to do . . . the kissing, with the teeth, like that.

But she is *fierce.* Perhaps an independent thought would make her like me more. Perhaps she likes the argument.

Which is it?

"Look, you've got her twisted up and tongue-tied. Let the fledgling *be.*"

"Nahhh, she's *cute* like this. Don't stop."

And as I blush and squirm the conversation drifts and twists, meanders, and I find myself watching them, the easy way their laughter falls right from their lips, the closeness as they all lean in together, the way jokes bounce from one to another.

I think I am in love with all of them.

And I'm so caught up in that that I barely hear a word until the sound of my name snaps me back into the present. "What is it that *you* desire, Neo? What is it you *love?*"

This.

Music.

Song.

This.

Love.

Tale nudges at my shoulder. Or perhaps I just imagine it, imagine her closer, warmer breath, the longing of a voice that wants to climb into your soul and learn its tune. "Music."

"Ahhh, see, I knew it. We have another muso. What about it?"

You.

"Voice. And story. Song. I . . . like the power music wields, to temper hearts and change the minds of thousands. The way it can ensnare and set you free."

"Mmm, she's powerful, all right!"

"Hush, you . . . just be careful, hey? Music is a *hungry bitch*, and she is not afraid to feeeeeed."

Bottles raised, they clink to that: a toast to hungry music. And then there's a lull while everybody swigs and everybody contemplates.

And then Zebra cocks his head and frowns right at keyboard guy. "This guy is *hot.*"

Everybody's focus shifts as fingers rise and fall across the scale.

"He *is*!" Jed nods, then, "Wait." Jed turns to Zee. "Hot how?"

"Oh, you know. Musically. But he has a certain . . . quality, elsewhere."

"Hush, you."

"Oh, come on."

"*Cha*, no. I'm a one-man guy." He snuggles up to Zebra, and they melt into one another.

So *easy*.

"So, Neo," Jed says, from his cocoon, "what music do you like?"

Another question, so simple and so hard.

"Everything."

I watch the distrust ripple round the table, and I realize how that sounds: indifference, or a big fat dirty lie. "Okay, no. Not everything, but every *kind* of music, as long as it's true."

"True?"

I nod. "Real. Felt. Not constructed solely for performance' sake." I almost add, *like you*, but Cap nods thoughtfully beneath his baseball cap.

"Yeah."

And as we sit there with the beer and twinkling lights and closeness, it occurs to me that this is the greatest conversation I have ever had. That I feel *right*, for the first time since Janet and I discovered *The One Love Movement on Bantu Biko Street* and listened to it on repeat, lying beneath the BigTall tree, carried away by the comfortable rhythms and the rustling leaves and dappled sun.

I drift again, warm and safe with Tale pressed against me, until Jed and Zebra move as one and lift their drinks high in the air. "To *music*!"

"And to grabbing what you love and *running with it*!" Tale adds, raising her drink too.

"To music, the only sharp thing you should ever run with!" Jed grins.

And I lift mine, Cap lifts his, and it doesn't matter who kissed who or who can hear or who can't find the words, we're here for the same thing, and we salute the music, one and all.

I have to stop before I'm home, lean back against a neighbor's wall, hands upon my knees, and remind myself to *breathe*.

And I catch myself trying to breathe Tale, hoping that my jacket soaked up something of her, of them, of the whole night. But all I smell on it is soap.

What *was* that? What just happened?

Something happened tonight that I cannot put into words. And I want to, but it keeps its distance, hides just out of sight, and I don't want to pry. And anyway, why tie it to these *words*?

Breathe, Neo. Breathe. It's good.

Tonight, I found people like me.

There are some things you should know about boys and how to handle them . . ." My sister lands her step beside mine as we trudge the Monday walk of doom to school and suddenly the road feels so exposed. I glance back at Jeso, talking Cherry's ear off, but I think they're far enough that they can't hear. "They're a football chant to your CD collection. One-track mind." I cannot believe she's saying this. Not here, out on the school road, where boys who are not brothers appear every few yards, spilling out onto the road to join the walking chain. "Make nice. Makeup, hair, you make an effort, like wrapping up a package, giving them the feeling of that they'll be opening a present later. It's like a promise.

"And you want the good sex, none of that thrust, thrust, done; all about them. Make him do it slow. Tell him *I'll get up right now and walk and not come back if we don't both leave happy.*"

Even in the open I imagine asking Tale to go slow, imagine her . . . How does it work? I imagine her thrusting up inside me, rough and gentle all at once, all chafing thighs, all full and close.

I know it isn't right, *that* isn't right, but it feels truer than anything I've ever known.

I blush.

"And hey, Nee, I get the urge, but really? In the streets at night?"

My sister's gone from know-it-all to deep concern in half a second. My blush deepens.

"I know. Sorry."

She chews on her bottom lip. Hesitates. "I heard you leave on Friday night."

My insides freeze.

"Listen, Mama's an old prude. She doesn't get it. But she's right . . . It's dangerous at night. There's more than your boy out there."

Nope. No. This isn't happening.

"You knowwww, you don't *have* to be a night walker. There's . . . other ways. You can always slip away on market days. Tell Mama one of the old hags was haggling too hard or she forgot her numbers. And water takes an *age* to collect, don't you know? And homework club . . ." She winks. And she wraps an arm around my shoulders. "You'll work it. There are secrets. Moments in the day you never knew you had. You just gotta work the system, baby girl."

I reach up for her hand. Squeeze. Give her a smile.

But in my head I'm thinking, *It's another world.*

"I got you, Padawan," she says. "Now for *goodness'* sake, do something with your hair."

With days gone by and nothing said, I thought I got away with it, that Mama's words and the shock and shame of being caught was deemed enough. But I was wrong.

That evening, after finishing the salon clean and beating Jeso (just) in a goalie-off, we come home to Mama whistling at the door, with a screwdriver in her hand.

And now I'm a prisoner.

We all are. Mama's added a padlock to the heavy, oil-slick night bolts.

"No one *needs* to leave at night." She nods, as though the matter's closed.

"But Mama"—Jeso's lip wobbles—"what if there's a *fire?*"

"Then we'll rip the shutters off and knock out all the window bars. This whole place would fall down if you lean against the walls. You're *fine.*"

And she takes the chicken from the side and plucks it with such force that nobody dares say another word.

Something changes then. My world becomes a little tighter-lipped, everybody watching and resentful.

I am trapped.

Trapped in Mama's world of expectations. Trapped in Jeso's fear and Linda's knowing *You're a woman now* ideas.

They all hate me.

They all *know*.

But they don't, because the boy they think I've found does not exist, and if they knew—

What?

In the school yard, people joke that if you're a bad girl the first-grade teacher will show you what's what. And they don't mean that she'll stripe your hand with willow cane.

Everybody laughs at her, but they're afraid the teasing might be true.

It can't be. She would never have a job. But that's the worst thing they can think of. Making you do . . . that.

And now I'm trapped inside this cage of judgment that isn't mine, and I can't say, because that would be worse.

I'm trapped.

I'm never getting out.

I so want to be like my best friend: so sure, so in control. I want to step into the night and run: to *her*, to them, to safety, but even if I knew where Mama kept the key, her finding me with Tale would be worse than if I lined all Khayelitsha's boys up round the block and took them one by one.

She'd find a priest and find a boy and together they would pray that I was fixed before the wedding bells.

And I'd never hear her song again.

You do not trap a fly by buzzing at it, Mama always said. *You sweeten water with some honey and you wait.*

So that's what I will do. I'll wait. Do as she expects. And I'll charm the lock right off of that door.

I turn blind to my sisters' heavy looks and half smiles. Choke down Mama's too-long glances. Outwardly, I am the perfect daughter, my words and thoughts and deeds as starched-polite as Sunday best.

But just because I cannot *take her*, sing her song, it doesn't mean I do not want her. Everywhere I turn, Tale is there. In everything I do. I imagine bringing Tale home for a Sunday dinner, in a different world, sneaking glances across bowls of sweet potatoes, meat, and gravy. I imagine her beside me in the pews, singing her heart right up into the rafters as our fingers lace.

And I try to forget, to focus on my studies and the salon and the things a good daughter is meant to think about, but every time that I think *Mama would be maaad*, or *Stop*, my heart splinters and I cannot breathe and I have to pull myself back in and let my brain replay her voice.

It wasn't only her. She did something to me in the magic of the bar light, and now I found myself listening intensely, searching for that same experience, the weight and lightness of the music, the way it grounds you and it takes you to the sky. She changed the way I listened, and it changed the way I heard.

Perhaps *they* did, the whole band. Wondering about connections and togetherness. Wondering what music without sound is really like, when it's all you can get. But mostly, it was her.

I noticed things.

The aspiration of a singer's words, just a little breathless.

The twang of desperation or the spring of joy.

The way a whole band moves together: one beast, many voices.

Depth and nuance I had never heard before.

But still, there was Tale. The singer on my CD holds a note above her backing singers and I play over one long *different* note, watch her scan the crowd, singing, singing, singing, ever closer, coming for me with those—

"Neo!"

Someone yanks my headphones out and the bright, bright voices disappear.

Linda and Cherry and Jeso *stare* as Mama towers over me.

"Neo Elisabeth Mary Mahone?"

I wince. Stay quiet.

"Well? I'm waiting."

"Yes, Mama?"

"What exactly are you doing?"

I glance at the headings on my textbook. "Business Science."

"And *Business Science* requires no concentration? I could hand you the salon tomorrow and I'd sleep at night?"

My eldest sister opens her mouth in protest, but we all know Mama doesn't mean it. She would *never* trust me with her business.

"No, Mama."

"Well."

She holds a hand out for the CD Walkman resting in my lap. Leaves me with an open textbook, longing, and a half-finished refrain.

Outside of Mama's nighttime jail, everything goes on exactly as it was before, the world still bright and loud and full of itself. And music? It's still here, and I am still in love.

"She still keeping you prisoner?"

I nod.

My best friend rolls her eyes in solidarity.

She squirmed when I told her of my mother's jailhouse—although I left out Tale and Mama's imagined boy—declaring it all her fault for *ever* coming up with the idea to go see Umzi live.

Of course it's that. The only reason my Mama would do something so wild. Perhaps somebody told.

And I knew that I should set her straight, but in a way she had it right. She started this. And having my best friend feel a little guilty, more aware of me, for once, was nice.

"Here." Janet sits, holding out a shiny silver disc. It flashes rainbow in the midday sun. "This'll help."

"What is it?"

"Summer songs. Something to cheer you up."

"Ehh, you know that even with this weather it's not *actually* summer, right?" I pull at my cardigan sleeves to illustrate, hook the wool over my thumbs.

Mama would be mad to see me stretch it out like that.

I stop. Gently pat the sleeves out flat.

"I know, I know, but summer has the songs of looooooove."

I laugh. "It what?"

"Really. All that *fun*. It's *exactly* how it feels to be in love." She thrusts the disc at me emphatically.

"In love?"

"Yah, right."

"With . . . Max?" I almost say it without the beat, but she catches me off guard. And Joseph Mthandeni has been *close* of late.

"Yahhhh."

"You're crazy."

But she thrusts the disc toward me and gives me that *look*. The one that's as much full of pity as it is affection. The one that says *Let me lead you to the promised land, and teach you.* So we listen.

Bright, bright tones and bouncing beats.

Sun, encapsulated in a melody.

Surf songs. Reggae. Reggae surf. Dance songs. Beach songs. Lying-underneath-the-stars songs.

All love and saccharine adventure.

It all sounds manufactured to my ear, but Janet, lost in crush-feels, positively beams.

I try to imagine Tale singing this, but it becomes a satire. The two of us sitting in a back booth at the bar and *mocking* it.

"This is how he makes you feel?"

"Uh-huh."

"He makes you *high*?"

"Oh my stars, we need to get you laid."

"No," I say. "We don't."

"But, sugar, you are *missing out*." She grabs at my face and squeezes like an old-and-insane aunt.

"Gerroff." And then I realize what Janet just said. "Wait . . . are you? Have you?"

Surely, my best friend would have told me the *instant* something happened. Right?

". . . technically? No. But I think I might."

"With—"

"Max."

"Er . . . Have you met him yet?"

"No. But I joined his fan page. And it says he's *single!*"

". . . so you're going to what? Introduce yourself? Leave a message on his wall?"

"Oh, no!" My best friend looks horrified. "I can't go to him first. God. I will not present myself to him as a *hick*. I will be suave and I will be experienced. I'll know *exactly* where to touch him and how to make him squeal."

I cringe. "But—"

"School crush. He's been fawning around for weeks, haven't you noticed?"

I shrug, suddenly aware of just how *dry* the earth is. Dusty. I stare at it harder.

"You know . . ." Janet nudges at my foot with hers. "Khwezi kind of likes you. I bet he'd take you for a ride if you'd just ask him. Bat those golden eyes at him."

I cannot imagine quiet, awkward Khwezi giving *anyone* a ride.

I don't want to.

"No thanks."

"C'mooooon. If we find you one, we can obsess together."

I pull away.

"Yah, coz that will *really* impress Mama."

And honestly, I *almost* say. I do. Just to hush her up. But I don't want to cheapen Tale's sound with thoughts of scoring points on dance cards, or with boy-lust or with summer songs. Tale deserves more than that. Tale deserves *soul*.

What Tale deserves is "N'kosi Sikelela."

Every version I could find, carefully arranged one after the other so they tell a story: the many moods of Africa.

Because what else is so much soul-of-Africa as that?

My favorite, right now, is a Miriam Makeba, Ladysmith, and Simon live recording. Not the anthem, just the Xhosa lyrics. Slow, acoustic, and the whole stadium pauses, takes a breath, and sings. A prayer wrenched from the heart.

If I could stand upon the beach beside her, I would hum it just like that. All sorrow-hope. Longing and remorse.

But there are others. Just as much a part of it. The hymn as it was first intended. Protest songs. An anthem held up strong and proud and striving. Everything we could be, everything we should be.

Shona and Swahili translations, the *pan-African dream*. And the hybrid anthem of our own proud lands: the Xhosa-Sotho-Zulu-English-Afrikaans all coexisting so that human lives would follow.

And Boom Shaka's solid beat, taking every bit of pride and history and connotation, and framing it as something new, something that my generation could throw out across the streets.

Schoolkids, choirs, stadiums, projecting the same words for a hundred different reasons in a hundred different ways, every single day. It's *part of us*.

Music changes. Brings the history of every incarnation past. The way we use it each time tells a story, adds to it. But the biggest tale of all is that it's *there*, permeating everything. It's *live*.

This song isn't Tale. But it's everything she makes me feel, and it's the best I've got.

"What you listening to?"

"Huh?"

"A . . . music and association thing."

"Couldn't get a signal on the radio?"

I shrug. "Not trying. This is *good*."

"But *Max*—"

"I know, I know. But . . . there's so much *here*."

Janet takes an earbud, listens in as thirty schoolboys blend their bright-and-hopeful voices at the morning chorus.

"You're listening to *school stuff* instead of the golden voice?"

Eish, sometimes she *doesn't get it*. "Yes."

"Really? It's Friday lunch. He's doing the top ten."

I shrug. Resist the urge to rip my headphones back and pull away.

"No thanks."

And my best friend rolls her eyes, and today we do not share. We sit, leaning on each other, in completely separate worlds.

It is not enough.

Janet might not recognize the longing in my face—it's not like hers, all sugary and light—but it is there. I'm *restless*. Like wire brushes whisked against a drum skin. How has it been a whole week, and only a week, and *how will I see her again? When?*

I spent all my money on those beers, and Mama sure won't give me more for credit. There's not enough to call the band's number, but enough for one text.

Just one. So I wrote her a message:

Thank you.
Let's do it again?

Careful. Nothing telling, unless you know. Unless you read between the lines, unless you read around them.

Just like the best lyrics.

Stevie Wonder's "Happy Birthday" chorus. A celebration, best of wishes . . . protest.

But is it enough? Everything I want to say?

I draft another:

Tale,
You make me feel. You make me
listen.
What? You ask. To what?

And I say EVERYTHING. To
everything.

And another:

Stuck. Trapped by woman who
Knows nothing of real love.
Send help.

And:

Meet me by the BigTall tree.
Tonight.

They sit hot in my hand, glowing too bright in the dark, too solid in the day. And I delete them all. It might not even be her phone. It could be *anyone* reading my words.

It could be her.

I don't know which I'm more afraid of, and I know I'll never, ever send them.

But in the still of night, as Cherry snores and Max and Sammi visit the constabulary live on air, I retype them all, and I imagine my so-silent song twisting up into the air and dancing close with Tale's.

"But you must get a *lot* of distressed people walking through these doors."

"Mm-hmm, mm-hmm. In a place like this, it's busy, busy."

"I can imagine . . . so how do you deal with that?"

"With—"

"The constant stress of responsibility."

"Yah. Someone told me we're built on our choices, and in this work, sometimes . . . it feels Khayelitsha's built up on mistakes, you know? But this is our *community*. It hurts, we hurt. We try to heal it, help those folks whose pain bleeds out into the street. But we're small, y'know; there's only so much we can do.

"We're also *strong*. We get up and we come to work and walk the beat because we're strong. We have to be. This is our community. Our people."

My parents are firm and constant:

> *Music is no life.*
> *Boys?*
> *You go to school, you get good grades, you* listen. *That's your life.*

But this life is not enough, and I grow desperate under its constraints, desperate for anything that hints at something more. I listen, desperate, to UmziRadio. I dream of Friday nights, replay the raising of glass bottles and her thigh pressed against mine.

Once, I thought that I saw Cap in the fridge aisle of the minimart, but bar light and baseball cap meant that I could not *really* tell, and I did not dare to ask. Still, I went back and trailed the aisles more often than I care to say, hoping for a better angle, hoping that the others might just shop here too.

No luck.

I linger over every flyer-plastered tree, every papier-mâché wall of advertisements, hoping hoping hoping that there will be one with TALE AND THE STORYTELLERS bold across the top. Something I can hold or fold under my pillow. Something I can keep and hold in secret. Something *mine*.

I find:

The Cornfields
Your Superman
&
JACKRIP

9:30 on. Free entry before 8.

And:
Gazelle VS. Buffalo

There's:

The Wailers: Tribute Band.
& Open mic—unleash your inner Bob!

And:
Khayelitsha United Mambazo Choir
Ngobunye ubusuku! One night only!

There are new posters in black and green detailing heavy-metal folk, and age-gray sheets I cannot read. And there are other things. A whole building, boarded up, the doorway scattered with empty bottles and foil packets, and the walls covered in the same poster two hundred times: SAFE ABORTION: QUICK SUCCESS, and I wonder whether that happened here, or the posters are all incidental, simply pasted up on an abandoned canvas. There are football matches (MANCHESTER V. ARSENAL. ALL YOU CAN DRINK) and day-care adverts (ALL YOUR CHILDREN'S NEEDS AND LIKINGS TAKEN CARE OF. NO MORE TEARS!). And for a moment my heart stops for the family of RUSZANI BHEMBE: MISSING.

But there is no Tale. And I'm lost without her.

P ass the combs." My mother long released the others, but I'm stuck inside her tin-can salon, wilting underneath her sprays and glues and muttering.

"Yes, ma'am." She could just as well have reached across for them herself, but I stretch across the three-chair shack, pass her the long-handled combs, and watch her as she works.

It's quiet. For a moment you can hear the teasing of the hair. But it never takes my mother long to get the people talking.

"There's an overflow again." Mama sniffs in theatrical disgust. "Of course there is."

The customer—a familiar face although I couldn't name her— nods, although how anyone can smell slurry in here, over Mama's products, I don't know. "There's always an overflow."

"Ain't that the truth. Always swimming in the shit."

She's right; more often than not you'd have to walk past three or four or five latrines before you find one that's not filled right up, and sometimes . . . sometimes, you're too desperate to walk.

Khayelitsha makes a lot of shit.

"Someone should complain. I don't know what we pay them for."

"Seriously. Before the drowning happens all over again."

The familiar woman frowns, and I wonder *how* she has not heard the legend, so old a warning that it's bandied round the dinner table, a warning that administrators in the fancy houses do not have our backs.

Mama sucks the air in through her teeth. "*What* her mother

was thinking letting a seven-year-old out around here at night I'll never know. But it was dark, and . . . slippery, and the scrap-of-a-thing fell right into the hole. Left nothing but a skid mark and a single shoe. What a way to go. *Imagine* it."

She grins at the woman's shudder. My mother, when she tells her stories, is the visciousest narrator. She pleasures in reactions.

Cutting your hair at Madame Serious is guaranteed a show.

I listen for a while as she weaves from rats (*as big as babies, fierce as dogs*) to education (*Africa will* rise!) to the rotting state of our society (*It will only rise if lazy kids and useless men would realize what they've got*) and I stand quiet, ready for the wash, the dry, the sweeping.

Today, I am Mama's lackey. Today, and every day until I learn my place.

I try to learn. I do. But I can hear the *show* in Mama's voice, and my mind wanders to another stage. And I stand trapped in a box of my mother's wishes, and I pine.

Finally, finally, finally, after six or seven hours of standing, sweeping, quiet as a mouse, Mama releases me, with strict instructions to go to the market and go home, and she'll see me in an hour.

The sun, already level with the rooftops, blesses Khayelitsha with gold-light. The streets feel roomy, loud, alive, and I stretch out and fill as much of this wide open space as my small body will allow, free from Mama's judging gaze.

And in the middle of the red-wide street, there is a *battle*.

Twelve boys, one tight circle, and a beat. And all around, the market traders *scorn*.

I stop as the smallest one steps into the middle, challenges another.

"*Mornin' yawnin* everybody *fornicatin'*
Khayelitsha *mornin'* predawn noise.
As ya *baby* brother *wails*, the *early* bangin' *pales*
In comparison.
To the *garrison* of *last night's dreams*."

The circle jeers and cheers and cajoles in the half breath as the challenged boy steps in.

"Last night's dreams? Man, what are ya *on*?
This *garrison* ya *thinkin'* of is *nothin'* but a *jailhouse graveyard* nothing but a *cage*, of your *mind*,
Of your *own constraints* and complaints. It's *sugar-free no victory*, endless piles of *essays* and a *math test*, that ya didn't *study for*. You wanted to *party more*.
Quit throwing your life away and *fight*."

"For your *right*?
To *paaaarty*, party to the *top* don't *flop*, and by *party* I mean *go to school*. Coz it's *cool-er* to be a *sharp* suit than to be a *brainless* brute, lootin' shootin' drinkin'-sinkin' *down*.
You *fight*."

"The Khayelitsha noise is *growth* and it's *family* it's *music, use it*, take it in your *heart* and wrap it *up* with a *ribbon* and you *carry it, marry it*, make Khayelitsha *proud*."

And the challengers dissolve into companionship, high-five, laugh, melt back into the circle as another boy puffs up his chest and walks into the ring.

That's music.

And even if the older folks don't know it, scenes like this, they make the produce ring a little brighter, and they let the city *breathe*.

A little farther down, by the orange stand, a group of women in brightly patterned skirts and turbans sway, crooning the old songs.

And as I walk, radio spills out from every shack and chip stand. Dance beats, rhythms, smooth jazz, and springy pop, permeating *everything*.

And underneath that is the rush of cars, the honking rustling bustling of a hundred thousand people as they talk and walk and haggle—for oranges or car parts or affection.

Underneath that, wind, so gentle that you have to *listen* for its hum. And the warm and ever-steady beat of sun against the earth.

As I wander through the market with my mother's shopping bag I'm serenaded by this arrangement of life.

All around me, Khayelitsha *sings*.

But the feeling does not last.

Mama sits across from me, calloused fingers working the potatoes with a skill and grace I've yet to master, two and a half of them for every one I peel.

My knuckles *ache*.

There *is* a rhythm to it, it is true. But it is tight-lipped, disapproving, stilted by a hundred disappointments.

Scrape, peel, scrape, peel, *plop* into the water.

Scrape, peel, scrape, peel, *plop*.

My mother does not speak, just turns her spuds around with the precision of a music box or a rotisserie.

Not even a whispered hymn tonight. Just quiet.

Beside us, Linda shells the peas. The *thllllllp* of a thumbnail in flesh, then *pop, pop, pop*, they land.

And everything feels dark and small and the rubber headphones sit *so heavy* in my pocket, make my palms itch and itch to reach for them. But I do not dare.

"'mon, baby. Let me show you how it's done." Joseph Mthandeni steps in close, with swagger, and he puts his arms around my neck.

I feel the heat of him and instinctively inch backward, knocking right into the desks.

"No, no, no!" Janet steps between us, breaking us apart, and I am grateful. "No, Neo." She waves her book and pencil as she talks: her pages full of stage notes. "You're excited. Nervous, sure, but you've got this far; you're finally going to know what all the fuss is. And you love him."

Working with my bestbest friend is hard. She has this vision in her head that only she can see, and she's *demanding*. Try as I might, I cannot play the hungry-for-it teenage girl she wants. "Honestly, Neo. How hard is it? Look, just"—she muscles farther in, grabs Joseph's arms, and drapes them round her own neck—"look him in the eye. Look keen."

"I'm trying."

"Uuuugh!" She pulls out of his embrace, steps back, throwing her arms up in the air. "Impossible! You. Are. Impossible."

We stand there staring, unsure what to do without her barking her instructions. And my best friend breathes. I watch the anger flooding out of her as she exhales. But the irritation stays. "I *know* you've never felt a thing inside that trunk of yours. I know that you have *no idea* what this is. That's okay. It isn't real . . . Think of him as *music* if you have to. Think of his embrace as beats, if you are so in love with that. I don't care. Just make it believable."

I know that I should step back into our tiny fake-stage ring. I know we're acting. That it's school, with a whole class working in this room, and that I'm safe.

If I could just see *Tale* standing there, I'd win SAFTAs for my weak-kneed, doe-eyed acting. I'd make my best friend proud.

And nobody would know.

But everyone would see. I can't.

I stuff Tale back deeper inside my chest and I step forward, stiff as the pastor in his starched-white neck.

"Okay," I say. "I'll try it again."

J anet and I *argued*.

It was stupid.

I knew it was stupid.

We're listening to an old spiritual, with six-part harmonies and voices running like a river, and piece by piece it's carrying away the ugliness that's sitting on my chest. And Janet hits pause.

"I just love the way he spoke about these guys."

I nod.

"So *cerebral*, all that stuff about traditions and how taking us back to our roots is the *only way* we'll ever see our futures in the face of all this Western culture."

It *was* a good speech.

"That's exactly why we're here, folks. This little space on Friday nights, it's *ours*. It's *us*. It's *yours*. And it's okay to pull inspiration, but let's keep reminding ourselves who we are."

And I think of Tale's lips upon my skin, how that's exactly who I want to be.

And I think of the band.

The music.

". . . don't you think?"

Janet is staring at me.

"Eh?"

116

"You can see them, right? My father and Max, standing over smoking beefsteaks on the *braai*?

". . . He couldn't wear his hair like that, though."

Max's hair? What did I miss?

"*Why?*"

"Come *on*. You saw him that night. And it's longer now, I swear. He posted pictures from this week. Posing with the nurses. With that half smile he does . . . How could I keep my hands off him like that? I'd just want to reach right up and run my fingers through it all the time. So *tousle-able* . . . Maybe he should wear it plain."

I nod. Eye roll. But she doesn't notice, and I don't know whether that annoys me more. I *want* her to notice. And I really, really don't. I want her to know how much I *long* for Tale. I want her to sympathize because the things we want are so very unreachable. I want to compare muscles, or their voices or their hair: to rate them out of ten and argue argue argue over whose choice is supreme.

I want my best friend in the world to *know*.

But it's not something you share.

"You think? Short? Something you'd want to take home to Mama."

And suddenly I'm *mad*, at Janet and Tale and Max's stupid hair and the whole *world*.

"Something you can't *grab*?" I am so, so done.

It's all about Max and boys and keeping up appearances. Always. Always Max this, marriage that, isn't this the *best*? And:

"No one *cares!*" I yell, snatching my earphones away and already I'm up and running.

She follows.

Everybody knows you do not follow someone when they're mad. But follow, Janet does. And then we're scrapping. Full-on. Like two snarling dogs. And the lazy school yard turns into a fight cage as the whole school crowds around us. All I see is uniforms: wool and pleats and jeering. And my best friend's face, ready to explode.

"What's your *problem*?"

"You are. It's always you."

"Eh?"

"It's always you. And always boys and there is so much more, you know?"

I don't remember what was said. Not really. But I do remember "prude" and *"kindie,"* and feeling anger, hot and fierce. And then it was gone and I felt wrenched as though she'd pushed me—though she didn't—watching from above in horror as the fabric of our friendship tore.

Without my best friend nattering into my ear about her perfect future, I sank further into music. It was comfort. Conversation. It was all I'd ever wanted.

Think of him as music . . . if you're so in love with that. It still smarts. But she is right. I am.

In the living room, the TV blares, all proclamations and canned laughter intertwined with Jeso's howling glee. But I have music.

"And tonight we have a very special show," I say out loud, to the empty room, "*filled* with special guests as we talk about Living the Dream."

I imagine that the dresser is a desk, lined with screens and microphones instead of Linda's hairbrush and a row of nail polish, and through the mirror there's a seat for Maximillius, room for Tale and the band to crowd around the mics.

"First up, we have Umzi's Max, perhaps the most famous voice in all of Khayelitsha. Good *evening*, sir."

Hi. I imagine his confident reply.

I imagine asking him exactly what it feels like to be living the life that everybody wants, and how, exactly, someone gets into this business:

"How does it all *start?*"

And I imagine him, so charming, sharing anecdotes about his first day, junior-Max all small and shy and wearing boots three sizes too big, and bigger tales: his favorite moments so far; who or what has made him nervous; the weirdest thing he's done for Khayelitsha's entertainment.

"Now"—I turn to the Storytellers—"you guys have a little bit different experience, the other side, if you will, as creators of the music. Tell us a little more about your . . . process, I guess. How does something go from an idea to a song that we hear on the stage?"

I picture them all huddled in the bar, lit by their excitement as they think of something new, and then later, on an empty stage, rehearsing, practicing the same bars over and over until the rhythms and the speed and the emotion are all etched into their bones.

"And one for all of you . . . How do you juggle all the *real-life* stuff and the music?

Oh, honey, this is real life.

Yeah. We don't have to.

Music *is* the real life. Everything else is just mortar.

And that is all I need: I sink into a daze of butter-smooth guitar riffs, and drums that sound like Khayelitsha streets, of harmonies and pipes and dirty lyrics popped out—not quite spoken, not quite sung.

When I fail to wow the crowds of businessmen and parents with my acting skills, and Janet flounces off to renounce everything we shared, my parents sigh, loudly disapproving of my efforts.

But they let it go. And I slip quietly back to my dreams.

When I show less care for polishing my mother's mirrors, I'm given extra hours before release.

And in them I hum tunes beneath my breath.

When I come home with an F marked on my schoolbooks, I *expect* the lecture. I expect my parents' angry faces towered over me, full of disappointment. I expect to lose my music, to be banished to a world of silence, not even a radio switched on if I am in the room.

But you cannot stop a songbird any more than you can halt the rhythm of the sun.

My father *sighs*. Loud and hard and put upon. And Mama hovers at his shoulder, all drawn face and angry bosom.

I sit. They do not need to ask.

"I—" I start to defend myself, but there's nothing to say.

"Explain." Papa pushes the offending page toward me.

But I can't.

He steeples his fingers underneath his lips, leaning, heavy, like I've made him *tired*.

And here it comes.

"What is this?"

It's an F.

A fail.

"You're a bright girl, Neo—"

And my stomach ties itself in knots of guilt.

"So explain to us just *how* you manage this."

"I—"

"It's this *music* again, isn't it?"

Yes.

I stare at the wood grain of the table. Do not speak.

"It is not good enough. This"—Mama swallows, sneers the next word—"*music*, Neo . . . It is not the career that you think."

I have heard this before. *Get a* real *job. Music is a risk. It's fast men and* tsotsis *playing at a grown-up life.*

Bitter old folks' lies.

"Baba *works* because music is solid!"

"Your father works for the man, Neo. This Mr. Sid, he is a businessman."

"Exactly. Running a business. Music."

"*Neo*," Baba's tone warns, but I can't stop.

"No. Baba. The big house with the windows filled with glass, the fancy suits and hat? Mr. Sid bought those with profit. From the station . . . And DJs and musicians? The ones on MTV and going to America? They make money to do that. People want to be informed and entertained."

Baba sighs.

"It is not the path you think it is."

"Oh, I know it's work. I know there is no glamour in the ghost hours and I know the money doesn't come in record sleeves. But it's *music*, Baba. It's what moves this city."

"What moves this city are the thousands upon thousands of

blue-collar laborers. The servicemen and scavengers and men with barrows full of slurry. The women like your mother who raise kids *and* businesses from nothing. What moves us is the *work*, and this lush music life is not for you."

"It's so unfair! Hundreds do it. Mr. Sid did it from nothing just like us! Just let me *try*." You never raise your voice to Baba. Never. But my traitor lungs squeeze out my words with everything they've got.

And then I realize, and you can see the silence bounce from wall to wall.

I'm doomed.

My parents sit across from me stern-faced and sad and worldly wise. But for a moment they say nothing.

Finally, Baba sucks the air across his teeth and lets it out again with force. "So. Since you *clearly* do not care about your future—"

"That's not—"

"*Whsshtt*. You do not see what life will be like if you don't succeed. We want better for you. And perhaps if you see what this life is really like . . ."

My skin buzzes with thick disbelief. Are they saying what I think they're saying?

"You mean—"

Baba nods, without even the hint of a smile, and says, so weighty, "Yes. Forget school. See how you will cope without it: Tomorrow morning you will go to work with me."

I t's late when Mama knocks upon our door and enters. Linda is in front of the mirror, wiping at her face with something that smells just like Mama's floor polish. Cherry is asleep, and I'm trying not to wake her with the *clack clack clack* of plastic casing as I *desperately* flick through every disc I own. Do I remember the tracks? The release dates? What if someone asks?

"Neo." She hovers in the doorway. "I need a word with you. About tomorrow."

In the mirror, Linda mouths, *You're dead*.

Mama sits us on the doorstep, looking out across the street, and sighs.

"You're a good girl, Neo Mahone. I know that. But sometimes you lose your way."

What is this? I try to let the night air calm my thoughts, but all I feel is guilt and fear.

What did I do? Is she going to pull the radio right out from under me?

She sighs again, all heavy, like she's come to a decision. She *is*. She's going to tell me I can't go. "We're done."

I frown.

"This boy thing, this music thing, we're done."

I still don't understand, and when she pulls the padlock from her pocket, I am *sure* she's going to tell me I can never leave again.

"If we're putting you out in the big wide world, I have to trust that you will make good choices."

I nod, staring, terrified.

"You understand? Your Baba and I . . . We do all this for you. I have to trust that somehow it's enough, that our example is enough. That you'll . . . Listen. Tomorrow . . . I need you to mind your father. It's his place of *work*, and if I hear a single incidence of you getting too loud or sure, too big for your boots, we'll go backward so fast that you'll spin. You hear me?"

I nod again.

"Good girl." She nods, leans in almost close enough to hug, just for a second, and she's rising—groaning—to her feet.

And the padlock goes into my mother's apron rather than the door.

I could go right now. I could run to Tale and the band *right now*.

But I still have a box of CDs to look through, archives to replay before the morning. And anyway, there is a voice—my mother's—*We are trusting you to make good choices. Trust you. I trust you. Trust . . .*

The next morning, my mother shakes me awake a full *hour* earlier than usual.

I step into my school skirt and blouse. Given a choice, I would wear jeans. My letter jacket. Something young and hip and *Umzi*, but this is my father's watch, and this, he says, is education. So I step into my uniform and out into the kitchen.

Mama stands over the stove, boiling up the tea. "In the real world," she whispers, barely audible over the bubbling water and the loud, loud silence, "you'd wake to stone-cold water or an empty bucket."

But she smiles as she sits opposite me with her own mug.

Some days, I would curse my mother, the tired, tough old hen; proclaim her fit for nothing but the stew pot. I'd wonder how we were ever related, because we couldn't be the same blood, we just couldn't, but then there are moments like this, away from all the disappointments, when the world's too busy sleeping to be watching us.

"Mama?"

"Yes?"

I feel like I am standing on the edge of a high stage, a microphone in front of me, an audience below. And I wish I could explain how scared I am. Excited. How I want to make her proud.

But I've heard the *you can't*s one too many times. I know how that song goes: with the sucking of the cheeks, the kissing teeth, the frown. And this moment of softness would be gone.

"Nothing."

She almost says something. Almost reaches out to squeeze my arm. But Baba stumbles in, and Mama's up and pouring tea and packing bread into a tuckbox.

Baba sips his tea in silence, frowning into nothingness.

Finally, with Cherry and Linda still wrapped in their blankets, dreaming of prom hair and dresses and mountains of homework, Baba slams his cup onto the table, kisses Mama roughly on the forehead, and we're on our way.

To Umzi. Land of dreams.

The sun is lazing in his bed, as well. It is still dark. And I'm surprised to find that it feels different: not the fun, exciting dark of Friday evenings, but a sleepy dark that prickles at your skin.

We walk, and I miss my sisters' babble. Jeso's energy. The endless growing conga line of students on their way to school: a road full of uniforms, each with stories of the day before. Baba does not talk, so instead I listen to the streets: TVs and radios whispering apologetically, a baby fussing. Somewhere out of sight the harsh creak of pumping water and the plastic slap of plakkies against earth as someone else steps out into the dark. And above it all, one determined cockerel, braying warning that the day shall dawn.

Baba grunts at it, and I wonder whether he is always like this, or he just resents me being here.

I'm sorry, I want to say. *Thank you. Take a chance on me—you'll see.*

But Baba has his head down and he does not look as though he wants a conversation.

And as we pass the still-closed grocery and Mama's salon and the Cokes café, Khayelitsha *stirs.* You can almost hear it sigh and drag its feet up out of bed.

In Khayelitsha shacks and formal brick houses lean together side by side, but toward Umzi the corrugated iron grows less and the buildings stand up tall—two, three stories high. They *gleam*, even in the dust and with the litter trailing gutters.

And suddenly, we turn a corner, and even though it's familiar I'm surprised as Umzi stands before me looking different. Looking new.

J anet and I used to fantasize about running Baba's lunch at exactly the moment that Max and Mr. Sid came by.

We tried. Walking past the gray-smoke glass and glancing quick, but Baba always frowned, and neither of us ever dared open the door.

Once, we staked the place from behind someone's car across the street. It was Janet's birthday and all she wanted was to catch a glimpse of Max. An autograph, if she was lucky. A shake of the hand. And so we sat there hidden on the curb, tracing hearts into the road dust with our toes.

After three hours, we ate Janet's birthday cake from squares of pink-striped tissue.

It was *good*, all butter sweet.

And on a sugar high we laughed and laughed and I told her that she could have Max—I would marry them myself, become a pastor—if I could have a show.

"Whoever heard of a religious DJ?" she laughed. "DJ Godlovez. Slammin' Prayer Queen."

I shrugged.

"Worth it. Anyway, I'll be unique."

She sighed, all happy, and she leaned against me and she whispered, "You're certainly that."

And we'd have waited more, long into the dark, our parents' wrath be damned, but the car's owner saw us by his precious ride and chased us, yelling such vile things and promising to find our mothers.

We never dared to try again.

All that to say that though I've wandered past Umzi HQ a thousand times, hands in pockets, dreaming of a future far too big for me, I have never pushed against the heavy door. Never been inside.

UmziRadio smells *different* than I'd imagined. Of paper and old coffee mugs and not the busy hub of *cool* I had concocted. Still, I breathe in deep as Baba leads me through the door.

This is *it*: where all the songs hang out and play.

Welcome, welcome, listeners, to the Neo Show. Today is all about success, and boy, do I have a lineup for you.

We're starting with Blk Sonshine's "Building." Because everybody needs something strong to build on if they're going to make it.

And as we walk across the foyer, I feel exactly like the tree that Masauko Chipembere sings of, growing from a seed, roots firming with every step.

I'm *here*.

In the foyer. Staring out across the desk onto the street. Mama would be pleased to know that my first hours of work at UmziRadio were not spent on a big grand tour or playing with the mixing desk or *fraternizing* with the stars. No.

I stood with Baba at the desk, so close that I could almost feel the scratchy polyester of his one and only suit.

We stood and stood and stood.

There's a radio half-buried under a haphazard stack of red-spined log books, dials just waiting to be turned. But it's dusty with neglect and Baba scowls deep when he sees me looking at it. The radio is not part of his day.

And so we stood beneath the buzz-hum of the lights and ceiling fan, and Baba told me, with the reverence of secrets handed down, how to greet a person coming through the door:

"Good morning, sir. Good morning, madam. Fine day, isn't it?"

How to check for ID hanging around people's necks, and in it's absence, ask if I can help.

How to read the In/Out book. The *big responsibility* of not letting just anyone walk through those doors. And how to phone upstairs, to the offices and newsrooms and the other places locked away.

At eight, Baba signed for a delivery.

At nine, another.

And at ten the door opens and in steps Mr. Sid, bigger than I had imagined, all gut and suit and cowboy hat and sharp sharp suit. With him comes a gust of outside air that smells like pink camellias.

I imagine passersby laying the winter flowers at his feet.

Mr. Sid was kind of a big deal. The township *hero*, risen from the ranks and proving that it can be done.

Everybody loved him.

I loved him. And now he's here, not five meters away.

"Good morning, sir."

My father has always filled the room, big and loud and sure. But somehow, standing before Mr. Sid, he's no more than his role. A man behind a desk.

I flinch at the thought, even as I stare in awe.

The big man does not even look at Baba, and I *know* he hasn't noticed me. And then he's gone, past the desk and through the doors into the inner sanctum of the station, and I'm left with an emptiness I can't describe.

Baba coughs. Adjusts his stance. Shuffles papers.

I follow his lead. Straighten up my shoulders. And we stand.

This place is not what I imagined. It's too quiet. The wrong sort of big. Perhaps Baba was right.

Soon after Mr. Sid, the door swings in again, and this time the noise enters first.

Laughter. Jostling. All the warmth of Umzi.

"Shaaaame. There's *no way* I am eating that."

"Come *on*, the listeners will *love it.*"

"So you do it, then."

"I'll treat you."

"Yah? Treat me to what? Gold Ferrari. Oysters on the beach?"

"Noooo—"

Max and Sammi and another girl walk in, all draped across each other, slurping coffee through tall straws.

And suddenly I feel like I am really here. They're gone in seconds, through the doors, but I imagine that the music's in the building, and it reaches even here.

I stand a little straighter. Listen harder to my father's breathing, his occasional instructions. And I feel the rhythm of it in my bones.

Upstairs, in this magnificent place, the golden voice brings music to the city, helps it move one foot before the other. And I'm part of it, the first face that suitors see, guarding the doors.

By the time we're home, I'm *starving*. I've never stood in one place for so long, and my calves burn and my feet ache, and all I want to do is sit beside my father at the table and dig into supper. But Mama has me heading for the tap in seconds.

The streets are full of Khayelitsha evensong: cooking pots and families, children running wild in the last dregs of the sun, and people drifting home.

If you listen hard enough, there's birdsong too, and crickets: everywhere the settling in and heralding of night.

I lift my hands up to the pump and push-pull-push the handle.

The mamas and the grandmothers, they make this look easy, but it's not. It takes my weight to make it move at all, and all the water's settled deep, with a long way to travel.

Push-pull-push—Finally, in a great sputter, there is water in the bucket. And when it's full I pause just long enough to catch my breath and switch the buckets underneath the spout, and then I start again.

Push-pull-push—

"Eh, chica, looking goooood."

I tense. Look up.

He's tall. Not much older than me, I'd guess.

I want to tell him to mind his own, but he walks with a swagger and a mean look in his eye, and suddenly the streets seem bare of anyone to see. I swallow down the fear and irritation, and keep pumping.

"What's up? Can't take a compliment?"

Eyes down. Don't look.

"Ehhhh, you no good anyway." He spits, and swaggers down the street.

Cherry and Baba are deep in conversation about tax, its benefits and pitfalls, when Jeso turns to me and asks around a mouthful of potato, "How was your first day?"

"It was—" I think of all the standing standing standing, and the staring and the silence, but . . . the first line of defense. And Maximillius behind those doors, the pulse of it right there. And a smile tugs at my lips.

"Nothing special," Baba growls. "You'll see one day. Isn't that right, Neo?"

I lower my gaze. "Yes, Baba."

And the conversation moves to other things, but Jeso has this look of curiosity upon his face, like he knows there's something more.

I almost text Janet. Tell her that her dream man fills the room with a *buzz*, that he smells of sweet coffee and aftershave, that I was there.

I almost ask her to come meet me at the BigTall tree.

I want to. But I remember circling like dogs, and anger rises till I'm hot around the ears. And anyway, what would I say? I got into the building . . . and was stuck behind a desk? He didn't even look at me? That Baba's right, I am a desk troll? When you think about it, getting through the door is nothing. Anyone could get that far.

It's hardly the studios and picket fences of the futures we always imagined. So I switch off my phone, and just wish that she was here.

It's late when Jeso burrows in beside me, underneath the blankets.

"Hey," he says.

"Hey. What's up?"

I wrap my arms around his skinny body, feel the warmth and weight of it, and wait. "What was it really like today?"

I wish that I could tell him that I'd seen the studios, had tea with all the stars. But Jeso knows a lie. "Okay, Baba's right, it's awful: standing, waiting, no one even looking at you. But . . . it's not. It's like . . ." I stop, try to find words that Jeso might understand. "It's like football. When you're on the field, you don't always have the ball, isit? But when you score, you score, and the *team* wins. You don't always kick the goals, but you're still part of that team."

He thinks. "Which player are you?"

"Tryouts, I guess. Or pre-tryouts. Or the water girl. But I'd like to be out on the pitch."

"Neo?"

"Yeah?"

"We are still talking about music, right?"

"Yeah."

He snuggles deeper. "Then you'll be a star."

"Thanks, bru."

We're quiet for a moment, until Jeso moves. My brother is transparent even in the dark, and I can feel the grin wave right through his body. "I scored a hat trick today. In real football."

"You did?"

"I did! In five-a-side at lunch. Big William was in goal and he's big and never misses."

"Except he did."

"He did. It was beeeautiful. Like I couldn't even believe it."

"A'ight, it looks like we both had a good day, then."

"Yeah." He melts into my arms, already half-asleep. "Nee?"

"Mm-hmm?"

"I'm glad."

The next day I wake with a single thought: *There's always music. Everywhere.*

And I am going to find it in the silent, too-big world of work.

I start on the way there, counting footsteps, waiting for the beat. And there it is: I find it in a memory. My bestbest friend and I walking down this selfsame road and singing marching singing, each in turn.

Shay shay coolay—
—Shay shay coolay
Shay shay cofisa—
—Shay shay cofisa

The two of us laughing all the way, slapping hands and knees in time to the old nonsense rhyme, then always, always breaking out into a run when we reach one . . . two . . . three . . . four . . . five . . .

Running faster faster, till our hearts raced with excitement and we crashed into the classroom, breathless, and we'd won.

I should have known when Mr. Sid stopped in the entrance hall and looked at me, that this was not like that. But it felt like winning everything. And it sure felt as though the music led me where I had to be, past the constraints of school and the objections of my father right into the arms of destiny.

And I suppose, as a minor key leads on and shifts into another, brighter key, it did.

But this was then, and I knew nothing but the stomach flip of Mr. Sid looking at us.

"Who's this?"

Baba looks at Mr. Sid's chest as he answers, not quite daring to raise his eyes. "My daughter. She needed a lesson in a proper day's work."

The founder of Umzi flicks his gaze to me, and I feel his eyes move up and down and back again, taking stock.

I pull my face into a smile, and Mr. Sid smiles back, too wide.

The next day, Mr. Sid does not just bustle through, he stops at the front desk, and he looks at me, and looks at Baba and looks at me again.

"Still here?" he says.

"Yes, sir." I try to push the pride up to the surface of my skin, to let him see how much his station means to me in those two words.

He nods. "And your father, he's working you hard?"

I glance at Baba, unsure what to say.

"It's quite a sentence for a girl, eh? In this dusty old station instead of chilling at the beach with all your friends?"

My father shuffles papers, does not quite meet Mr. Sid's eyes as he says, "She won't be a nuisance, sir."

"Ohhh, a pretty thing like her couldn't possibly be."

My stomach squirms at that, and I rush to put him straight before he thinks that that is all I am. "Actually, I'm quite a fan."

"Oh, really?" He pushes his cowboy hat farther up his forehead, revealing one quirked eyebrow.

"Yessss. I've listened to Umzi for as long as I remember. It's . . . an honor to be here."

"Ahh, yes. Well, that's good to hear." He licks his lips. "You know? There's more to this station than the doorway, and a fan should see. Why don't you both come upstairs? We'll talk."

I hear "foolish notions," "school," "education," and "responsibility." Then Mr. Sid, big and sure and clear even through the door. "I don't give rocks who you are—if you're in this building, you are mine. And that includes your daughter. . . . Send her in, please."

Did Mr. Sid—*the* Mr. Sid—just stand up for my dreams?

Mr. Sid sits in a leather chair behind a desk.

He's *big*. Bigger than he was out in the hall. Or at least his person fills the room.

He's sitting right in front of me.

Breathe, Neo.

Mr. Sid looks up. I meet his gaze, hope my hunger and my dedication show. But the way he watches as I cross the room, it does not feel like recognition. It feels like being stripped down and trussed up and weighed.

Nerves.

That's all it is.

Just nerves. Mr. Sid is *wonderful*.

"Biltong?"

He takes an ornate silver knife from his desk, fingers it lightly, turns it over in his hands before he *chops*, strong and precise, as though he held a miniature machete. He grins, pops a bite-size piece of peppered dry-meat right into his mouth, and *chews* as he holds out the plate to me.

"No, thank you."

He shrugs, sets the plate and knife neatly in front of him.

"Soda, perhaps?" I notice the minifridge behind him. "Beer?"

"No thanks."

"Suit yourself."

"So. Your father tells me that you want this life." He waves a hand casually across his office.

I nod. I don't trust myself to speak.

"Hm."

He watches me. Stares. And I feel small, but at the same time, there's this true pure golden nugget of my soul, glinting from inside me, and under Mr. Sid's eye it feels precious and appreciated.

"You knowww"—he draws it out—"UmziRadio was *top* in rankings this year. Best commercial station, voted by the public. Best show, best presenters, best best best."

I nod again. I *do* know.

"That does not happen with small thinking, small people, small ideas."

"No, sir."

"All right."

All right? What does that mean?

"So tell me." He smiles, sort of, as he leans back in his chair. "What is it that makes you one of us? What makes you a radio rat? What makes you Big Thinker Neo?"

Now's your chance. Impress him. Tell him how you've always wanted this. How you've practiced in your room and with your friends, and you've listened to all of Umzi's archives at least twice.

"I, er . . . music." I wince at my stupid words. "I mean to say . . . yes, I love music. I love the way it means something. Tells us something about us. And if radio distributes that, it's like we make connections, and it tells us who we are together."

Breathe.

Mr. Sid just sits there, eyebrow quirked. Waiting for more?

"I like . . . not specific artists, actually. I like *everything*. I like that different styles are like a different *skin* for music heart.

That . . . that's what I think Umzi is. One-size-fits-all *skin*, for everyone. The whole community."

"Mm-hmm." Was that a smile? A twitch? Masked disapproval?

"And . . ." What more does he want? "If I can be useful, I'll be the best . . ." What? "The best that I can be. You won't regret it."

He waits, just a second, then leans forward and sucks the air in through his teeth. "UmziRadio is *passion*, Miss Mahone. Passion for this Khayelitsha life. It's young and hip and relevant—"

And I *know* he's going to say that I'm a fool. Too bone-heavy and brain-dull to be of use. That I clearly don't have what it takes.

And I'll be back downstairs with Baba, invisible to those who do.

"And you might just fit in. Not, of course, in place of school. Your baba's very clear on that." He winks, and for a second I feel *wrong*, but he continues: "After school. And I'm afraid there is no pay. This is an internship. It's work. The bottom rung."

I nod. "Yes, sir. Thank you, sir."

I'm on a *rung*!

I leave that room on *air*, so high that I barely notice the Mr. Sid licks his lips and reaches for another piece of meat before I close the door. My mind is elsewhere, in the studios with music in my ears.

Y
ou know . . . we should double-date."

"Eh?"

"You and me and Tsimo and whatever his name is." My sister grins conspiratorially at me over her freshly painted nails. Or rather, she grins at my reflection in the mirror.

I pull out my headphones and stare. "What?"

"Oh, come onnnn, you *are* seeing him again now that she's let you out, aren't you?"

I freeze. I can't even think about it. It's too risky. And of *course* my sister takes that as a yes.

"Well then. It'd be *beastly*."

I picture Tale, sitting in the sand beside me, legs wrapped in a silk sarong. I see her poking at the meat upon the braai, the air thick with the smell of it against the salt of sea. I see her laughing with my sister—

And Linda falling shocked into the water, drowning at the shame of it.

Mama with her trust.

I shrug.

Linda raises one perfectly shaped eyebrow. "Afraid to be seen with me? Think I'll show you up? Come on." She launches across the room onto the bed and *pouts*.

"No thanks." I *can't*.

She pushes her face right up next to mine. "Please please please please please? I'm just *dying* to meet him."

I can't. It would ruin everything.

"I'm sorry. I just have to focus on the *music* for a while."

Linda flops beside me in disgust. "You're *hopeless*. Have I taught you nothing? You don't have to choose."

But she's wrong. I kick her away, shove my earbuds back in, and ignore her. Because, yes, I really, really do.

Baba is all, "You will not miss a class, you hear?" and, "The man says jump, you jump, and make damn sure you land on both your feet and don't step out of turn. The man's your boss now, and you'll take instruction or you're back with me."

But in my head there's *music*, high-pitched, humming in my ear. UmziRadio.

A station built with Khayelitsha hands.

And I hear Max and Sammi and the news guy welcoming the new recruit with open arms: *Come, be part of it. UmziRadio is you. It's yours.*

That night I do not sleep. I lie there in the dark, staring at the ceiling, listening to the late show, and let the voices wash right over me. And I'm not staring at the ceiling, I'm staring at my future: buzzing bright, all headphones and pitch monitors and music. Music *everywhere*.

My best friend and I have dreamed of this day: the day our futures rise.

And I almost text her sorry, almost tell her everything and ask her to come meet me at the BigTall tree. But my best friend would see Max first. She'd see parties and the gossip and the street cred. Not the music.

And just for a little while, I want this to be all about the sound.

chool is *stifling*. Time is slow, and all this energy inside me builds and builds and builds and there is nowhere I can let it out.

This classroom is too small. And for the first time I *reeeaaally* notice the old, paint-flaked tables and the long cracks in the walls. For the first time I *really* notice just how dry and dull the teacher's voice is.

There's music waiting for me outside of these walls, and I just want to leave.

Janet sits across the room, right in the corner, next to Cebile. Good, sweet pastor's girl Cebile, who thinks that friendship is fried iced-sugar donuts and cat's cradles and notes passed underneath the desk. A girl so not-like-us. My best friend must be really *mad*.

I try to catch her eye. If I can just catch her attention, make her look at me, maybe we can catch what we once had, and I'm waiting for my bestbest friend to ask. Waiting to share the *oh my goodness* nerves.

Because she'd get it.

Not everything, maybe, but my bestbest friend was there for my sixth birthday, and the karaoke party where I insisted on making every song choice.

She was there when I worked extra hard for three whole months to buy the Walkman with both radio and CD player; when it broke, and my heart shattered with it, and Janet—headstrong, ballsy Janet—took it to the store and argued until they gave her another. She was there when I bought my first reggae beat and she's the one who pictured every frame—in detail—of the beachside video that she imagined we'd direct.

She *knows*.

But Janet does not ask.

And as I sit there in the classroom with this space between us full of the not asking, part of me is mad right back. Mad that she doesn't know. Mad that she wasn't right beside me, camped outside the door or hiding underneath the desk or listening in on her cell phone. I'm mad for everything we've lost and everything between us and I'm mad because *Cebile*. And by the time I'm done with all the reasons that I'm mad, I'm almost glad that my best friend won't look this way.

Walking down the same old streets today, it's different. The rich sun bounces brighter off the pavements, trees glow greener than they should in winter-leaf. That winter blossom smell that followed Mr. Sid hangs in every street, and everything is warm and fresh and new.

I want to fit in this new world, but I feel small. My legs shake underneath me out of nervous pride, torn between bouncing confidence and *Quick, let's run away.*

I do the only thing I can: turn my thoughts to music. To the beats of fresh young kwaito kids and the strength of voice of singers old. To the solidarity of it—the band and I, our bottles raised as one. And then, as my feet begin to find a rhythm, to rooms and rooms of music: endless walls built out of old cassettes; machines that run on sound waves; servants of sound, paid in tickets to the most exclusive gigs.

Music is religion, and UmziRadio a church full of disciples, honoring and celebrating, preaching to the world at large.

Baba makes a show of handing over an ID badge, pointing out the place I have to sign for it. Disapproval fills the foyer, and when I step into the corridors it's like walking out into fresh air.

I'm here.

In UmziRadio.

I am a disciple.

ll right. Lesson one."

I'm concentrating so hard that it almost feels like dreaming. Mr. Sid raises a finger. "I like my tea *milky sweet*. The way the British do, but boil it with the milk, not water. Mmm, the British know their tea."

I know it's only tea, but up here, in the inner rooms of Umzi-Radio, the staffroom with its woolen couch, the electric kettle and tiny stove, and the posters signed in silver Sharpie, a room that smells like coffee and exhaustion, that you can imagine sitting in at midnight, arguing over the playlists . . . I feel like Mr. Sid is *trusting me with secrets*. Letting me into this secret world of musical success.

Which room is this in Umzi's church?

Community or prayer?

After learning which special-leaf tea is Mr. Sid's, which mug he likes, where the paper and the business cards are stored, I spent my hours in a cupboard.

"It's not much"—Mr. Sid grinned conspiratorially at me as he pushed open the door—"mostly junk. And there's probably spiders in the actual records. But it's been a while since anyone looked at this stuff. Who knows what we are hiding?"

My job: to take the CDs and the vinyls and separate them from the dust and wildlife and the props, and *order them*, make sure everything is catalogued—artist names and tracks and albums— make sure everything is findable.

I blink at the dim-lit rows of shelves, stacks of paper, jewel cases and record sleeves, tumbled into one another. Boxes piled up to my shoulders. Music *everywhere*. And as Mr. Sid retreats I breathe in the warm paper-plastic-dust of it: the smells of songs lost in the dark.

In the almost dark, the bare, age-yellowed bulb above casts more shadow than light, and the blue-tinged glare of the computer screen makes everything look dead. I guess they don't use this room much. But it's enough to see by, so I step forward and reach for the first box.

CDs. Mostly from the eighties.

The job is endless.

Artist, track, album, year, record company, key words.

Artist, track, album, year—

Mama would be pleased. It is the kind of task she'd want. *Find her something boring. Physical. Find her something dull. Find her something so mundane that when her eyes fall out from boredom she will see the error of her ways.*

There is *everything* in UmziRadio's collection: old spirituals and psalms and gospel adaptations, and pop and rock and soul and jazz of every era, and there's rap and heavy metal, kwaito, choral pieces, techno, metal, everything in every hue and combination. Each box is something new. A treasure.

Sometimes there are notes, hand scrawled. Set lists and annotations. Once, a love note and a shopping list on two sides of a menu.

Vinyl. The musician's dream, the music's past literally worn into the record with each listen.

This job could take me years. And I don't mind at all.

When we were six, Janet and I fell out over something. I don't remember what. But I do remember she was wrong and I was right. I knew it the same way I knew that fire's hot. It *burned*.

I stomped around for weeks. I hated her. I *practiced* hating her, over and over, under my breath.

But I missed her, and that ate away at me. I missed her bossiness and the way she always knew what we should do to fill the day. I missed her wild and crazy stories of the palace we would live in and the princes we'd bewitch. I missed sitting beside her and knowing we were friends, knowing she was there and fierce and loyal, and mine.

I broke, placing a yellow sorry note into the wall.

When we were eleven, Janet noticed her first boy. Really noticed, I mean—not the games of innocence.

She giggled when she saw him. Passed him notes in class. She wrote his name into the dirt a hundred times, and sat there starry-eyed and sighing.

I didn't get it.

One day we were talking music, passing her brand-new phone back and forth to beat each other's scores on Angry Birds—she was better, always; her fingers knew the weight of it, exactly where the buttons were, by instinct, where I had to concentrate—and the next she'd changed.

At twelve, she tried to dress me. Nothing new. We shared our wardrobes freely, although more often I raided hers—my own pickings were smaller, older, let in and let out and worn a thousand times before. Besides, I didn't care so much—but that day, I was sick of it, self-conscious and resentful of my best friend's *everything*.

"Here." She tossed a lightweight blouse across the bed. "This might soften all that fierce. Get you noticed."

I stepped back from the growing pile of clothes and glared at her.

"I. Am not. Fierce."

"Yahh, sure."

I left. We did not speak all the next day. But as Janet drifted toward a circle of our classmates, my chest hurt, and when I scored a copy of *Kulture Noir*, I wanted to share every lyric, every sliding rhythm, with someone who'd see where it marked my heart.

I wore that blouse for a whole month to say *I'm sorry*.

I miss her. And the entire journey home I try to make the words fit in my head, the words to drag her back to me, the words to tell her that my dreams are coming true. But the words aren't there.

Eventually, I just text: I have news.

Nothing. No reply. So I add: Mr. Sid has goat-breath.

Janet replies sixty seconds later:

WAIT

WHAT?

Send Message: J

Meet me by the tree?

• • •

The Cape air has that damp-and-stormy winter quality to it, and laps cold at your skin.

Janet's late, of course.

I wait. I always wait, itching for things to be right between us. But it makes me nervous. What if she doesn't show? What if she's *dragging* herself here, already done with us.

I lean back against the tree trunk, feel the roughness of it grounding me, as solid as a lullaby.

Janet's *always* late.

"Sorry, sorry, sorry!" Janet bursts into view. "Oh my God! Mr.—Tell me *everything*."

I wait for her to catch her breath, but my best friend is restless, shakes my arm impatiently.

"Okay!"

And I tell her everything, from needing music, needing more, to Mr. Sid's eyes moving up and down and judging, right up to the cupboard of secrets and dreams.

"I'm *in*!"

"Oh. My. God. OhmyGod. You're in! You're actually in the building, up the stairs!"

I nod, and a flicker of realization crosses her face. "OhmyGod, was Max there? Did you see him?"

You'd think that this would be the end. The final, desperate note: my best friend unable to see what really matters. But that one line, Janet's—in her way—excitement, was everything I needed, and the air between us cleared. We know this road, and we are okay.

I spend all week in Umzi's cupboard after school, gently opening one box at a time and witnessing the songs of yesterday. The shelves, too, are thick with jumbled piles. I clear off the top one, start an *A* row of CDs, and then start piles for *B* and *C* and all the rest, stacked up on the floor.

After an hour I switch and catalogue the things I've found, absorbing names and dates and filing them away inside my brain. There's so much new music I almost cannot bear it: so many names and tracks and live recordings, and I want to hear it all.

When you sit in a silent, empty room, you notice things, and in this one, I can feel the music breathing, leaking out from every box, every jewel case, whispering in the walls.

Listen, it says, *Listen to my story.* Desperate and longing.

And I try.

I borrow Baba's radio, and when I'm not listening to the CDs I'm adding to the files, I tune in to the rooms next door. It's strange to think that just a few meters away someone is *actually* saying everything I hear, that it's not some robot or a distant and untouchable star.

Strange, but *perfect.*

So I sit there and I sort and catalogue and listen, and at the end of three hours I boil Mr. Sid his tea.

His door reads EXECUTIVE CEO, and I wonder, as I knock, why his name is not below it. But every day before I can surmise, he grunts, and I place the tea upon his desk and ask him whether that is all he needs, then he shoos me home.

• • •

I try telling Janet that it's not as glamorous as she thinks. That I am *literally* in a room of boxes, with spiders and dead skin for company. And no, I haven't met Max at the water cooler, and no, I will not have my own show in a week or two.

But I don't think she believes me.

"What do you *do*?"

"I listen to the music that's forgotten. And I file. I am, in fact, a secretary."

"Yes, but what else? What's it like? Who have you met?"

"Nobody . . . unless you count the *A*s: the Abaqondisi Brothers to Amampondo, so far."

She shakes her head. "No, I don't." And then, "Wait, really? Nobody? You're inside the place of all your dreams and you've done *nothing*? What *are* you, a mouse?"

I shrug. "I'm learning. And I'm busy. And—"

"It sounds like a waste to me. Get out and introduce yourself. Put your ideas on the boss's desk. Find *Max*."

"It's not like that. I can't—"

"Why?"

It's already everything. But I don't know how to put that into words. It's something that you feel. And I want my bestbest friend to know so badly that the words are out before I even hear them in my head: "Why don't you come with me?"

"*With you?*"

"Yes!"

"To *UmziRadio*?"

"Uh-huh."

"Won't you get in trouble?"

But once we get past Baba the hallways are empty and I've barely seen a soul, and I want my bestbest friend to understand.

"C'mon. It's Second-Monday Take-a-Friend-to-Work Day."

Janet *laughs*. "Oh well, in that case, it'd be rude not to, hey?"

"It would. Umzi would be *mortified*."

We buy Cokes—Janet buys them, but I am not saying no—in the MotoloCafe and we drink them as we walk toward the station, dawdling as much as time allows.

I am excited-nervous.

"You remember the plan, right?"

Janet rolls her eyes. "Yah."

"Yeah, sorry, just checking."

Janet pulls the collar of her shirt up tall. "Just like in the movies."

"You look like an idiot."

"Eh, *fine*. Serious. We're serious."

I dig an elbow hard into her ribs. "We don't have to do this."

"Sorry, sorry. I want to . . . but why don't you just *ask*?"

I could ask Mr. Sid, it's true—tell him my best friend is his station's second-biggest fan, after me, of course. But this is work, and I want to be the grown-up intern, not a girlish fan.

Besides, we'd have to get past Baba, too.

I squirm, and Janet sees. "Ehh, all right." She stops just around the corner from the station. "Ready?"

"As I'll ever be."

I push open the big glass door and step into the station.

"Hi, Baba."

My father grunts and waves me past. He still won't really look at me; no congratulations, no asking how my day has been. It hurts, for as long as it takes to cross the foyer and push through the second doors. And then I'm home, safe in the inner sanctum, and phase one is complete.

I wait for five minutes, then text Janet:

Send message: J
The cuckoo bird has landed.

Now it's all on her: my bestbest friend, SAFTA winner.

I slip into the hallway and I wait, imagining that I hear her stepping into the foyer, telling Baba that she has a *ton* of homework I forgot: She'd be quick. Just business.

I imagine Baba standing taller, straighter: *See? Neo cannot do it all. I told her.*

And then I hear her, *takkies* squeaking on the plastic lino stairs. She did it!

Janet bursts through yet another set of doors into the corridor, all triumphant smiles. "Hi!" And then, "Wohhh. Neo. This is *UmziRadio.*"

"I *know* . . ." Janet and Neo in the palace, right where we belong.

"C'mon. Show me where you work."

It's quiet. Quieter than usual, as though Janet being here is muffling the music in the walls, and I *wish* that there were speakers everywhere, or that a huge winning team would spill out of a meeting room, all victory and jostling and hurling rugby balls across each other's heads.

Or that a street crew would break out before us, challenge the two rookies to a duel.

Something.

Any sign of the life that leaks out across the airwaves.

Anything that lets her see.

But the halls are like a silent breath.

A church.

And if the station is a church, the dusty archives room is a shrine. Catacombs, except that its inhabitants are very much alive.

We step inside the cupboard.

"You weren't kidding?"

"Nope."

"You work in a *cupboard.*"

"Yes, I do."

She breathes, takes it all in. "Look at all this stuff!"

"I know!"

"Is it like . . . old?"

"Some of it, I guess."

I show her the catalogue, and it feels like I am baring something of my soul. "Just *look.*" I breathe. "It's like . . ."

Janet blinks. "A shopping list."

I grin. "Yes! Only the produce isn't beans or cabbages, it's *everything.*"

"You," my best friend proclaims loudly, "are a *massive* geek. A freak. *Nobody* gets that excited by a list of old dead guys who sing."

"I know."

She grins. "Glad we cleared that up. So what do you *do*?"

"I told you. I'm clearing out these boxes, trying to make sense of it, make space for everything, and make sure nothing's lost forever."

"Ehhh."

For a moment, Janet stands among the boxes, saying nothing. And I am afraid. What if she doesn't like it, doesn't get it? What if all she sees is the cupboard and the spiders and the sincere lack of Max and glamour and celebrity?

She looks at me, and looks back to the stack of boxes at her feet, and back to mc again.

"Can I help?" She grabs a box, pulls it open eagerly. And together we work.

"Records?" She pulls out a cardboard sleeve, gently turns it over. Pink Floyd.

"Yeah." I breathe.

I pull another from the box as Janet says, "My grandparents had a record player."

"Yeah?"

"Sure. They danced and danced to it, right in the living room, every Sunday afternoon right from the day that they were married."

"Mmm." I close my eyes, imagine it, two young things, growing old in their embrace, swaying to the music as the world spins forward all around them.

Janet pulls the record from its sleeve, strokes the second paper casing, then pulls it free from that as well. She turns it over in her hands, and back again.

"It's weird, right? All that music on this *thing*."

"I guess."

"Come on. It's not exactly practical, is it?"

I laugh. But I rather think that is the point. It makes you stop and think. It makes listening an *act*. A choice, in a way that radio and MP3s do not. Even CDs, you just click in the disc and there it is.

"Hey." Janet's voice is sharp. "What's this?"

"What?" I lean over to look at the vinyl disc she's holding.

"Someone's scratched this out. Look."

She's right. There are deep, angry lines etched the wrong way right around track three.

My chest tightens at the sight of it. "Who'd do that? How could they?"

"Maybe someone really hates these guys?"

I nod. Swallow. And my heart beats hard.

I *want* to believe that it is only one. An angry fan. A terrible mistake. But I spin the box around and there in big, messy letters is marked DO NOT PLAY. I take another LP from its sleeve, and it is the same again.

There's another.

And another.

The third has notes in thick black pen upon the sleeve: INDECENT. INDECENT. FOUL.

Another: PLEASE DO NOT PLAY TRACK 6 ON SIDE B.

And: SYMPATHIZER.

There's Miriam Makeba, Stevie Wonder, Mzwakhe Mbuli, Diana Ross, Abdullah Ibrahim . . . name after name of stout musicians with their work defiled. I let my fingers trace over the damage, imagine the crackle of a bouncing needle finding nothing but broken lines and static, the smooth-strong voices gone. The singers, with everything they have to say and each swelling emotion, silenced. I imagine the listener, desperate, wanting; feel their frustration at the silence. And my heart breaks into pieces.

Why?

Finally, Janet drops the last record back into the box.

I sit back on my heels and let the air out slow across my lips. I'm shaking.

So much music, gone forever.

Why?

"So, this stuff . . . it's like, history, right? A . . . musical grave-yard? A museum?"

"No!" Instinctively, I pull the box of broken records closer. "Music doesn't *die*; it remakes itself every time it's played."

That's why it hurts. I cannot shake the fact that *these* tracks are slashed and buried in a cupboard, lost forever.

"Huh." My best friend frowns. "You know, you're pretty wise sometimes."

"Thanks?"

"Yeah. Stop it. It's making my head hurt. 'S like being at school all the time." I think she's joking, but my bestbest friend falls quiet, chews upon her bottom lip, and suddenly there is that deep ravine of nervousness between us.

She doesn't get it. After everything.

And then it rushes out across her lips: "You know what educa-tion *I'd* like from this place?"

And I can't help it. I look at her nervous, worried, blushing face and *snort*, and gasp for air and then I'm laughing. We're laugh-ing. Together.

"C'mon," I say, when finally we stop for air. "Wanna see where the golden voice works all his magic?"

"Yessssss."

The light above studio one flashes orange. Show in progress. But down the hall, studio two sits empty.

"Here."

"Woh, really?"

"Yessss. Want to go in?"

"*Do* I?"

I'm glad.

Without my bestbest friend I'd sit inside my cupboard-shrine and that would be all. Wonderful, but limited. And here I am; we stand inside the smaller-than-you'd-think-it room, breathing in the wires-and-plastic smell of monitors and microphones, and if there were any room I'd *spin*.

"Eh, it's pretty tiny."

"Yeah, I guess."

"Hey, Nee, do you think we're breathing *Max's air* in here?"

I shrug. Perhaps; or perhaps in rooms like this the music and silver-tongue charm float in the air like dust motes. Maybe we're both breathing in raw talent.

"Oh, c'mon, it's a *joke*."

"I know."

Janet sinks into a high-backed chair. "All right, so, hit me."

"Eh?"

"C'mon, there's no one here. Hit me with your dream show."

"Eh?"

"YO YO KHAYELITSHA! THIS IS NEO AND I'VE GOT SOME *MUSIC* FOR YA! You know . . ."

And I grin, open my mouth to share a million and one ideas, and I *want to* but there are so many possibilities, all tangled before me like old forgotten cables, and I don't know how to even start.

"Uhhh."

"C'mon. Anything. What do you want to share?"

"I don't know! *Everything*, I guess. All of it. I want to take that catalogue and lift out all the old forgotten songs that meant something to someone once, and give them life again."

Janet leans back in her chair and grins, wide and in control. "I'd just like to remind you that we had a deal. I've been your manager for*ever* and I'm not going to stop just coz you've got a taste of the life." And quieter, she adds, "And . . . I think someday you will."

The whole thing, from the cupboard to the heart-wrench of the ruined tracks to this, takes less than fifteen minutes—the time we figured we could claim my best friend was explaining our assignment—but it changes everything.

I fall into a rhythm, Janet and I comfortable again, the music all around me. And it's good.

Have you ever thought about it? *Rhythm?*

The day in, day out? The ticking slipping sliding of the hours?

The way you move in time with it, sink into it, accept it?

Chores, lessons, Umzi, homework, chores, sleep, work, church.

Chores, lessons, Umzi, homework, chores, sleep, work, church.

Chores, lessons, Umzi, homework, chores, sleep, work, church.

Mama kept me busy. I am *sure* it was deliberate: every moment planned and executed. I'm sure she thought I'd hate it, that I'd turn my back on work in favor of the thrill of aimlessness. But I want this. I want to be just like Mr. Sid, to bring the music and the soul to people's lives. And I'll do anything to get it.

Besides, life without a rhythm is like *music* without rhythm. It's not music, it's just noise you cannot follow or control.

All around me, the piles of rescued, sorted music grow:

D, and Mister Devious's lyrics fill my ears as I list his catalogue, mingle with Errol Dyers almost comically as Cape-jazz-rap. And I realize *this* is why I love our music. Why I love this rainbow nation full of difference and tolerance. Because we live here side by side, and we take one another's rhythms and we twist them with our own.

It's *beautiful.*

F, and Deborah Fraser's strength sings clean, and Brenda Fassie stands there proud as though she's ever ready for a fight. These two women *own* those voices, make me glad-indignant standing here beside them. And then Freshlyground reminds me of lazy summers lying underneath the blue, blue skies with Janet at my side.

In the *I* pile, there is IppyFuze, *dirtier*, with Siya Makuzeni's gravel voice and discordant attitude delving deep and taking us down with her. And there is Izingane Zoma, *maskanda* music, Zulu folk with tradition at its heart, full of the rhythms of pasts and presents, full of undulating joy.

I keep on moving, adding to the declarations of who we are and were and who we'd like to be, bearing witness as I catalogue.

But there's a song missing. Silenced. Not by someone with a knife, but by expectation and by fear. And suddenly I'm desperate to hear it, because it's a part of *my* catalogue, of who I am and who I'd like to be.

Music's an addiction. Hits you hard and fast as blind-and-foolish love. And I had both afflictions.

And I know it's risky, I know that Mama wouldn't let me leave the house ever again, but I have to find her. I have to know whether that song still plays.

I try to hear her as I walk into the dark, but my mind is filled with the white noise of doubt.

And then, the warm folds of the bar, light spilling out into the street. And chatter. Real noise. Life. And there she is, sitting in the fairy-light booth beside the others, exactly as I left them.

I pause in the middle of the crowd, people catching up, laughing and leaning, and drowning the week's woes in beer and whiskey. A pianist in a straw hat sits upon the stage, filling in the spaces with rising scales.

I let the hot-tin wonder of it settle in my lungs, let the safety wrap itself around me. *Even if she doesn't,* I tell myself, *this, here, is enough.*

I breathe. And breathe again. And then I match my stride to the piano and step forward.

Cap sees me first, waves me over from under his baseball cap and hood, then goes back to the conversation as Tale leaps right to her feet. She meets me two steps from the table. "Ahhh, chiquita, you came back!"

Arms around me. Soap and sharp beer breath and rubber scent, catching in my hair as she kisses at my cheek. The whispered first notes of a song.

"Of course."

She hugs me for a second longer and then drags me back toward the booth. "We thought we'd lost you after Jed and Zebra's little show."

"Jed and Zebr— oh, that?" Heat radiates out from my face as I remember: teeth and tongue and hands. My gaze flicks toward them. Zebra waves. "No, you were *fine*."

"Uh-huh. And you, my princess, are as rose red as that sleeping beauty."

Eish.

"So hey, we *missed* you."

"Really?"

"Yeahhh. That pretty little face of yours glowing up the place?"

And I blush even harder as my insides shrink against her words.

"Oh, shush. No. I missed you. Really. Where've you been?"

"I . . ." Standing in the bar light, with Tale's rawness right in front of me, my news seems small and flimsy. I'm a glorified cleaner-secretary. Not even glorified. It's nothing.

But she's standing there and asking, and somehow, answering is easy, just because it's her. "In a cupboard, mostly."

"Eh?"

"Oooh, *closets*." Zebra squeals. "Do tell."

And I slide into the booth beside them and explain. I them all about Baba's work and how he's never let me go before. I tell them that it's all I've ever wanted, and now, sure I'm unimportant, but I'm *there*.

"That's great!" Tale beams as though she really means it, and I swell with pride.

"So, this Mr. Sid . . . He's getting what from you?" Cap asks.

"Eh, labor, I guess. But I'm there. I get to be there when it happens. I can learn."

Cap nods.

Underneath the table, Tale's fingers find mine, wrap themselves together, and we sit, for a second, comfortable together. And then she pulls away and suddenly her hand is elsewhere, resting on my thigh. Warm and solid and electric, and it's like her voice is running up and down my skin, all over it.

"I'm taking it and running!"

Tale *laughs*, sudden-strong and loud. And, oh—

Do they know?

"That sounded better in my head."

She chuckles. Leans in closer, soft and patient. "That's okay. And yes, you are."

I fall back in with them as easy as counting to ten, as easy as leaning in to Tale's touch. It's like I never left. More than that— almost like I've always been there.

We talk, about nothing in particular: our weeks, all the mundanities. And halfway through the night, as I watch them match each other's moves, bat judgments back and forth across the table, so close and so familiar and happy, I realize I don't know a thing about them. They're all older. So much cooler. And they're . . .

They . . .

Do things that I did not know you could. And it should feel wrong, shouldn't it? Sitting here beside them?

But as Cap leans back all casual, and Zebra shrieks more than he talks, and Tale's hand strays just a little higher—as the beer flows almost as free as the laughter, it does not feel wrong at all.

I worry for a moment that it should, that something's wrong with *me*. And then again that maybe they will see I don't belong. That I am not like them: too young, too . . . not enough. But when I tell them—laughing, joking—that my mother *literally* locked me up for running with a boy that exists only in her head, not one of them tells me to go back home, where I belong. They only smile, warm and reassuring, and Zebra, reaching up to squeeze Jed's hand, says, "My father and I . . . *argued*. All the time before I left. It's better now."

The conversation moves. We talk and laugh and talk some more, and in this tiny booth, among new friends, the song still sings.

Ehhhh, all right, let's play."

Half the class sits underneath the tree, legs extended in toward the center of the circle. Only Cebile and the quiet ones sit out, hiding in the classrooms.

These here are my brothers, sisters.

I am not a quiet one.

And so I sit beside my bestbest friend and play.

Truth alphabet was first invented in the first grade, all of us in turn naming a thing we hated: anger, bees, cherry cough drops, right through homework, funerals, the teacher with the crooked nose.

It looks a little different now.

A: What attracts you?

(A nice one)

B: Who is your *best* friend?

(Jeremy)

C: A condom, yes or no?

(Eh, no. Where'd I get it?)

The questions pass around the circle amid fits of laughter and the drumming of heels and occasionally shrieks of disbelief and lectures (*You* know *you can get them at the clinic, right?*).

I sit here hoping hoping that they'll stop before they get to me.

When Joseph, six places away, answers *P*—favorite position— by leaping to his feet and thrusting his hips back and forth, I realize. Six places. That leaves me with *V*.

My stomach drops. My toes curl tight, digging right into the earth.

I do not want to answer that.

I can't.

Janet answers *U*—underwear?—with confidence, as though she does not even care. "Blue," she says, "and lace."

And there it is, the only question she can ask.

"I'm sorry," Janet whispers, reaching for my hand as she announces the next question to the circle:

"*V*: Virgin?"

And I get up and walk away.

I pull away that week, claim homework and the station's work and tiredness.

No one says a word about it, but I know they know. I know they're judging.

Janet does not push.

I hide, fall into the life I want instead.

I lose track of time two nights in a row, lost in memories of the closeness and ease of company who does not care who has done what with whom, and lost again in piles and piles of musicians I've never heard of: bands who produced one album and stopped. Demo tapes and live recordings.

This playlist fills my ears, my heart, my brain, and I just wish that I could play it out where everyone can hear.

"Heyyy."

Janet crashes to the ground beside me and takes up an ear.

"Hey."

Do not judge me. Please.

You know *I haven't . . . that I'm not—*

"What we listening to?"

I breathe. "The latest from the *M*s."

M is delicious. *Full* of treasures.

Arthur Mafokate, "King of Kwaito," who brought us "Boss . . . You would not like it if I called you a baboon"; Vusi Mahlasela, soft and sad and easy. And Hugh Masekela with his bright bright horn.

I lean into her, clinging to this ritual of ours: We've been sharing music since the dawn of time. We know this move, and every-thing's all right.

Mango Groove swings breezy in our ears, and I feel lighter for it.

"Howzit at the station?" she asks after a moment.

"Okay."

"Really?"

"Yes."

And we fall quiet again.

We *are* all right.

"Y'know . . . *M*'s my *favorite* letter."

"Yeah?" And for a moment I think that maybe *All About Love* has sunk into her bones.

"Yaaah, doll. *Obviously.*"

Of course. It's not the beats at all, just Max.

Have you ever thought about *rhythm*?

The way you fall into it, play it hard until it leaves a groove?

The way you move in time with it, sink into it, accept it?

We know this move, just like we know the others. We've been friends forever.

But still there's Tale, sitting there, and still I cannot say.

I off-load to Tale. We sit by the bar with icy beer in hand, and slowly all my nerves unravel.

Tale gets it. She gets the music and the hiding and the wanting more. We talk. I tell her about finding treasures in the archives. She tells me that standing on a stage is all about becoming who you want to be, in front of the world.

She laughs when I tell her about the truth circle. Not unkindly—out of recognition, sorrow, comfort.

"Sounds like a fun game," she whispers. "Tell *me* what you can't tell them?"

And then I try to tell her about *A*: attraction, and the growliness and soaring and control.

"I just *love* a voice that drags me through the ditches," I say. And she leans into my ear and whispers low, "Like this?" Then breathier, as though the moment will expire if we don't taste it, "Come with me!"

And she moves *fast*, and I have trouble catching a hold on her fingertips and following. And then we're outside in the soft-damp of the shadows and I'm up against the shack wall and that isn't soft at all—it scratches, sharp and rough and dangerous, and *I don't care*. And Tale's standing before me, close, her fingers on the waistband of my jeans and her breath at my throat as she leans in and whispers, "Just like this."

I nod, helpless, and she moves again, closer, pulling, pushing, and I *want us to be one* and want her to stop and I never want this thing to end. And then she *kisses me*. Not like before, chaste and lips to skin. She *kisses*, and her soul climbs into mine and makes a nest, and together we *sing*. Great choruses, two voices forming a whole choir. She *kisses* me. And kisses me. And kisses me. The sound inside us rises, higher, higher, soaring, and she kisses me, and I kiss back and our two voices *play*. And suddenly it thrums inside me, deep and desperate. Raw. And I will never, ever get enough of this, this more-than-sound.

She shifts. Kisses me harder.

And her fingers find their way inside my jeans, letting in the cold-damp night. I *freeze*, and Tale shifts again, stroking, murmuring a reassurance at my neck, and I give in to her, relax, and—

"Tale." An apologetic cough, and Cap, looming round the corner, seeing Tale and me up against the wall. "Uh, sorry. We're up, like, now." And Tale *groans*, just loud enough for me to hear, and then she's gone, and I'm left outside in the dark, breathless and unfinished and alone.

L ust," the preacher says with relish as we sit in wooden pews and listen, "is inside us all."

I *squirm*. Feel him staring at me, judging. It's as though he *knows*.

"Lust! People, have you noticed that this generation—your children and your brothers and your sisters—has no *self-control*?"

Beside me, Mama mm-*hmm*s in agreement, and I wonder whether she can see into my mind the way she used to do when I was small:

Neo Elisabeth Mary. Someone ate the butter cake.

No, you can't. Don't even ask.

Neo Elisabeth, get in here. I can smell the trouble on you.

Pastor Simphiwe carries on:

"It's not their fault. For we are *made* of sin, and this world—this Western world—we live in, is out of control. Everywhere they look, there's *more*. Billboards everywhere: every restaurant, every store, vying for your money. And it's *easy*. It's easy to see these things, all big and bright and in our neighbors' hands, and to think, *Yes. I want that.*

"And we surrender to it. As much as we can. We have the nice shirts and the big big hair. We have the phones. We have the good, neat yards because we saw that ad for Weedokill.

"And we want more.

"We cannot have it without living well beyond our means, but that does not stop us *lusting*. We want *more*.

"*What's wrong with that?* I hear you say. *What is wrong with working for nice things?*

"But, friends, this marketing is like Lucifer saying to us, *Look, that apple over there? So ripe!*

"And we *know* we do not need it. Know we shouldn't. But we sin. And sin. And sin again, because in this battle between spirit and the flesh, we're never satisfied.

"I want to introduce you to a word." He pauses. "Temperance.

"Taste it. Sound it out. It's good, no?

"Temperance.

"This *temperance* is the thing that stops us. It allows us to choose: Say no.

"Say *no*, I'm not going to choose to worship at the house of Coca-Cola. I am not going to work and work and work for an iPhone. No. I'm going to spend my time with *God*. For I am a spiritual being, and when I die I cannot take my fancy heathen goods to heaven. No! I will not let the things that rot rule the eternal. I will not even let them rule today! I choose *temperance*. I will be drunk only by joy, and fattened only by the weight of love. My passion is for faith, for scripture and for goodness. *I choose self-control!*"

But "passion" spouts forth from his lips, loud and sure, and I feel Tale's lips on mine. Her hands on mine. Her music in my ears. And I want *more*. And I wish my mother were not next to me so that I could trace each place she's been. I don't want temperance at all. I want Tale's skin on mine and her voice wrapped around me, in me, through me, over and over, more and more, forever and ever and ever and ever, amen.

After church there is the gathering. A table is laid out beside the pulpit, laden with juice jugs and plates of malted rusks, and everyone shrugs off the obligations of the service. Laughing. Hugging. Swapping news.

Mama settles in beside the juice table and everyone—I do mean everyone—seeks her out. My mother, as the congregation's stylist, is *hot property* on Sunday gatherings. Everybody wants a piece of the week's latest.

Usually, this is my favorite part. The *family*. But today the crowds of earnest-happy people make me want to run. I feel like an impostor, and I wonder how nobody sees through my disguise.

I back away, head for the exit, and make excuses as each of my Mama's friends leaps out of nowhere asking after me.

I slip out of the big wide doors, but the gathering has spilled into the street, all *So-and-so's not doing so well; maybe we could, y'know* and *I have* no idea *what to do with him, sure, I have tried everything* and people pull their heads in close and favors out until every promise changes hands, each problem has a meal or untorn suit or workforce, and every troublemaker has a guide or two or three. Some days, I like to watch this busybody magic, but today I head left, right around the building, seeking quiet. And clearly I am not the only one; there's the squeaking moaning fast togetherness of a couple from the choir, still in their robes, all over each other, hidden from their parents' eyes.

I resolutely do not look, keep walking, and at a safe distance I drop to the ground.

Mama would belt me from here to hell and back if I brought headphones with me to the service, but now, sitting with the taste of Tale on my lips and the sound of strangers mating in my ears, I wish I had them, just this once.

I lean back against the church wall and close my eyes, dream myself back to the bar, leaning up against *that* wall instead. And Tale standing over me the way they're standing, over there.

Hands and growling voice and fingers strayed.

And in the church behind me, *someone* strikes up on the keyboards.

Amen Siakudumisa,
Amen Siakudimisa,
Amen Bawo, Amen Bawo,
Amen Siakudumisa . . .
Amen, Siakudumisa—

Just the keyboards at first, and then voices, one, two, three, six, ten. And I picture them inside, pulled in by the sound of praise, raising voices. And at my right, the couple raise theirs too, in different praise, and I'm caught here in the middle and I do not know where I belong.

eo, Neo, Neo!" Janet steps into the school walk, loud and grinning.

"Morning."

"Notice anything?"

I frown, and Janet steps in front of me and twirls, gesturing at her outfit, with the skirt hiked up a touch too high to be appropriate, and the top three buttons of her shirt undone.

I frown.

"I'm trying something new. You like?" She links her arm through mine before I have a chance to answer, and picks up the marching pace. "Tell me all about *you*. I miss you."

"We see each other all the time. Five days a week."

"Yeahhh, but we don't *see* each other. How's the station? How is Max?"

"I . . . don't know? I haven't seen him."

Janet purses her lips like a disapproving mother. "Neo Elisabeth Mary. Are you telling me that you live—metaphorically speaking— *right next door* to the golden voice and you've done nothing about meeting?"

"Yeah . . ." And at that moment a group of seven or eight boys, all from our class or the one above, step around us on their march to school. Someone in the rabble *whistles* and another jeers: "Good *morning*, ladies."

I almost tell her. Almost stop her in her tracks and ask her, *What about me? D'you see anything new?* but the words choke out before they hit my tongue. Not here. Not now. "Anyway, he's *yours*, right?"

"Damn straight . . . but you have to introduce me. How can you do that if you don't make the effort?"

"Okay," I sigh. "I promise that *when* I meet the golden voice, I'll lure him in for you. Okay?"

Janet nods. And as we walk to school, I wonder whether this is what we have become.

usic is religion, and Tale is its god.

If there was any trace of doubt left over of where exactly I belong, it vanishes on Friday night.

I sink into the empty booth just as the Storytellers take the stage. And Tale sings.

She sings the way she kisses: fierce, affectionate, and always in control.

And *oh*, I want it. I want *her*. So badly I can almost feel her fingers at my jeans.

She sings. And it's like slipping my hand in hers and walking on a summer's day to somewhere wild and overgrown and *ours*.

She sings. And I see underneath the cockiness, just for a second, just a flash of something raw and naked. And I see us climbing into one another, seeing everything. The flesh and soul and everything.

She sings, and *I* am flesh and soul, and suddenly I'm *sure*.

Flesh begets flesh, and I want it so.

When she's done, I have to bite my tongue and *not* call out for more, to bring her back to me. I want it so.

The band comes crashing back and Tale slides into the seat beside me, grabs my hand.

"Heyyy, Princess." And she kisses me all long and slow and raw, right there, with people everywhere. My stomach crawls. I almost pull away. But Tale's teeth are at my bottom lip, scraping hungrily, and instead I pull back *just enough* that she can feel it, and she reasserts the pressure, takes a hand to guide me back to her, and *grins*, widening everything.

"Wohohhh," Zebra squeals in delight. "Those tables just turned."

And Tale stands, and because she is still kissing, one hand at my neck and one around my waist, I stand up with her.

And she breaks away, just for a second. "We should—"

"Yeah, you should take care of that. Nice to see you, Neo."

But we are already gone.

Tale's faster this time, up against the wall, kissing, kissing, kissing, and her fingers at my waistband. And I can hear our voices running for each other, desperate to join.

But as I blink her in, I notice yellow bulbs strung up along a rooftop three stores down. And that light ruins everything, tempering the blanket-dark and holding it at bay. Reminding me that life exists. I *can't*.

I break away, pull back, out of her air.

She bites on nothing but the night, sucks in oxygen where there was flesh.

She's hurt. And I do not want her to stop. I want to give her everything.

"Not here."

She shakes her head, leans in toward my neck, all teeth and breath and asserting control.

"Not *here*," I breathe again. "Please. Somewhere private."

She *groans*. But then before I can apologize, she nods, and pulls me out into the exposed night.

I stumble after her. One step, two steps, three, her hand on mine. I don't know where we're going, but I'm *desperate* to get there.

My lips feel enormous, broken and alive and lost without her, and I *almost* tell her it's okay, that I was wrong, that out here is just fine.

There is a queue.

Waiting in the dark beside the bar.

Two queues, boys and girls waiting outside each small wooden shack.

People who can see us. And I almost pull away and run, but Tale stops and turns and she is there—right out the open and she doesn't care—breathing all the air out from my lungs, pushing her air down into the very depths of me, and I would follow her to Kingdom Come.

She *laughs*, a sound that peals against the silence. And she's shoving me right past the crowds and through the door.

"Sorry, ladies, sorry. This is an emergency."

There's grumbling, and fists banging on the door, even as it closes.

"I—"

"Shhh." Finger to my lips. And as she hooks the latch she *kisses* me.

"Hey!" Someone in the line is *pissed*.

"Occupied!" She breaks the kiss and calls out brightly, "Consider it out of order!"

"But shouldn't we—" I start.

"Shhhh. It's fine. They'll get the idea in a minute." She kisses me again, and I can't hear them anymore. And if you do not breathe too hard, all you can smell is fresh-dug earth, deep and old and clean. And if you do not look too hard, you do not see the gnats and blueflies battling the light; there's only Tale's body right in front of mine.

And then she kisses me again and I don't care.

I feel her undoing the buttons at my neck, working down down down until my shirt flaps open in our own imagined breeze, and I just *stand there*. For one second I feel *judged*. Vulnerable.

And I realize that I feel naked and I *am*, or almost, and I cannot help but giggle.

Tale quirks a smile and reaches to unhook my bra, and then she kisses me again, softly. It's a kiss that says *You're beautiful* and rips a whimper from my chest.

And then she's *everywhere*, a furious explorer, trailing nails and tongues and, *oh!* She runs a hollow rhythm up and down my ribs that makes me dance beneath her feather-touch.

She grins. And then she tires of it and *stops*. I arch my back, push my chest toward her, begging silently for more, but Tale *grins*. And then she *growls* and there is something new, teeth right where my bra should be, and biting-sucking, hard.

I throw my head back and I *scream*. And Tale works her tongue in circles, nibbles, *pulls*, and it is all that I can do to stay upright and not land one foot right in the latrine.

She stops. Switches to the other side and I feel *loss* and *longing* as the cold air bites, but then I'm swept up in a second round.

I breathe out the scream this time. Slow. Controlled. And Tale takes it to mean "more."

And then somehow, just when I think I might die from dizziness and pleasurepain, she's pulling off her vest and there is *muscle*, skin exposed. I fumble with her bra. Apologize. And she takes pity on me, reaches back and frees the catch herself. And I want to give her everything, but *how?*

She nods, her eyes all twinkle and encouragement, and I bend in to taste her neck, her clavicle, and run one fingertip along the bone right down her chest and to her belly button, and I let it hover there.

I *want* to walk my fingers lower. But I do not dare. Not yet.

She moans, pushes into me, and gives me confidence to take a nipple in my mouth. I test it, roll it round my tongue, and Tale hisses, "*Shhhhhhh.*" But I do not think she's asking me for quiet.

But this feels weird. I stop. Return to nuzzling her neck, and Tale opens her eyes wide. "Nuh-uhh," and guides my head back down to finish off the job. And so this time, as I suck, I let my fingers wander. Trace her waistband. And she *squirms.*

When anybody asks of my first time, I will tell you of the dance, the to and fro, the way she led. I will tell you how I did not *once* feel so lost that I wouldn't find my way. I will tell you that I loved her, that I wouldn't change a thing.

I will not mention the latrine, with the flies hitting the bulb, or how somehow, at one point, I *swear* my white shirt hung right in the hole, and sure, it might only be earth, but that shirt was never the same again. Because none of that matters. What matters is the dance beneath the light.

The dark feels different after that, like an echo of the night before. A safety net of memories. The ghost of skin on skin.

I longed for dark all day. As Mama had me scrub and clean and reorganize the hairpieces by length and weave and color. As we peeled the butternut and shucked the beans. Fetching, carrying, and everything too loud, too bright and unromantic in the sunlight.

And my feelings grew, soft but strong. And by the time night came and we all fell into our beds, I'm *ready* for it. For the dark. For Tale.

Cherry's breathing stills. Then Linda's. And finally I'm left alone.

I stare at the ceiling and I *breathe*. My skin shivers at the memory of her feather-touch. I breathe. I feel her kisses, hard. And I remember crawling into her, safe and warm and wanted for exactly who I am, and in the dark, I smile.

Music feels different too. As though every song has extra layers and I can see them all. As though it's right.

I sink into love songs and to bouncing ska and gravel voices singing of the hardships of this world. Everything I hear feels more alive.

It's like I've found my lyrics and stepped up onto the stage: the me I'd like to be. And I never want to step down to the floor.

J anet's waiting underneath the BigTall tree. I see her from a hundred yards, and suddenly I'm *nervous*.

Will she see the difference?

Sex is meant to make you glow or something, and she is my bestbest friend. She'll know.

And I want to tell her. I want to tell her everything. But there are people everywhere.

Someone drags a goat past on a rope, as if to illustrate. He's flustered, and the stubborn creature weaves and ducks and digs its hooves into the earth as though it knows its days are up.

Friends slap hands, goods make their way into pockets. Three men sit upon the curb and pass a brown bag back and forth: They look a little worse for wear.

People. Everywhere. And I can't tell her. But it's more than that—I cannot tell her because if she leaves it is the end of everything.

I slow my breathing as I walk. Breathe shallow, hoping that a lack of oxygen will turn me gray and ordinary.

"Hey," I say, landing beside her.

"Hiiii. Hey, did you hear? Max and Sammi are covering the Khayelitsha Pageant."

"Oh. I . . . guess that makes sense. It's a big event."

"Yeah . . . I thought I might enter."

I lean back against the tree, and then, because it seems like she is waiting for an answer, I ask, "Why?" Janet looks at me as thought I'm stupid. "I mean . . . you're smart. You don't need that."

Beneath the stare of disbelief, my best friend crumbles. So

unsure. And I want to pull her close and whisper that it's all okay, but that would make her tumble faster. "And you don't need it to get to Max, remember? You've got me."

She smiles, and I almost believe her.

"Here. I brought you something." I pull out a bag of Mama's sugar cookies, swiped from her customer stash, because somehow I thought today I might need them.

"Won't Grandma Inkuleko miss these?"

"Probably." I shrug. "I'll blame Jes's sweet tooth."

Janet laughs and takes one, and another, and another.

Better. This is almost normal. We can do this.

"Do you think I'm beautiful?" Janet asks, brushing golden-yellow cookie crumbs off of her lips.

"Of course," I say, without even thinking.

"I mean, *really* beautiful?"

We've had this talk before, Janet wondering aloud what kind of castle her strong jaw and smooth skin and straight black hair will win her, and I've never understood. My bestbest friend has everything.

Lust—Pastor Simphiwe's words sound in my ears—*breeds lust. Everything is not enough.*

"Really."

"Like, good-wife beautiful? Good enough for . . ."

"What?"

She shakes her head. "Not for what. For who."

"Then who?"

She grins raw, all embarrassment and fear as she changes the subject. ". . . What d'you think it feels like?"

". . . sex?"

"Yeah."

Teeth and hands and give and take and hotcoldlonging trust.

I want to tell her. Tell her that it will all be okay. That even in the dark, with sewage at your feet and bugs ahead, it's whispers of *You're beautiful*. But that's not what she means.

I shrug. "I think they say it hurts."

"Yeah . . . so . . . why does everybody want it?"

Music. Music made with bodies.

"I dunno, Jan. Old biology or something? The survival instinct?"

But it's so much more than that. It's safety.

I find Tale in the shadows, and she takes me by the hand and we climb up the night, up and up and up toward the moon.

We fall into a rhythm, Tale and I. One of music and of shadow and of riding in the space where both things meet.

Every time I see her, my heart strengthens. Every week her voice renews and restores me.

It's *fine*.

And I never ask her anything. Why would I? Tale bares her soul up there with every single song, and I know everything I need to know.

"Mmmmm," she says, lying spent beside me in the patch of dry grass just around the corner from the bar.

"Mm-hmm."

She laughs, rolls over, traces something—grass, I think—across my stomach.

"You're not really one for words, are you?"

"I guess so? I could say the same for you." And it is true. Around Tale I am not. Words fail me. Around Tale I don't need the words to tell her who I am.

"Yah. That's why I like you. It's . . . uncomplicated."

And she flips onto her knees and she's on top of me, sitting at my waist.

"Hold still," she says, pulling my hands up behind my head. And she leans down and kisses me, and starts the song again.

ometimes, I wish that we had more. Not only shadows, but the daylight. Open spaces.

I asked her once. There was a movie showing in the football club on Sunday night. James Bond. And I thought, everyone will be there, and no one will be watching us. We could just go as friends. I thought—

I don't know. But I wanted it, and so I asked.

And where she'd lain there open, our hands curled up against her chest, she pulled away, closed off.

"No," she said. "Not out in the open. No." And then, small and sad so that I have to listen with no room for anger, "Isn't this enough?"

And I wonder have I *ever* seen two girls together? There are friends, of course, leaning on each other's shoulders as they giggle over boys. But not . . .

There's distance. It is not the same.

Have I ever heard of two women—not sisters, aunts, or work-mates—living underneath one roof?

I've not even heard my best friend compliment another girl without a chasing insult.

I've heard *You know what she does?* about that first grade teacher, and there were rumors when someone quiet from Brenda's class just disappeared. Pregnant, they said. Because she was . . . y'know . . . by a woman.

Which doesn't even make the slightest bit of sense.

So ashamed her parents sent her to the village.

That's it. Two whispers on the playground, nothing more. Because we all know how it goes. You grow up, find a boy, get married. There is space for nothing else.

But here, in the shadows we have made our space. It's ours, and nobody can touch it.

Everything is good.

Better.

I'm almost halfway through the boxes in the archives. There is room to move. I've even come to an agreement with the spiders; they stay quiet when I'm in the room, and I won't try to hit them with the corner of whatever CD is at hand.

Music hums right through the walls, louder every day. This groove is good.

I knock on Mr. Sid's door, holding his tea and a fresh, unopened bag of biltong.

"Sir," I say, placing both things on his desk.

Mr. Sid looks up. "Oh, Neo."

"Hi."

"You're done?"

"It's six. Mama will expect me home."

"Mmm, mmm, yes. A good girl *never* disappoints her mother." He reaches for the biltong.

"No, sir."

"Very well. I'll see you tomorrow."

He goes back to marking something with his pen, and I move toward the door.

"Oh, Neo?"

"Yes?"

"It's nice to see you looking fresh."

The music, it works wonders.

I 'll trade you these candies for your apple," Janet says.

She's feeling fat today, or far from baby-skinned or something. And I'm taking full advantage. "Yesss!"

She tosses me a handful of sweets wrapped in orange paper and we fall upon our break-time snacks, glad of the cool air upon our skin and the chance to rest our brains.

I press play on the CD, filled with old-school kwaito.

"You know, this guy was the *first*. The very first."

Janet bites into her apple.

"How do you even do that? Take everything that's gone before and invent this whole new thing? D'you think he knew as he was doing it? Did he know that this was it, that it was big?"

She puts the apple down. "Woh. You . . ."

"What?"

"That Mr. Sid does not know who he has. You know that, right?"

I blush. "Eh, I'm interested, that's all."

"You're *brilliant*. You know, you should show him. Tell him you want something more. Make him use you."

"Nahh."

"I'm serious. Sure, Max has that smooth voice and all the charm, but you . . . you'd add something else."

I swallow, hard, and the orange sweet scrapes down my throat.

"You really think so?"

"Yes."

S he's right, you know."

I squirm underneath the bar-light as Jed and Zee suck teeth in matching approval.

"Absolutely. Girl, you've *got it*. Why not flaunt it?"

"Mmmmm."

"But," I start to argue, "I'm at school. And I've never had a job except working for Mama."

"Uh-uh . . . tell me three things about young Yusef up there." She nods toward the stage, where a guy in low-hung jeans and gold-rimmed sunglasses riffs into the microphone.

I watch him for a moment, listen to his lyrics, free-fall words on grief: losing his mother to the great disease.

"He's good," I whisper.

"Anyone can tell me that. What else?"

"The way he pops his words out, you *know* that they burn. They're real. And you can see it in his eyes, as well."

Jed nods.

"And he's following the greats. The rhythm he's got going, I've heard that before. He's building on it, though. Stretching it out slow to make us feel the pain of every single word."

"Don't you want to get up there and give him all your money?" Jed asks, and I nod.

Zebra turns to face him. "Or adopt him. Honey, d'you want a kid?"

The conversation moves, but I sit watching Yusef for a moment more. All the pain and comfort flowing back and forth from stage to audience to stage.

I imagine playing that out across airwaves, imagine Yusef's words hitting a hundred other heartstrings; more. I imagine our connections growing stronger.

And I wonder if they're right.

I sit among the boxes, scrolling through the list of every artist housed inside these walls, and *shake*.

They're all in my head at once, Mama, Baba, Janet, Zebra, a hot mess of *This lush music life is not for you. Music is not real,* and *You can do it. Prove it. You take the scissors and you run.*

No child of mine—

Do it!

But there are boxes all around me, photos on the walls of people who can. Who have. Who will for years to come. And in my head is Tale, bright and fierce, her hands on mine, talking of the stage and who she wants to be. And somehow that's enough.

My mama always said that when things are swingin' you don't step in front of 'em, just let them tick. If business is good, why change all your prices just to beat next door? You let it swing.

But even Madame Serious can sometimes get it wrong. And I want something more.

Have you ever thought about rhythm? The way it changes from inside a song? The way it picks up pace or drops and takes you somewhere new?

Rhythm is the *key*, but sometimes rhythm shakes and shimmies, shifts and emerges all mermaid-new.

The next day I linger as I place Mr. Sid's tea upon his desk, change the rhythm, nervously clutching two doughy fried *koeksisters* wrapped in paper which already drips with grease and syrup.

"Yes?" He looks up, all confused.

"Your tea."

". . . so?"

"Ibroughtyousomething." I thrust the pastries at him and then I wish I hadn't because now I have nothing to hide behind. What does one do with one's *hands*?

I drop them to my sides, clench and unclench. But I feel so lost. Exposed. I wish Tale was here to take my hand and pull me through. To make the drummer *chase*.

"Huh." Mr. Sid peers at the pastries and then back at me.

And I settle for folding my arms across my chest. A shield.

"You want something?"

What if he fires me?

What if he sends me home for arrogance and cheek and having a rock-star ego?

Baba will be *furious* if this goes wrong. And vindicated. Both; this music thing will be forever *irresponsible* and I will have to listen because Mr. Sid, the master, will have spoken.

But if this goes right . . .

"Yes, sir. I . . . Did you know that sixty-eight percent of your audience is under twenty-one?"

He stops. Pushes his papers aside and looks at me. "I did."

"And did you know that all your presenters and jockeys and musos are well *over* that? They're *old*." And as I say it, my heart stops. *Please don't hate me, please don't. Please.*

"Old?"

"Sorry."

"Well." Mr. Sid reaches underneath his desk for biltong, bites and swills it down with tea, licks his lips all hungry-like, and never once do his eyes move from me. "What do you suggest I *do* about this aged and decrepit problem?"

"I . . . You have me in a cupboard. And I'm so so grateful for the opportunity, but why don't you *use me*?"

"Use . . . you?"

"I could research. Talk to people. Load the CDs in the studios or live-tweet everything that happens here." I would have to ask my best friend *how*, but I could do it, if he wanted.

And honestly, I can't even believe I'm asking. But secretly, deep down, I'm thinking, *How can he refuse?*

I brought him pastries *and* free labor. And I'm right. I'm good. Surely he can see.

You take what you love and run.

Mr. Sid just sits there with his steepled fingers and his sharp sharp suit and *smiles*.

"UmziRadio..." he says it like he is giving a speech, "UmziRadio ticks over like a Cadillac. She purrs."

I nod. Not understanding.

"Why?" He pauses, reaches for the biltong, bites. "Because she's made up of the best parts. Yes, we oil them regular and take them to the good mechanic, never to the cheap one, but you cannot service *rust* and make it purr. You understand?"

"I . . . not exactly."

He smirks, rallies, carries on. "You cannot drive on crooked nuts and pointed tires. You won't get *smooth* unless you build her well. UmziRadio is the *Cadillac* of entertainment."

I nod.

"And would you have a 1956 collectible housed in a garage alongside a child's toy made from coat hangers and tire scraps?"

"Uh, no?"

"No indeed, you would not . . . I *like you*, Miss Mahone. You've got *balls*. But Umzi cannot cozy up with toys. We're not at play."

And my resolve crumbles right there with my world.

I'm done.

Never. You will never do it. You are just a girl.

"Look. I like you. And maybe you're right. Maybe we *can* use you. One day." He grabs a strip of dry-meat, sticks the end of it between his lips, and *sucks* before he takes a bite.

Chew, chew, chew. All the while staring at me, and you can see the hungry plan forming behind his eyes.

And suddenly he swallows. "But finish in your cupboard, eh? You're just a girl."

S o," my father asks, before he's even seated, "how is it?" And from his tone, I'd swear he knows.

I do not want to talk about it. Not tonight. But Baba's waiting for an answer. *Everybody's* waiting.

"All right."

"Mr. Sid working you hard?"

Did Mr. Sid call him in to talk after I'd gone?

Did they sit and laugh over my dreams?

"Yes, sir." I swallow, hard.

"Good, good."

I'm hungry despite feeling sick with everything—as though I have been hollowed out by Mr. Sid and now I need to fill the space with something. Anything. We fall upon the sweet potato stew like starvelings, and for a moment there is nothing but the sound of spoons on bowls. Scraping. Slurping.

And then Baba coughs in that polite assertive way, and says, "What does he have you working on?"

I freeze, spoon in the air. Is this a trap? My father does not ask without a reason.

He waits, and as I watch I swear his eyes gleam happy.

"Still updating the music records. Clearing boxes. It's a big job."

"Hmm." He stabs at a potato without shifting his gaze.

"What?"

"And you like this work?"

"It's interesting."

He leans over his stew, toward me. "And you're being *useful*?"

"I think so. Mr. Sid wouldn't have me do it if they didn't need it."

"Mm-hmm."

Mama eyeballs Baba with her *careful* look; the one that says *You're right, but don't you dare cause upset at my table.*

The kitchen is Mama's domain, and she is *fierce*. But Baba does not have to say it. You can hear it in the silence:

See. I told you so.

It's not so easy, isit?

You'll never amount to it. You're not Mr. Sid; you're just a girl.

You *are just a girl.*
You are just a girl.
You are just a girl.

Those five words lace through everything. I hear them in the silence, in the movements of the day. I see them in my mother's hustling, the pitied smile from Grandma Inkuleko, the gentle exchanges with the men at market. Everywhere: *You are just a girl.*

It laces, and it tightens until it squeezes every breath from me and it is all I am.

I *mope.*

To the outside eye it's probably not there. I do my mother's bidding, and I go to school and empty boxes at the station. Everything goes on. But underneath the motions I am broken. Shut off from the dream.

I stop bringing new music to the playground. I stop listening to Umzi late at night.

I do not slip into the night and to the bar. I can't.

I am nothing but a girl.

After a week of this, Janet finds me at the far side of the yard and sits. She dumps a stack of papers in my lap and sits, and sucks the air in through her teeth until I look at her.

"Hi."

"As your manager," she says, all bossy, "I'm telling you that it's enough."

I drop my gaze, watch a lone ant march out across the earth.

"I'm serious. Enough. That Mr. Sid, he doesn't *know*."

I cringe.

"He doesn't. I've been doing research."

I don't want to know. Mr. Sid says no, and he is right. But Janet does not budge.

"Who. Needs. Radio?"

That jolts right through me like an untuned violin. "I do."

"Eh, I know, I know." Janet waves off my concern. "Mr. Sid and Max and airwaves. Our show out across the world. I know. But you don't need them."

"Eh?"

"Podcasts."

"What?"

"People post their own shows to the Internet, and everybody listens. . . . Think about it. You could sit here, sad, or you can prove him wrong. Rise up. How'd you think he started, anyway? I'm not denouncing Max, but we should switch sometime and see what's up."

I do not know how to answer.

My best friend *believes*. She's here. But Mr. Sid said no.

But always there has been this plan, Neo and Janet on the airwaves and owning the world.

My best friend reaches out, taps the giant stack of pages. "Think about it, Nee. Our *show*."

I nod, dumbfounded.

"Theeeere we go. That's better. Get back on the horse and show him."

T hat afternoon I stare at artist names and styles and key words. I flick through websites for the major stations, try to figure out what music is, why I am doing this, what I'd even have to say.

Just a girl's still there, but there is also radio, right at the heart of everything, playing everywhere you go.

There's *fun* and *energy* and everydayness.

Khayelitsha.

And I know what I will do.

"Now I learn my ABCs: all the things you never knew about our homegrown music talent. Twenty-six podcasts exploring music and what makes it *ours*," Jed reads, one painted eyebrow raised up high. "And you're qualified to teach us?"

"Yes." I nod, *hoping* that I sound more confident than his question makes me feel.

"Mm-hmm." He flicks through my notes. They all do, crowded round the pages.

NOW I LEARN MY ABCs: All the things you never knew about our homegrown music talent.
Host: Neo E. M. Mahone

A: Attraction. Feel the *heat* and *longing*
B: Bubblegum and other '80s influence.
C: ~~Control? Power ballads/ protest songs?~~

Children of Africa? CHILDREN OF THE CAPE: *Really*
local bands
D: Dance dance dance daaaaaance

As they read through the ink-scrawled sum of my inside, I can't help but squirm.

What if they see this and they do not want me? What if standing up and singing does not always get applause, even from your friends?

K: Kwaito vs. American hip-hop—why we're different.
Why we're better.

L: L♥♥♥♥♥♥♥♥♥♥♥E SONGS (Obviously?) "Pot Belly"
(for J/ because acceptance is key) Masekela—who
doesn't fall for that horn?

M: <u>Mandela</u>, Bringing SA's plight and it's music to the
wooooorld. Feat: Protest songs, "Biko," Mandela, Live
Aid, Live 8, and the things we *wish* they'd heard.

N: New beats. Hot hot hot new music. What should
you be listening to?

All the way up to the *Z*s, with notes on who and what and why.

On the last page, Tale pauses. Frowns.

"We need to talk about this V entry."

"Ooh, yes! I want to talk about the ways a venue makes the

music, shapes it. The way it feeds into the players on the stage, reverberates or swallows sound. The way live music is always, always something different from a studio recording," I babble, excited.

"Yah, not that part. The part where it says 'explore theory with Tale and the Storytellers.'"

"Yesss! I thought we could illustrate, tour together for a week or two and really show the differences."

Tale stiffens. And I should have known. I should have stopped right there, but this was *everything*. My career, my friends, that voice: the perfect melting pot. And so I kept right on.

"Because . . . it's so, so different. Even you. You *know* what your sound does to me, right? But when certain factors get in the way of that, like in All the Rage . . . You felt so far away and—"

"What?" Tale stares. "When did you go out to Rage?"

"I—"

"No. We're not doing it. And you stay away from there, you hear. You never, ever go there. It's not the same as here. It isn't . . . They're not like us." And she pulls away, her face a sudden storm.

I know that. And I have no intention of going back, but Tale does not listen long enough to know.

"Jeez. I don't. I didn't . . ." And I don't know what I said, but Tale's *freaking out*, all tense and jittery and unable to look at us.

What did I do?

"It's okay, T." Cap leans across the table, and his voice is strong and slow and stops Tale in her tracks. "Neo can just *talk* about the difference, right? There must be *millions* of live tracks to compare."

I nod. Desperate to fix the thing I broke.

Slowly, Tale breathes, and nods, and picks up my list to finish.

I sit there, shaking, waiting for an explanation. But it does not come, and except the staticky discomfort in the air, you'd never know that anything had changed.

When they've flicked back over my plans, digested it, they nod approvingly, and Tale slides across the sudden, unexpected gap, slips her hand in mine and whispers in my ear, "It's brilliant. You're going to do *good*."

I t's not fancy like the studio. There's no red blinking light and no RECORDING sign. But Janet's Mama's office does just fine.

I've been here once or twice before, but never stayed. It's *nice*. A whole wall lined with books, and a big framed picture of the mountain, and a corkboard bearing schedules. And on the desk there is a potted flower.

It's the kind of room that fits their life. Peaceful even while it works.

"Where is she?" I ask, feeling just a little strange planning to fill this quiet, adult space with *vibes*.

"Lecturing till late. She has a class on Neoclassicism."

"Eh?"

"Don't ask." And then, "She won't mind. Hey, she won't even *know*."

We sit in high-backed wooden chairs, beneath the gently clicking ceiling fan. Janet sets up the microphone and MP3s and whatever else this thing needs. I watch in awe, and try to breathe out through my nose and not throw up.

"Okay," she says, finally. "You ready?"

"No?"

"Nn-nnh, of course you are. You have your script. Water? You need water? Tea?"

Tea seems right, somehow, and Janet runs to make it, black and sweet, leaving me alone for a few moments.

I run over everything I want to say. Try to hear the pauses and the stresses in my head.

And she's back.

I wrap my fingers round the tea for comfort, and we start.

"*A-B-C-D-E-F-G*, come appreciate the songs with me?" I rap the school rhyme. Pause. Cringe. "Ugh, can we delete that?"

Janet nods. *Thank* goodness *this thing isn't live.*

"Music has the power to change the world. *My* world, anyway. And yours. Here's the thing. It doesn't matter that I'm *just a kid*. Us fledglings got our finger on the *pulse*.

"I'm Neo, just your average schoolgirl muso with a bigger crush on *sound* than on the cornrows or the slick shirt or the smooth tongue of the boy next door.

"And this week, *A* on the alphabet timeline, we're kicking off with just exactly why. This week is *attraction*. Let me take you for a *ride*."

I lead with a hot-and-heavy song that everyone will know, with the poster boy singing of bedding her and moving mountains. Obvious and familiar. Foreplay, if you will.

And from there we move to *quiet* sexiness. A love song, full of simple rising-falling riffs that slip bright from the tongue and make you want to *dance*, hand in hand and cheek to cheek with her.

Fast-slick lyrics; words so clever that you'll fall over yourself just to crawl inside the song and learn from them.

Fractious syncopated rhythms, drums and finger-plucked guitar together, whipping hearts into a frenzy. *How far can we push you? How hard will you dance?*

And then a growling gravel voice, scraping at your insides like musical *teeth*. Slow and low and teasing. Deliciously sore.

And an a cappella, *rich* with harmonies. At first you hear the voices as distinct—leaping, playing, running up and down the stairs—and suddenly they *find each other* and they blend, embrace, and together they *expand*. And you could not, *would not* separate them out because you'd break the sound.

Always, always, they are in control: the gravel voice and fast and low and soaring high, the solo and combined. Control. Leading, bending, molding you.

And finally there is the afterglow. Something still and pure, uncluttered.

And suddenly our half an hour is *up* and I'm left breathless and amazed.

J anet sits there just as stunned as me, and then it all slinks out across her lips; a "Yessssss." And then she's up and busy, clicking things and dragging things and typing, and she's cut my face out of an old-school photo and attached it somehow.

"Okay. I think we should run it like that. It was perfect. Yes?"

I nod, and there it is, uploading to the Internet. And suddenly I feel *exposed*.

I can't believe I did that. In my best friend's mother's office.

I squirm at the thought of her hearing my handiwork. And then harder at the thought that someone—anybody else—might.

What if they don't like it?

What if no one hears?

And what if they can *tell* whose voice it is inside my head at night? What if they can tell that she's a *she*?

I was careful. But this raw part of my soul is on the Internet for everyone to find. And maybe careful doesn't matter: Your protection only has to break the once.

I shoot out of the chair and dash outside and *vomit*, until every naked thought is spilled into the street and there is nothing left to feel. And then, as I straighten up and wipe my lips upon my sleeve, pride floods in to take its place.

I did that.

I put all my music-feelings into something I could share.

Like radio.

You'll never make it, eh? Well, Baba? Mr. Sid? I think you might be wrong.

My Facebook page—neglected since the day that Janet made it years ago—is *hot*. And it feels huge. The moment that you step up to the mic and people hear, for good or bad.

Comments: 33

Smooth beats girl

Eh! NEO. I dint know tht u cd do that. You got WORDS.

She looks good too? Don't you think?

Yeah. You scrub up gud.

Less get between the sheets. I bet that ass can *dance*.

Niiiice. I love the way you didn't stick to just the classic crooners.

So true about the growlin

When's the next one?? Count me IN!

And one, from the Storytellers fan page:

That's My Girl.

"What now?"

"Now," Janet says, typing furiously on her phone, replying, telling everyone to share, "we do another. We alert His Highness, Mr. Sid, that there's a new queen on the block."

I don't know how she did it. I still don't, and I doubt I ever will, but when my bestbest friend has an idea, things *move*.

Mr. Sid is waiting the next day, sitting with this *look* upon his face, all hungry and amused.

"Mmm, mmmm. " He leans back in his chair and smacks his lips together. "It appears I have misjudged you."

"Sir?"

"Your show. Quite innovative, putting it out like that. Of course, it isn't clean; the sound is terrible. But there's a rawness there. . . ."

I practically jump at him and offer him my soul right then and there. But something stops me. Maybe it's a hint of Janet or of Tale rubbing off on me. Maybe it's the gut-pull of the *You are just a girl*—a petty, girlish need to win. But somehow, I keep all of that behind my teeth and shrug. "Thank you."

"You know you have to take it down?"

I what?

He sees the shock, and now *he's* smiling. "Copyright, my dear. All those songs—you have no right to use them."

Shit.

All our hard work, all our *We'll show him*.

"Unlesssss . . ."

I force myself to look him in the eye, to swallow back the tears. And Mr. Sid, he draws it out, tears off another chunk of meat and chews before he speaks. "I'd like to offer you a deal. You keep making them, *for me*, and you can use whatever songs you like under the Umzi license."

I—

I what?

Relief floods through my veins like oxygen. It *worked*. We showed him.

And I'm going to accept, whatever terms he has to offer, but Janet's stern voice bursts into my thoughts and something stops me.

I smile as sweetly as I can and nod, as though considering. "I'll have to ask my manager."

Sometimes, when you know what's coming on your playlist, you anticipate. You see how one song leads into the next. But when it's new you can't see what's in front of you at all. That moment when the next song plays, all you have is what you hear. Moments to make up your mind. Sit it out, or dance.

I like this beat. And I'm ready to move.

And this one has a beat that you can dance to.

I t's a whole big thing. Publicity, they say. Good news for every-one: I'm going to be a *star*.

Mr. Sid's car is sitting outside school at two, a full half hour before the lessons end.

Everybody *whispers*:

"Who's it for?"

"Where is it from, an expensive car like that?"

"Why is it here?"

Beside me, Janet grins, tears the back page from her book, and scribbles something on it.

Umzi 905fm!

She passes it to Joseph Mthandeni, who passes it to Candice, who passes it to Jeffery, and soon it's been in everybody's hands and the whispers turn to something louder, more excited.

UmziRadio is here!

Our school.

Someone ululates when the teacher's back is turned: *"Alielielie-lielielie!"* And finally she calls the lesson off.

"All right, all right, since you're all so keen and since this is a special day, you may all beautify yourselves, practice your hellos."

The class breathes out the tension, only to have it rise again as pure excitement.

"Eh!" The teacher's voice cuts over everything, sharp-sure. "Remember that you represent the school, please."

. . .

When the bell rings, no one knows quite what to do—pour out of the room and run, like always? Stay? Do we sing and dance a welcome, or sit stiff and wait for questions like when doctors come to talk to us about all the ways we're most likely to die, and how to maybe not?

The crowd pools in the doorway, pushing, shoving, and eventually we flood into the yard and wait, all of us, a giant circle of anticipation.

Mr. Sid steps out of his car and, straightening his hat, he walks toward us.

"Never have such well-heeled boots walked across this earth," Janet whispers in my ear, impressed.

Headmaster Zuma shakes hands with Mr. Sid and leads him through the crowd toward his office.

At his nod, Janet and I follow, leaving everyone behind.

The sound guys follow not long after, joining us for juice and malted cookies laid out on a tray.

"So, Neo." Mr. Sid is watching me intently. "How exactly did you think to do this show? Where did the music come from?"

The sound guys tense, pushing the two fluffy microphones a little closer.

I stare at my knees. They're chapped and dry against the winter cold. "I've always wanted to, you know? The music's always been there. But this show, that was all Janet's idea."

Mr. Sid raises an eyebrow. "Ahh, of course . . . this is Miss Janet, I presume?"

She nods. "Yes, sir."

"Mmm-mmm-mmm. You two make quite the team. And a *credit* to your school, as well."

Headmaster Zuma preens and cuts across the conversation. The mics swing wildly toward him like two eager bees. "St. Nicholas' Hope is here for its community. We foster innovation, creativity, entrepreneurship. And as such we are *delighted* to welcome you today. It's a privilege for us, our students. Thank you."

"Not at all." Mr. Sid's chest puffs as he waves the compliment away. "The privilege is ours: it's all for the community, right? And where would we be without the future generations?"

"Quite." Headmaster Zuma offers him another cookie.

There's an interview, of sorts, where Mr. Sid explains the partnership—school and station supporting the exploits of one plucky teen who might just make it. Celebrating talent.

Good publicity for everyone.

And when we step back out into the yard, there's *singing*. The whole school—or everyone who could afford to stay behind—lined up, dancing, swaying, singing thanks.

"Get that," Mr. Sid says, and the sound crew nods. "And speak to one or two about the opportunities here and the music that they like. For color."

Someone dances up to us and drapes a garland of bright yellow flowers around Mr. Sid's neck. He bows, quirking a smile, and watches gracefully for just a moment before Janet and I walk him to his car.

He slips into the driver's seat, legs still on the pavement, and sighs a sigh of comfort. Bliss. And then he turns the key and grins like Jeso on the football field. "Listen to her," he says. "How she purrs."

I nod. Try to shove my hands into pockets that aren't there.

How do you say good-bye?

"This is a *car*, Neo. Worth something. Worth working for."

I nod again.

"And you *will* work. Yes? You'll make me proud."

And then he pulls away, judders down the street, a smooth car on a potholed road. And Janet and I breathe.

I t all moves so fast after that. No time to take air, to plan, to celebrate. Suddenly, I'm sitting in the hot seat opposite the golden voice himself.

Janet's waiting in the lounge, of course: She'd *never* have forgiven me if she were not allowed. And I am ushered in midsong and handed headphones as the numbers count down, three, two, one. No time to even say hello.

"All *right,* you guys. It's time. It's time. We have our special guest right here. The newest of our crew. It's *Neo.*"

It feels different in here: There's that Umzi energy that I've been looking for. The air *sings* with it. And as Max talks, my eyes glide across the room, looking for the cause of it, and I find myself watching Max's lips, his face, full of contained energy, just like a music box, slowly winding up and up and up.

"Hi." I sound so small, as though the room is not a cupboard but a stadium I can never fill.

He laughs, easy and relaxed. "Hi. Welcome to the show. Welcome to *Umzi,* I guess."

I'm sitting next to Maximillius, *on air.*

I freeze. I have no voice. Nothing to say except for *wohhhhhh.*

"Although you're not really new, are you, box girl?"

I shake my head. "Uh-uh."

"So you're the *newest voice* of UmziRadio. How'd that spin?"

"I . . ."

He laughs again. "Clearly, it's your way with words."

"Uhh." And then it *clears,* whatever fear has gripped me vanishes, and I am *here*, exactly where I'm meant to be. "Yeah, something like that. I *asked*, at least. But it's like I said in that first show, music has all the control—I'm just the monkey hitting play."

"Uh-huh. That first show, ladies and gents, was Neo in her living room. We've linked to it on Umzi's site. But we were so impressed that now she's ours."

"Oh. My. God. OhmyGod. Oh my *God*!" Janet *squeals* as I step through the door and *breathe*. "Neo! You were *faaaabulous*!"

I grab a cola from the fridge and flop onto the scratchy couch. "Thanks."

"Where's—"

And Max walks in behind me. Janet *freezes*, bug-eyed, with the words stuck in her throat.

"Great job in there," he says, crossing the room to fill a mug with water.

I nod. "Thank you. It was fun."

"Yeah. Well. You're a *natural*. You make it easy."

"Really?"

You can see the nervous *oh my God* rising, building inside my best friend. She stands there silently vibrating. Staring at me and at him like, *What?*

"Sure. You wouldn't be*lieve* some of the rescues I've had to make. Fish-mouth terror is a natural hazard in this business. *Especially* when you spring them with a question which demands some *realness*."

"Yeah?"

"*Sure*. And then there's the jackasses."

I grin. Because surely that implies that I am not one, and because if Janet were a pot she would be boiling over right now. "I'll bet."

"Chhh, yah. I should tell you sometime." And with that, he nods at both of us. "Anyways, I have to get back." And then he's gone.

The door closes behind him and my best friend *screams*. Breathy and half volume, but it's definitely a scream. "Whuuuuuut? You whut? You—I—whuuuuu."

And for the first time in forever, I feel right and good and true.

It takes her a full fifteen minutes to stop hyperventilating in my ear. I have to make excuses to pop into Mr. Sid's and thank him, and when I get back, she's still there, barely gasping air.

When she finally regains control, we sit there, in the hub of UmziRadio together, two best friends.

Leaning on my shoulder, Janet looks up at me. "I'm so freaking proud of you."

"Heh. Thanks."

"I'm serious. You *killed it*."

"Thanks."

"So . . . now you're, like, a real celebrity—"

"I'm *not*."

"Whahhhht. Yes. You are. And now you get your pick of crushes. *Obviously*."

I groan. "I don't *want* anyone. I'll leave that to you."

"Oh okay, I don't know how you couldn't. Look at him! But, good, so Max is still mine?"

"Of course. Yellow wedding dress and half a dozen babies, isn't it?"

"Yes yes yes." She laughs. "And you're going to help me catch him."

I'm still in the cupboard, but now it's not just boxes. Now I have a microphone, a script. A mug of tea all of my own. And I still fetch Mr. Sid his drink before I leave, but it feels like an exchange.

Janet has her own badge too, and Baba has to wave her through.

When he phoned up to Mr. Sid to clear it that first day, you could see him bite his tongue, the words all puffing up his cheeks until he swallowed them.

That night, he's full of warnings.

"So they're using you behind the scenes. Careful, hey, a place like that they'll chew you up and spit you out, no questions."

"It's *good*, Baba. He's liking what I do. This could actually work."

I expect something. Recognition. Pride? A stiff apology? An argument? I'm not exactly sure.

But my baba merely grunts and does not say a word.

And Mr. Sid is *pleased*. The station received texts and comments, calls and e-mails, all lording the fresh new voice of Umzi:

Wow, she's *hot*.

Dear sirs, I would like to applaud your discovery and use of Neo, the girl behind the music ABCs podcast from Wednesday night. I look forward to seeing where she takes us and how her form grows. Good show!

Will you be my girlfriend? I will make you feel dat 80s vibe.

So much insight for a juvie mind. Amazing!

And as Mr. Sid sits there, all fat-cat sipping tea, I'm proud.

You know how a song can make you feel invincible?

UmziRadio did that for me. And Saturday, as Mama, Cherry, Linda, Jes, and I marched down to Serious Hair for the weekly deep clean, I sang.

"Why are you so cheerful?" Linda grumbled, not yet quite awake.

"I'm sorry. Some of us are climbing up and getting *out*. Come up and join me."

Mama *tschhh*s. "You climb all you want, but first you take this broom."

I do. But because I'm irrepressible, there's Tale-music-Tale right under my breath, and when Mama steps outside to catch some air and cross the street to swap news with the paperboy, I switch the radio from News Speak to Umzi. Turn it up a little.

Jeso looks up, all surprised, and then he melts into the sound of it, swings his hips, mock sings into his duster.

Cherry giggles, and suddenly this workhouse feels *alive*.

Mama lurches back into the shack five seconds later. "What is this?"

"It's music, Mama." Jeso grabs her hand and tries to make her dance.

"And this is not a disco. It's a business. Real work."

I flinch. And Linda steps up, puts her hands on Mama's shoulders as though maybe they are equals.

Linda: the defuser.

"Maybe it'll do the business good, Mama? Bring in the young crowd. All those hip and money-foolish boasters."

Mama knocks my sister's hands away and pulls the plug.

"Sure. And what boaster will be awake at this hour, eh? No, now's the time for the mamas and the nine-to-fives, those of us with cracks in our hands and lines on our faces." But she looks at us, my sister tall and calm and Jeso breathless with excitement, and she adds, "When the sun peaks, you can have your musics . . . if the customers don't mind."

Mama spoke to me that night, before Baba came home. Ushered the others into the bedroom, closed the door, and sat me down.

"You're safe, aren't you?"

"Eh?"

"With this . . . everything. You're being safe?"

I don't know what she means. Safe with music? Safe with Mr. Sid? Safe sneaking out at night, with Tale? But I reach for her hand and nod.

"And you want this?"

I nod again.

"You know, when the doctor says you'll have a daughter, your heart sings—a daughter! We're more complicated than the boys, us women, but it's worth it. But it sinks, too.

"The world is not kind to us. And I hoped—like your sisters— that you'd be a doctor or a lawyer or run a business one day. Something to prove to menfolk we are strong."

And suddenly I'm seeing her, wrinkles and faults and everything, exposed. She looks . . . sad, but not the same sad as she did before.

I try to say, *I will. I am,* but the words catch and fade, and Mama keeps on talking.

"But if this is what you want . . ."

"It is."

And it's her turn to nod.

"Then you must do it right."

My mama, she has warnings too, packaged up in freedom.

"If I'm to write this show, and do it well, I have to be out there with music," I explain. A risk. But I may never see this open, worried mother again; now's my chance.

Mama sighs, already fading back into her straighter, tighter self, and for a moment I think she will take it all away. But Mr. Sid is big. He's Baba's boss. Appearances are everything. And she doesn't like it, not one bit; it isn't . . . *becoming*, but if Mr. Sid commands, and she knows where I am, if she can see the plans and schedules for who's playing where, I'm free. No more creeping out at night!

And better than that, worth almost more than anything, I think my mother almost, maybe, sees what I could do.

I t's late, and I've spent the evening hidden in our corner, watching Tale and the Storytellers on the stage.

I thought that they might say something. Be proud of me or comment on my show. But they're all busy, kept up on the stage by keen customers and fewer acts to share the light tonight. And it turns out to be perfect. I sink back into the cushions and I lose myself to Tale's voice. To harmonies. To *everything*.

It's magical, the way they work the crowd. See them? Such control.

They move us right through the slow pain of unrequited love into the dizzy heights, through strong and hard, and gentle-soft.

I watch as Tale pulls us by the hand—each and every one of us—takes us in her arms and bares her soul.

And then it's late, and everyone drifts home, and what is left is quiet—that post-night quiet of contentment.

The bar staff are busy cashing up and wiping down. The band is piling their gear by the door. All business. And then Tale leans across the bar. "Hey, Tam. Can we get that cake?"

"Sure thing, sugar." And she straightens up and sets a bright blue cake upon the bar. A blue cake covered in what looks in this light like glitter, gold and twinkling. It reads: SUPERSTAR.

Tam pours shot glasses of beer—one for each of us—and Tale makes a toast. "To Nee, my blushing princess and our rising star!"

Everybody clinks, and Zebra adds, "Do they let princesses work like that?"

"They'd better. We need actual musos up behind the wheel."

"Oh my gosh, you guys." I blush.

"All Cap. This one's a softy."

"Hey, I just like cake." Cap shrugs, shrinks inside his hoodie.

"Doesn't everyone? Dig in."

We cut the cake using a handy beer mat, pass the pieces round. And when we're done and sugar high, Tale lifts my hand and licks the crumbs and cream and icing from my palm.

"Ooooooh," Jed teases, but he follows suit and sucks the frosting from his fingers.

Cap wipes his hands upon his jeans.

"Hey, listen," I say, snuggled in against Tale's muscled chest. "This next show is *local*. All about the music we make every day on Khayelitsha soil."

"Damn right." Zebra waves an index finger through the air, a proclamation.

"And I would *love* for you to join me. Come and play? Show this town exactly how it's done?"

"Yessssss, girl."

"Play a new scene? Yes!"

Tam, who's gone back to stacking things behind the bar, pipes up: "Don't you be leaving me, you hear. A show, great. But don't you get all big and famous and abandon me."

"Never!" Cap says, shaking his head, hard.

And there is sugar and there's beer and bar light, and everything is working out *just fine*.

But Tale pulls away. Kisses my fingertips just once, and then lets go and whispers, "No."

Everybody stops.

"Ehh, Tal', c'mon."

She holds up both her hands, surrendering or stopping us, or both. "No."

And, *We're not doing it. You stay away from there, you hear?* flashes through my brain, hot and angry, as Tale stands there feet away from me and she looks *small*, and sad, no longer Tale the big cat, the confident, the honey-milk, just sad.

"I'm sorry." She says it again. And there's this space between us, and I don't know how to cross it.

I want to ask, *Why not?*

What are you afraid of?

Aren't I good enough?

I want to take her in my arms and hold her tight and not let go.

I want to ask, *Why not?* again.

But it's Tale. The front-liner. My rescuer. And all I've got is "It's okay."

They rally, all of them, and we come up with the best backup plan for the third show. I'm proud even before we start.

It takes me thirty full, long minutes of staring at the business card before I actually dial. I just sit there, turning his card over in my fingers, over and over and over, spinning it in my hands. But when I actually dial, a gentle, friendly voice picks up. He's everything they said.

Show three is *on*.

Meet me early? he says. *If we're doing this, I want to show you something first.*

It *is* early. Jeso and my sisters are coiled together under blankets, and there's that selfsame lazing sun as setting off with Baba, and the sleepy dark, which prickles at your skin.

The same symphony of morning noise as Khayelitsha stirs, but today it sounds different. Louder, surer, with less dragging of the feet. Or maybe that's just me.

I wonder who I'm waiting for. Brother X, I know, but we have never met, and when I asked how I would spot him he just said, "You'll know." And I'm not sure, exactly, whether I'm supposed to meet him on the platform or the train. All I know is *6:02*.

Slowly slowly, people shuffle up on to the platform: suits and pale blue scrubs and boiler suits, standing side by side.

The music here is muted. No one dances. No one sings. People barely even *yawn*.

And when the train—all screeching, sparking metal—roars

beside us, everybody shuffles on, still silent. And they sit and stare, or stand, holding the metal bars above their heads and sleeping fast against their arms, only jerking conscious as the train makes stops.

It's *quiet.*

I always imagined growing up and working as a thing of freedom and of power. Like Max and those two girls, filled with laughter and with purpose.

I always thought my Baba was the exception to make the rule.

But nobody here sings. My commute is almost always filled with chatter—Jeso, Janet, Cherry, someone in my ears. But today there's nothing but the *shuk-shuk-shuk-shuk* rattling of the train and the sound of people bearing up and bearing down and bearing loads until it's so loud and so close that I can't bear the lack of conversation.

I stare out of the window.

It's strange, watching my world through glass, separate and distant.

I watch the young girls picking trash around the tracks, standing well back as we rattle past. I see smoke beacons heralding breakfasts where people can spare them. A truck unloading goods. I see people meeting-greeting in the streets, one woman close enough that you can see her bright pink dressing gown and unkept hair.

Mama would have a *fit.*

Shacks and lean-tos and brick walls all together, jumbled, rising up on top of one another like they're fighting for the sky. There's rust and garbage piles and peeling paint in overoptimistic colors, all under the washed-out gray of early morning light, all over the gray yellow of earth walked over far too many times.

Khayelitsha is a shit-hole. But it's *mine.* Like the stinky baby brother we all love.

And as I watch it pass, I just want to go home. Back to Mama and to Baba and to Tale, and the noise of it, because this silent window world looks older, sadder, and I miss its song.

But this box with the glass windows keeps us separate, *shuk-shuk-shuk-shuk-shuk,* it carries me away toward the wider, cleaner streets and smarter clothes and money, where everything is big and strange and out of reach.

I look away, afraid that if I don't I might just leap out through the windows and tumble broken to the Khayelitsha earth.

Breathe, Neo.

It is still too quiet, and my slow, deliberate breath melts into the nothingness.

Is this what our Brother X wanted to show? The *everything* of Khayelitsha? Or the broken quiet?

Why?

And then I know:

He appears at the back of the train—it must be him, right?—with the strum of a guitar, bright and solid like a shining light against the grind.

He pauses, grins as people turn to look. And the guitar speaks out again. A blues riff this time. A whole phrase. And he sings out above it. "A-babababa-ba-baaawap." He tests out the air, eases in, and a gray-haired, gray-suit man smiles as he moves to let Brother X step past. Now he stands right in the middle of the carriage, in the aisle, all laughter lines and lightness, color spilling out from underneath his green-wool tam. "Befooooore I start," he rips, his words all strung together like a chant, "let me just say good *morning.* Yessss, let me say good morning. Good morning, you, sir with the sleepy head." Not a chant, a *song,* and the gentleman beside him looks up, shocked, and everyone around him grins. "And *you*, madam with the pursed lips, I hope you're fiiiine today. And *you*, sir with the snoring, and you and you and"—he swings down the aisle toward me, left-right-easy as he plays—"you. Who here has the moooorning blues?" Someone whistles in agreement. And this strange train superhero sings.

And sings.

And sings. And he brings this dead, gray train right back to life.

"Mr X? Brother X? X?" I ask as he finally crashes into a seat across the aisle from me, still plucking gently at his strings.

"Ahhh, Neo? Hi! Did you see it? Did I show enough?"

I glance around the carriage, look at softer lines and unhunched shoulders. Smiles. I look at the way people move. Connect. Remember how to breathe.

And he did all that in fifteen minutes on an early morning train to nowhere.

"This is your ABC guide to S'African music, and today we're close to home with Children of the Cape. Music is for *everyone*, you guys. It's *yours*. And it's not just the affluent green-side Cape Towners, the ones in the big houses and the plane rides to the West. It's not just for the record labels. There's music right here.

"In a little while I'm going to play some of the *best and most successful* Cape Town music. But first I want to talk about *true* music. The sounds and opportunities, the *song* of Khayelitsha."

I hit play, and Khayelitsha sounds fill up the space.

My guest and I worked hard on this, walking through the streets and capturing the market traders' chants, the school-yard songs, the battles of the words. We rode the train and filled the carriages with songs that made the people smile. And then my guest—who does this *every day* and also runs a music shop for anyone and everyone—gives the footage to his kids and helps them string it all together with a narrative, walking through and seeing-hearing everything, a rhythm building up until it's all there, all together. And it sounds exactly like us. All of us. Together.

"Do you hear it? Mmm. I have this theory that music is in *everything*. Not just when it's sampled like this, mixed and churned out in your airwaves, but in every moment. All you have to do is listen, and the world will open up.

"And sort of following from that, let me introduce you to one Brother X, a true prophet of music. *Welcome.*"

"Thank you."

"So, Brother X, you are a music man yourself, and you recently set up a school right here in the township."

"Thassright."

"Wohh, that's *big*. Tell us a little about it?"

"Sure. The School of Musical Excellence is a dream. And it came about because one day I sat listening to the Michael Jackson on the radio, and I thought, *Man, that boy is fly*. And then I thought . . . I play. But I'd never *dreamed* of playing real, you know? And I sat there and thought, *Why?*

"And at the same time, my young nephew, he was getting into troubles with the street gangs. He's a good kid, but a good kid who was bored. And I thought . . . I have to fix this, to give him something to believe in and be proud of.

"That's what the School of Excellence is for . . . music, saving lives."

"Admirable. So admirable."

He laughs.

"Self-preservation. I don't want to live within a world where music only belongs to the strong, the rich, the lucky, and the old. Who's going to play *my song* when I am aged if that happens?"

I shudder at the thought of an elitist soundtrack. Because Brother X is right. Music should belong to all of us.

We move on, play a School of Excellence ensemble piece, kids on drums and keyboards and guitars. A choir.

And only once in the whole show do I wish Tale was beside me, that we could be shut up in here alone, with no escape and music all around and nothing stopping us. Just once.

We play to the successes of our own, with the Khayelitsha United Mambazo Choir, Freshlyground, and Ibrahim, Sathima Benjamin, and their American hip-hop daughter, Jean Grae. Sure, she hopped across the pond, but she was born right here and built of Cape Town jazz.

And then God saw the hour and he saw that it was good.

This rhythm, it is good: I've got music, I've got Tale, I've got friends. It's good. But if one thing's surer than the rhythm, it's that my big sister *never* drops a subject.

"So," she says, looking back at my reflection in the mirror as she files her nails, "how's that boy of yours?"

"My what?"

"Y'know. The boy." And I remember lying to her about where I'd been. Oh shit. I don't *have* a boy. "I suspect you haven't had much time for him with all this music stuff. Poor thing."

I nod. A get-out.

For a moment I think that it might have worked, but then she says, "You knowwww, you should make some time this weekend. We could double-date. Down at the beach?"

"Ummm, maybe not this week? But soon."

"I'm holding you to that."

And I don't doubt she will. Maybe I can put her off forever, one week at a time until we're old and gray and she has grandkids and I'm still a spinster, sitting in my yard, a blanket on my knees and a boom box at my side.

Otherwise, I need to find a boy.

I should be staring at my textbook, but instead I'm watching Joseph Mthandeni, chewing on his lip in concentration as he tips back on his chair, farther, farther, farther, teetering in the place of perfect balance.

No. Not Joseph. My best friend would never speak to me again. And honestly, I don't know what she sees in him—all brawn and confidence, no brain.

Khwezi, then? Mousy quiet. Awkward enough that he might just say yes. But I can't picture us at Monwabisi Beach, sitting on a blanket in the sand, or playing volleyball with Linda and Tsimo.

Tale, I can see, shoulder muscles rippling as she leaps up for the ball. I shiver. Swallow down the thought.

Boys.

None of them are right—the big, the small, the muscled or the scrawny, the brainy ones or popular. I try to imagine sitting with their arms around me. Talking. Leaning in to kiss. And my mouth tastes all bitter-wrong and my skin crawls.

Across the classroom, Joseph Mthandeni glances wildly round the room and grins, which sends him forward, back to four-legged mediocrity.

They're idiots.

And none of them knows music, either.

Maybe I should ask Janet for help. But I can hear how it would go, all questions and teasing. *I can't believe you took so long to ask* and *Let's fix you right up.*

I can see her making lists, eyeing up the hips and swagger of every boy in the school yard.

I can see her *glee* at how her bestbest friend has finally switched on the light.

And I see Tale, sitting in the bar alone, no music and no one beside her. And I can't.

Why would I need a boy when I have her?

I like our rhythm fine. When we're rising, falling, rising, falling, not too fast and not too slow, it's everything.

It swallows everything until there's nothing else, just Tale and the schoolgirl. The singer and me.

"I had . . . no idea bodies could do that."

"Yesss," she hisses, fingers still caught in my hair, "and they can do a whole lot more."

"Mmmmm." I arch to meet her, nuzzle close.

"I'm going to teach you," she says. "One thing at a time."

Sometimes, sometimes you find a riff that fits so comfortably, you wish it would go on forever.

It's like at a party with your friends, when you've found the *perfect* song. It's yours. Or theirs. Or maybe it just belongs to the night, but it is *perfect*.

And you dance and dance and dance, until you collapse to the couch with a big bag of Lay's and then you dance some more, your song still on repeat, so comfortable now that it is in the way you move. . . .

And then someone else steps up to the controls.

And in that awful, silent shuffle as the CD changes discs, you *freeze*.

Because the thing about the switch is that you never know what's coming next. Whether the next track will be exactly what you need, or it will suck your soul.

Nothing lasts forever. There is always the next song.

onight, Tale *sings*.

She always sings, but tonight I hear nothing but her voice in swathes, wrapping tight around my chest just like it did on that very first night. She *sings*.

The same song, in fact. Our first. And I sit there in the band booth and ride the wave as she sings faster, faster, making the band run. As she soars up to the iron roof and higher, higher, higher and—

She sweeps the room. And I think that she'll linger, that's she'll wink or smile or somehow tell me that this song, all songs forever, are for me. But she does not. She sweeps the room, meeting every pair of eyes.

And she *does* linger, but it's not with me, it's with the girl in a pink summer dress beside the bar.

She winks.

And she moves on. Leaving me behind.

I blink. And blink again. And then the jealousy floods into my gut.

Was this why she does not want me at some other bar? Why she wants nothing except Friday nights?

Does she have another somebody for other times?

Of course. Of course she does. Have you heard the way she wields that voice?

In the time it takes the band to clear the stage, I *seethe*. I go from grief to fear to *How dare you make me feel safe?* and back again.

And then Tale's here, sliding up beside me and kissing my head before she sits. "How was it?"

"What was that?" I say, barely audible over the noise of the next band taking the stage.

"Eh?" She frowns.

"You . . ."

"I what?" And she looks *worried*. Was I wrong?

"You . . ." I falter, but I blink, and I see her passing me right by. "That other girl. You were flirting with her."

She blinks, not understanding.

"The girl. In our song."

And her face flushes with relief. "Oh, honey girl, of course I was."

I— What?

She takes my hands, leans in to kiss me, but I move my head away.

"It's all part of the *act*. You've seen that song before, right? It's just how it goes. Gets the audience on side."

"Yes, but—"

"C'mon, sweets. This is what I do."

I think how many singers move among the crowds and single out someone to sing to. How many produce flowers. How all the best ones ooze with confidence, even when they sing of broken, softer things.

And I think, *Yes*. It works.

She's just doing her job.

And I shove aside the fact that I fell for that exact move, and stop pulling away, and her strong arm around me is such a relief that I fall right against her, my head at her neck. "Okay." I breathe. "I guess you're right. I'm sorry."

But the questions are still there. The *don't you go there* and the hiding and this desperate, small-voiced question: *Don't you love me?*

I sip at my beer, not asking, because the way she looked across the room, I'm not sure that I want the answer.

Tale shifts, look me in my eyes, and sighs like she's made a decision and she does not like it.

My heart breaks.

She's done with me.

We're done.

I should have stayed quiet.

"Hey, look, I've been thinking. I've not been treating you right. . . ."

"Eh?"

"I . . . I don't *do* this. Ever. And I swear I'll—"

What?

"But I want to treat you right. No more of this lying in the dirt to have some fun. Come with me?"

And it's not even a choice—of *course* I go.

Tale's house is less a house and more a *pad*, tucked away not two streets from the bar, in deeper shadow.

I'm relieved, somehow, to see she lives in iron walls. Familiar impermanence, as if we are the same.

Inside is one large room.

A stereo. An amp, wires running up along the walls and gathered at one high extension chord that disappears out through the roof. A TV resting on a set of drawers, and there's a rail running right across the wall at ceiling height, bowing under jeans and jackets and a dozen vests in black and white.

She pulls me through the door.

"You know . . . that first night," she says, and my gut tightens, nervous, "most people, they don't look away." I flinch, and Tale hesitates, but then, "Mostly, they look at me with this . . . hunger. Like I'm theirs somehow while I perform. But you? Not you."

"I looked away."

She grins, shyer than I've ever seen. "You did. And when we met, you were so flustered, and I knew right then that this was real. That we could—" She breathes. "So yes, I work that song, but not like that. Like this. Not ever."

And she looks so small and vulnerable in this space that is all hers, that it takes my breath away. I stand there staring. And then I see her space, a wall covered—absolutely, no inch spared—in festival flyers, posters, lineups.

There's Barleycorn 2012, Ramfest, and Rocking the Daisies. There's the Forbidden Fruits Fest, Rock the River, Up the Creek, and K Day.

And I find my lungs.

After a moment, Tale's shoulders drop and she shucks off her shoes and jacket, kicks them both beneath the bed. And then I see how *huge* it is. At least a triple sleeper. And I grin as she pulls me over to it, sits, and pulls me with her. And I grin as we lie back and Tale kisses me. Because the people in the bar, they don't see this. The inner sanctum. The true Tale.

This place, this is ours. Just ours. She's mine.

eo?" a small voice whispers from the doorway. "You awake?"

It's Jeso, and I roll onto my side to see him hovering in his pajama T-shirt.

"Mm-hmm. What is it?"

He pads across the room.

"Can I sleep with you?"

"Jes—"

"Please?"

And much as I want to float away on Tale dreams, my brother's *here*.

"Bad dreams?"

"Uh-huh. Can't sleep. I can't stop *thinking*."

"*Whsshhht*," I soothe, lifting up the blankets to let Jeso burrow in. "You stop that now, you hear? No thinking. This bed is a thought-free zone."

He nods, and snuggles in, all knees and elbows and affection, and he sighs.

"Nee?" he murmurs, moments later.

"Hmm?"

"I miss you."

I wrap my arms around him tighter. Squeeze. "I'm right here, stupid. Go to sleep."

"No. I mean, I *miss* you. With the radio and school and . . . I just miss you."

I search for the answers, an apology and promises that we'll hang out, but Jeso's body slacks before I have the words. He's already asleep.

J eso's sad voice taunts me right through Pastor Simphiwe's sermon. And though I'm sure his words are good and truthful, all I hear is Jeso, chanting *I miss you* on loop: the sad song of a forgotten brother.

I wonder about offering to take him to the park one afternoon. To stand in goal and let his buddies shoot penalties at my head. But it's not enough. I need something more. Something that is not a *gesture*. Something big.

And then the choir sings. Block chords and repetition raised like cheers. And I have an idea.

"Hey, Jes." I grab him as he slides out of the pew. "Bro. I think I need your help with something. Please?"

I tell him of my plans for the sixth episode of ABCs and he looks up at me, all seven-year-old serious.

"You *really* need me, hey?"

"I do."

"I mean, you don't even know the offside rule."

"I . . ." I taught Jes to play when he was two. I taught him the rules. But today that doesn't matter. I need him. I need him on my side. ". . . *definitely* need you."

"Okay. Yessssss."

Wohhh. You work *here?*" Jeso tilts his head right back to look up at the UmziRadio sign hung above the door.

"Yup."

"It's huge!"

"Yup."

"Woh, cool!" And then, as we go inside, "You get to play with all those squeaky records, right?"

"Uh, no. It's not that kind of DJing." His face falls, and I catch it quickly. "But there's a fridge full of Coke."

"Yesss. C'mon, c'mon, c'mon, let's go, quick!" He bounces down the hall.

"Welcome back, my musical illiterates. It's time to learn your ABCs. And today, we're talking *F*, and I have for you a *veeeery* special guest. Jeso 'The Dirvish' Mahone, seven years old, up-and-coming footballist."

My brother giggles, and the sound rings out across the air.

"There we go. Hi, Jeso."

He kneels up on his chair and grabs the mic with both hands. "Hi."

"So today we're talking football. Specifically the role of music. Football chants and vuvuzelas and how they bring us closer to this most beautiful of games."

"Amen!"

"The *point* of all this music is emotion. It's letting your heart fly onto the pitch. It's letting your team know they're not alone.

All that with the raising of voices singing predetermined words. And every time we sing, it's *laden* with the past. Association. Success breeds success, and every time you hear that chant you are reminded of its past associations."

I talk, and Jeso listens, eyes wide and excited.

"Take that moment of the game when, *ugh*, the play gets tough. You're low. You're tired. And then you hear it, one voice, two, a thousand:

"Shooosholoooooza," I sing. And my little brother's voice joins mine. And I fade into the official recording.

"And with all those voices out there, telling you to *push*, just like the great true pride of S'Africa before you, what else can you do but rise?"

We move from there to playground football.

"Can you tell us, Jes, some of your favorites? Liiike . . . for when you want to psych out the other team, or when you score?"

"Uh-huh. There's 'Yooooou smell, you smell, you smellll. Your feet are slow, your pants hang low, you smell, you smell, you smell.'" He grins, and launches right into another verse.

"Ahh, the fury of the second grader. You guys are *fierce*."

"Uh-huh. No one beats us. We're the lightning feet."

"And the songs help?"

"Of course. They, like . . . bind us together."

We high-five over that, and I continue. "We'll get back to football in a second, but I just can't talk about the sports-field bonding without at least a nod to a *different* kind of field. Our *anthem* was born on the rugby pitch, you guys. A show of sportsmanship for nations. How powerful is that?"

Jeso's nose wrinkles. "Well, sure. But it's not *football*, is it?"

I imagine all the listeners at home laughing at my brother the precocious football head, and I am so, so proud.

"No. Quite."

We talk about the other teams, national and world, and their chants and the different rhythms—how everything has a strong beat and lyric, because football is no place for fanciness.

We play "Waka Waka," and I ask my brother what he thinks of Shakira joining our own musicians on the pitch to sing at the World Cup. He shrugs. "Football's awesome. It has room for everyone."

And then we played "Wavin' Flag" and Jeso nearly toppled from his chair from singing with such gusto.

"When I get older, I will be stronger . . ."

I left his microphone on for that one, drums and stamping feet and singers and the voice of one enthusiastic boy, all rising together to make something beautiful.

Jeso babbles halfway home, skipping, whirling, jumping from one foot to the other. It *might* have something to do with him raiding Umzi's fridge, the two cans that he downed right there, and *four* he's managed to cram in his pockets (Mama's going to *kill me*), but not even sugar gives you that much of a high.

I shove in my headphones. But today I don't press play. I don't need to. I have song inside me. I have Tale, Umzi, and my little brother at my side; I just want to block out all the other noise.

I push my hands into my pockets and imagine Tale's footsteps falling next to mine. Imagine walking her along the street, laughing at my brother's madness, slipping a hand into my pocket: *You did good.*

And I do not notice when Jes wanders back to me until he tugs upon my sleeve.

"Huh."

"What is it?"

"It's the music, isn't it?"

"What is?"

"The dreamy-face on you. That boy-face. You're wearing it now."

And he looks up at me with so much understanding I almost, almost tell him everything.

But I've heard the whispered hate. The scorn and fear and *Did you hear? It's just not natural. Yahh. Imagine? The poor parents.*

You hear it. Everywhere.

Or you *don't* hear, and that silence, it is loud.

What if he told? The lock would come back out. I'd be teth- ered to my room and church and school forever. I'd go *gray* before they set me free. And I can't. I just found Tale and I cannot lose her now.

So I just nod. "Is that weird?"

He shrugs "Better than a boy." And then, "Don't worry, I won't tell, not even Linda."

I look at him, hard. "You won't?"

"Nope! Linda's silly. And I like music too. Besides, we're part- ners. We keep secrets." And my baby brother holds a sticky hand out, and we shake.

"Partners," I say. "Always and forever."

The atmosphere at dinner is hostile to say the least.

At first I'm terrified that Jeso will let something slip. Whether he understands the girl who sings or not, if he breathes a word it is all over.

All it takes is one innocent word.

And then I see that he is just excited for his radio debut. So excited that there is no room for anything besides the details and the thrill.

"Will you listen, Baba? Will you? Will you?" He cannot stop babbling, about the studio, the microphones, the big wide doors. He barely chews before he swallows, and it is a wonder that he doesn't choke on his potatoes.

And inside I burst with pride. And then I see the rest of them and I just want to *yell*.

Linda and Cherry at least listen, make *That's cool, Jes* noises.

But my father, he eats slow, and cannot muster the enthusiasm, even for his son.

"Hey, Jes," he says, "why don't we go to town to watch the game this weekend? You and me."

And Jeso nods and turns to me, oblivious. "The game? You get *sweet* stuff when you're a celebrity!"

"Yes, sir, you do."

"So what did you get?"

Tale. Love. A purpose. "I got music."

He sucks on a huge chunk of potato as he thinks. So big that, at first, he could not close his mouth and curls of steam clouded his face. And then he grins and swallows. "Football's better."

Rising, rising, rising, muscles arched, entwined. We rise. And it's like we're split in two, singing high-high-high and grounded, growling, low. And even in the moment, I am wondering how. How can we—two flesh-blood beings—sing this song with nothing but ourselves?

And with the soar and rush and falling back on top of one another, all content, I think, *I love you. I love this.*

And lying back among the pillows, I think, *Jeso's wrong. Nothing can beat this.*

Ever since Jeso curled up in the big studio chair, I knew I wanted to share everything; I love my worlds: the music and my brother and the girl. But I want them to be one. I want them all to know about each other.

"I want to take you everywhere," I say, and Tale turns to me and smiles.

"Eh?"

"Everywhere," I say. "To school and to the station and the market and—I want you with me. I don't want to ever let you go."

She laughs. "I mean, we've seen each other in the bathroom, so I guess there's nothing left to hide."

"I'm serious."

She frowns. "I know."

"I just want you in my life . . . all of it, you know?"

"Oh yeah, I imagine that your mother would *love me.* They generally do," she says bitterly.

I imagine Mama's face, stone-still and twisted in horror as I sat my girlfriend at the dinner table.

"Maybe not. But Jeso would. My baby brother. He would be all over you."

She bristles and then sighs, frustrated. Stares up at the rusted ceiling.

"I think you'd like him too," I try. Soft and quiet.

Tale does not answer, and for a moment I just lie there, watch her breathe.

What did I say?

How do I fix it?

"No," she says eventually, spitting out the words like bullets. "I can't. You can't *complicate* things like this."

"Eh?"

And *finally* she looks at me. "No families, okay? Just us. Families just mess everything up."

I think of Jeso. Sweet, soft Jeso, and the way he always leaps to my defense, the way he simply shrugged at the girl with the voice, and I cannot imagine him ever, ever doing something of concern. But Tale is in front of me and she looks fierce and scared and broken all at once, and I just want to make her whole.

And so I nod, slide over, try to nestle into her.

"Okay," I say. "No families." And I want to ask, *Just us, then? Somewhere else?* But she's lying rigid as if there's a wall between us, and I do not dare.

Heyyyyyy, my dear preliterates. Today we're up to *I* on the music alphabet, and we're not, despite popular suggestion, discussing me, my favorites, *or* the private alone moments with our whispered music.

"Not exactly. Today, we're exploring isicathamiya, and in a way that *is* about the *I*: the way the solo voices blend and separate. The ways in which the 'I' becomes the 'we.'

"It used to be *mbube*. Lion. But the style shifted with time and now the focus isn't flexing muscles, it's walking lightly with your brothers. It's *cathama*."

I worried that our argument would change things. That Tale would be distant and the safe-and-warm of everything would no longer be mine, but it still hugs my bones as I walk in and over to our spot. Still feels like I'm walking through life with a backstage pass.

She's *beautiful* tonight, up there on the stage, glowing warm and bright like sunshine rising up above the dark.

Warm and bright and primal. Like she's where she's meant to be. Where she'll always be. The singer who will always rise. You can count on it.

And that makes me feel safe.

I sink back into the corner of our booth, lean my head against the wood, and let her warm the fear out of my bones.

By the time the band is replaced up there by the Marley tributes and their rasta-lovin' beats, I feel almost normal.

"So, *ladies*, what is it tonight?" Zebra bounces up. "Greens, Greens, or Greens?"

Routine.

Safety.

"Yes please."

Three more yeses, and the rest of us sit cocooned in our little world while Zee goes off toward the bar. The others are already deep in conversation.

"Everything we play has *edge*," Jed argues. "Can't we try for something softer? Something with more strength from the harmony?"

"Softer?" Tale scoffs. "Oh, honey. Don't you mean *commercial*?"

"And what's wrong with that?"

"Nothing." Tale forms the word, but I cannot hear the truth in it.

They go on, and I sit back and listen, just happy to be with them, in a world where tone and pitch and presence are all ordinary table objects, carried around with us for everyday use. I listen, and I fall in love with everything all over again.

Before they come to anything resembling agreement, Zee returns laden with drinks.

"Hey, Neo. I found the *best thing ever*!" he says, hands flapping with enthusiasm the *moment* they are free. "Ever!"

Jed *groans*. "No! Don't let him tell you! Seriously, man, you need to cool that shit. It's *sick*."

"Nuh-uh, it's *fabulous*."

Jed shakes his head. "No, it's not. We are not a unicorn. And it's probably toxic and you're going to have to explain yourself to doctors."

"Eh?" I cannot help it.

"Now you've done it!" Jed covers his eyes, and Zee *beams* as he pulls two sparkling capsules from his back pocket.

"Is that—"

"Glitter!" He grins wider, bounces in his seat. "Rainbow glitter!"

Beside him, Cap sits silent and aghast.

"Zebra is an *idiot*," says Jed. "He thinks that eating this stuff he'll become a bigger, better gay."

"As *if*," Zee says, "but look! Isn't it *brilliant*?"

"You . . . eat it?" I ask. "But—"

"Somebody has been planning his Pride wardrobe."

"Eish," Tale huffs. "Pride isn't for weeks. You just wanted to kink up your bedroom hours."

There's a ripple of snort-laughs, but Zebra protests. "No, really. Coz this thing . . . it's a rainbow, in a pill."

"You eat it?"

"Rainbow on the inside!" He giggles.

"Can you imagine if we *all* took them for Pride? Dozens of us. Hundreds. *Thousands?* All of us marching, rainbow to the core?"

Jed wrinkles up his nose and Zebra nuzzles into him. "You realize I'm getting you in flag pants for the march, yes? We shall call you Rainbowlegs."

"You will *not*."

When they're finally done arguing, the group falls into quiet comfort with their beers, and I find the voice to ask, "What's Pride?"

They stop, bottles hanging in the air.

"Excuse me," Zebra exclaims, waving a finger of disbelief, "did she say what I think she said? Uh-uhhh."

"Pride," Tale says gently, "is a protest."

"It's a party!"

"Wait, okay, *which Pride?*" Jed asks. "Khayelitsha Pride, or the Cape party?"

"Either one . . . whichever way you look at it, they're both *both*, in different proportions . . . And they're both a protest running through the streets. Gays and lesbians and trans folks, all marching for visibility and equal treatment."

"Which we do not have!" Jed cries, indignant. "At all!"

"It's all about education," says Cap.

"And costumes!" Zebra adds. "Everybody being fabulous."

"Everybody?" I say. Like, there's more than our little quintet?

"Yesssss."

I try to picture it. I've seen crowds before, of course. It should be easy. But the people in *this* crowd are faceless, and I cannot picture what they wear or how they move at all. My stomach churns the way it did at that first teeth-and-tongues kiss from the boys, when I realized you could. And I'm *desperate* to see.

I imagine people standing arm in arm, a human wall. Imagine kissing in the streets, right out in the open.

I imagine marching Tale right past Mama, indistinguishable in a crowd of people just like me.

Marching with such joy and color that everyone—my mother included—wants to join us.

"Can we go?" I whisper, and Tale wraps her hands around mine, squeezes, just a little tight, and says, "We'll see."

We're all about the loooooove here in the studio today. That's right, my little protégés. It's *L* week on the ABCs show.

"Love, you guys. That big, deep chasm we all want to fall down. Philosophers spent *years* waxing about its meaning. Poets spend lifetimes describing it. But music, music says it best."

I play them Watershed's "Letters"—a love letter in song—and Mango Groove's "New World (Beneath Our Feet)."

I get it, this sappiness, but it's not me, and it's not all that love can be, and so I switch a gear:

Malaika's "Kiss Kiss," all smooth phrasing and stroking voices.

The Flames, with "For Your Precious Love." "Because this message of love isn't new, it's been around forever."

"Pot Belly," sweet and light and full. "I know my bestie *loves* that song. And, hey, it's a good message, folks. Love comes in *all sizes*, hey." And I picture *crowds*, people out in force to show the world that they just want to love. "Oh! And do check the video for that one if you can. It gives it this, like, extra layer. It's beautiful. There's . . . You'll see, but the way they play with color, *eish*!" And I see rainbows everywhere. "Because that's the thing, hey? We're not all the same. We're different shapes and sizes, man and woman, all of us are different, and that shouldn't matter. Love just *is*."

Song after song of happiness and proclamations and I end it with Stealing Love Jones's "Kicks." "For all the lovers and the future lovers out there. Here's that Friday feeling. . . ."

And I let Esjay Jones and the guitar carry us out with style.

O h. My. God. Look at it!" Linda has me trapped, pacing angrily across our room. "Look at it!" She waves the Umzi Twitter feed under my nose, and there's a silky pale pink dress and tiara above *Play to win: MISS UMZI wins a prom—with all the trimminz—for her matric class!*

"Aaaargh!"

"I'm sorry!"

"Sorry? Sorry! Families of employees *may not enter*! You have to quit!"

"Eh, no. I don't. You'll get your prom without the station's help."

"Yeah, in the school yard with a string of lights and eighties music, in a dress that Mama fixes up. . . . I'll probably go to my prom in *takkies*."

Three whole hours I've been here, listening to this. How Tsimo would pick her up in a yellow stretch limo. How the class would sip juice from tall glasses, and there would be cake as tall and fancy as a wedding cake, and she and Tsimo, they would sneak behind the rented stage and feed each other icing, and then afterward, a moonlit walk along the beach.

I tried to tell her no, that what she wanted was a classic black, and canapés, and that what people would *really* remember would be the music, and a selfie booth. And I picture Tale and me there instead of her, making funny faces, kissing kissing kissing, and it being caught on film, wallet-size and perfect.

But it didn't matter what I thought—I was ruining it all anyway.

Apparently.

Umzi's search for the township's prom queen was not open to my sister. The prize—the sharpest prom in all of Africa, designed to the winner's taste—inaccessible. And Linda was so sure that she would win. How could she not, with her knowledge of hair and nails and how to charm a customer? She'd win, if only I'd get out of her way.

And I'm sorry for her. Truly. But I will not give up music. Not for anything.

I want to take my goddess to the ball, and back in Tale's room I tell her so. We're lying across Tale's bed, heads hanging off the edge so that they almost touch the floor, and with the steady rush of blood, the giddiness and desperation, I feel like I am seven years old, begging Mama to say yes to Janet's birthday party invite.

"I want a *party*," I say, "just for us but where everyone will come so I can show them . . . how lucky I am."

"I'm *not* going to a school prom."

I sigh. "Oh, I know. Even if it was my year, we couldn't. But I still want to celebrate with you."

"I know," she says quietly.

"C'moooon," I whine, and I'm not talking about prom at all. "Come on, come on, come *on*."

"I just . . . don't enjoy the crowds. I'm sorry."

Tale, she who deals with audiences every night, does not enjoy the crowds?

"Fine. I'll just go on my own."

She stiffens, and in one swift move she pulls herself upright and on top of me, hands upon my wrists.

"It's not a game, you know."

"I . . . know?"

"No," she says, "I don't think you do. We're not marching against secret meetings in the dark, and whether your mother will set an extra chair for Sunday lunch. People march for their *lives*."

I blink.

"Life isn't all sex and music and fun, Neo. It's just not. You can't . . . Once you're out there, people see. There is no going back."

But Linda gets a party. She gets to put on a nice dress and walk out of the door with the boy she loves draped on her arm, and I want that as well.

I want to know what it is like.

And if she's right, why shouldn't I march? It's my life too.

"I'm going."

And I hope she'll soften at the edges, that she'll laugh and tell me that of course we both are, that it's where we belong.

But instead, she flops onto her back, and even though she reaches for my hand, she does not say a word.

I t turns out, when you are planning to attend a very public march for equal rights and visibility, you have a lot of secrets.

Times and dates and meeting places passed around like songs of old; nothing written down.

It's strange. The whole point is to be *seen*, and here we are with secrets, leaning on Tam's bar long after closing, planning routes and where we'll meet, and how to spread the word without the whole world knowing.

I asked why, and first I'm told, "You'll see." But I really, really don't.

Tale does not join us as we plan. She'll be staying home. And though I am excited to be part of it, to find that space in which I stand, it feels as though I'm cheating, somehow. That *she's* cheating me out of it. Or life's cheating us both.

"What's *with her*?" I ask, as Jed once again goes over all his rules for safety.

He ignores me, carries on:

"Stick together, two and two at minimum: There is no exception; group with others if you can.

"If there's sign of trouble, run: meet here, or here, or here, whichever's closest."

"Is it really that bad?"

All three of them just turn on me with scorn.

"Last year," Caps says, "we were lucky. The police didn't stop us, and only two of us were followed home."

"But—"

"Followed home and dealt with. Threats. Violence. Xanthia was in the hospital for a month."

"I—"

"We're *loud*, Nee. This one day, we stop being invisible, and people can't ignore us."

All that silent hate with the stereo turned up to ten.

I understand. There's risk. Be careful. Stay in groups.

Cap promises to walk me home. I listen carefully.

We'll remember—

Water.

Good shoes.

Do not accept offers from strange men (or women). . . .

Safety in numbers. And we'll figure out a meeting point on Friday night, the night before.

Got it.

Still, it bothers me that Tale will not take the risk. That she won't stand beside us, proud.

"What's with her?" I ask again.

"Tale?" Cap frowns.

"Yeah. You know her, right? You get her. I've seen the concern between you, and she's so . . . I don't know . . . Why won't she *come*?"

He pushes down his hood, and he looks tired, and he smiles the smile of a man who has seen many moons. "Tale . . . Many of us . . . have not had the best of luck with sharing ourselves with the world. It's hard."

"But she's so . . . confident. So sure."

There's that smile again. "Here. Sure. Here is safe. It's all in her control."

"But—" What could be so bad that big, strong, charm-the-thing-you-want Tale can't win? "What happened?"

"Not my story. You'll have to ask her. But Tale *knows* it isn't safe. More than any of us. Be gentle, okay?"

"How can I? She won't talk to me."

"Then maybe you're not asking right?" And then he adds, a little softer, "My story, though, is that I live alone, and have since I was twelve. I'm broken, and my parents could not, would not see that I was also whole."

It's my turn to frown.

"My story is that once, my mother made me pretty dresses, but"—he pushes on before I can ask questions—"they never fit. This draws less attention. I can *swagger*, hidden quiet in this cap and hood, and no one bats an eye."

"So are you . . ." And I stop. He's trusting me with this, and the answer doesn't matter. I don't want to know.

"I don't know." He smiles, almost sad. "It doesn't matter. My story is that it is easier to be a man than to look *butch* or *femme* or something in between."

"Easier like . . . safer?"

He nods, raises a fist to his heart. "And easier here. I've learned—we all learn—how to protect our own weaknesses. We have to. We pull our secrets close—like Pride. We march. We're *there*, and we want to be seen, but we won't show them everything and we will not share until we're ready."

I sit in my cupboard listening to all the sounds a building like this makes. The whisper of empty corridors. The static seeping from the studios. The *buzz* behind them. Locked away but there.

I listen to the shuffling of papers. The chewing, breathing, typing of my boss.

I hear it all.

And footsteps, maybe, right outside the door. Twice I think I hear someone go past, and twice my stomach drops and rises to my throat at once. And then I breathe, and tell myself that I imagined it.

I've thought about this. Hard.

Mama's *tchhh*ed at me so many times this week that I lost count, because I've thought of nothing else.

This week is Mandela week. Full of politics and protests and standing tall and strong.

Tale's silence grates—all her fear and hiding, whatever it is for. I hate that she would not even look at me. That she will not march and that we have to. I hate that Tale, the woman with the panther voice so slick and powerful—Tale with the leading and the taking—could not even find her words.

And I don't want to bed down in that world.

I've thought about it, hard. Whatever it may bring, I'm doing this.

I unclench my fists and breathe, feel the nerves thrumming underneath my skin, and breathe again.

I'm doing this.

I'm going to fix it.

"Welcome, welcome, friends and countrymen. Today on this, your musical literacy show, I want to talk to you in seriousness. Here on ABCs, you're listening to the Ms, and today is Tata Mandela day. We're talking about *courage* and expressiveness and *power*."

And I play just one line: *Freeeeeeee, Nelson Mandela!* And fade out. It is enough.

"Music. Is. Power.

"Look at the movement allll around that period. So much anger and resentment and, at the same time, so much hope. Hope that *music* brought. Because it gave people a voice."

We go through "Biko" and "Asimbonanga"—this rendition from the Soweto Gospel Choir—and Masekala's "Home."

"These songs, they were carried like torches, lighting up the darkest times. And have you noticed, if you're standing in the dark, walking home alone at night, the rhythm of a song will keep you safe, and keep your footsteps true? You sing it to yourself and there's a voice beside you. You sing it, and remind yourself that you are not the dark; it cannot swallow you. There are all kinds of dark. Literal dark and metaphorical. And songs, they work for either.

"So these songs were carried, and these songs were shared, each one lighting up another until the chain stood strong.

"These were songs of solidarity.

"Solidarity, and the scattering of seeds. No one can police music. They tried—they banned all the big songs with the power from the radio. They burned them. Scratched them out. But the music lives, and you cannot capture it.

"They sang. Everywhere, leaving evidence on people's hearts.

"It's like that. Sing me a song and I will listen. Whether you speak of Mandela and politics, of poverty, consumerism, AIDS, discrimination, of black or white or rainbow, I will listen. *Really* listen.

"Talk to me of all our differences, and I will run. But sing, and we're on common ground."

And this is it. I'm doing it. For every mention of a boy, of marriage, of what men I don't want are capable of. For every time I *almost* muttered Tale's name. For Tale and her will-not-come. For *everyone* who's ever felt the weight of silence. I'm letting out the song.

I hit play on SA's out-and-proudest singer, Nakhane Touré. And his smooth angst—vocals and guitar—sing out across the airwaves, full of fear and guilt and longing for man he cannot-should-not have. Just like that, I'm labeled. Sympathizer at best. Proud, if they look harder. And my heart cracks and it's beautiful. I just hope that others hear it too.

I hope Tale's listening.

"I *believe you* when you sing of love. Whatever it looks like. I *believe you* when you sing of hate or sorrow. Music binds us and we feel it too.

"It's like . . . Have you ever listened to a sad sad song, and the lyrics are part of it, but all the history of your own sorrows, the slow and heavy phrase, the harmonies, just *break your soul*?

"Or had an upbeat cheer you on a dreary day?

"Music has the power to make us feel as well as make us think. And that is everything.

"And it is international. Music reflects us, sends our image and our message out to others, and shines it back upon ourselves. And people *care*, because there is that connection. South Africa's plight has traveled *globally* through music. Look at *Graceland*, breaking the world's boycott to show that music, love, and song are stronger than this banishment."

Paul Simon and Ladysmith dance happy in my ears.

"Think of everything that did, introducing us to a new audience.

"And think of Live Aid and Live Eight. Do we wish that they would focus on a different message? A different kind of message? Surely. But that will only happen if we sing.

"So today, my challenge to you all is . . . *sing*. Sing the lyrics that you'd like to hear spread out across the world, whatever they may be: Sing about your cool careers, your cars, your brand-new *takkies*, prom. Sing about the girl, the boy; love whoever, unapologetically. Sing about your dreams and histories. Black, white, gay, straight, ANC, or, IFP, dancer, singer, scholar, waster—I don't care. Sing a song that's you.

"I'm telling you that it's okay. That you're allowed to sing your own song and sing it proud."

Tale. Are you listening?

"I'm giving you the power."

It's fresh and bright and light outside. Unreal. As though somebody painted it, so close that it's almost right but not. And I stride out into the street and I feel tall.

Comments: 537

Woah.

Go go gadget BEATS.

Niiiice. I love the way you find the obvious and the obscure and you give us both.

Isn't that singer gay?
>GAY
>>YOU gay
>>>do you think SHE gay? Nice girl like that?
>>>>It's always the nice ones. -___-

What is this Gay-straight?
>*wink wink*
>> You'll notice that the presenter did an entire podcast before this on love without one reference to a boyfriend or her own feelings or dedications . . . Just that "love is love" thing. Bit ambiguous.
>>>Do you think she is?
>>>>It's LESBOS. Are u? SHAME.
>Don't think she mentioned any cock
>>Wil yu b mah gf? I sh u hw its dun.
>>>You're disgusting. How could you endorse that sick, sick man? God commands that it shall only be a man and woman.
>>>>>You know what Touré is singing, right?

>>>>>>Hush up. She's talking of Tata Mandela, and music as a revolution. Nothing more or less. Keep your filth away.

>>>>>>> Sick. SICK. You should die.

Dis is a family show. Ur propaganda is unacceptible. Dis is not da revolution. Lost a customer.

WHAT IS THIS
>Boycott
>>Yah, I'll not be listenin

Umzi? Not on my home soil!

WHO ELSE IS ON TOP OF THE WORLD? #music #MUSIC #POWER

It's . . . unsettling.

I know that it's the Internet, just strangers I will never meet, and I don't *care*.

But their words spread like a loa loa bite; harmless right until the worms start crawling around in your eyeball.

Only man and woman.

Shame.

I feel filthy. Wrong. But they do not understand. They haven't felt the things I do. It can't be wrong; it can't. And yet . . .

It starts there, on Facebook and in Umzi's comments. Questions. Speculation. Names.

And I don't look.

Janet texts me, once:

Got your back, bestie. Don't worry.

And then she does not say another word, just sweeps them all away.

But there's whispers in the real world, and then I come home and find Mama waiting, cheeks sucked in and hands upon her hips, and she says, "Is there something that you want to tell me?"

"No?" I say, not catching on. Mama does not do the Internet, any more than she does radio.

"Mm-hmm. I heard something today."

"Oh yeah?"

"Yes. I heard a rumor."

"Oh?"

"This show of yours. There are people saying that it's devil worship. That you're . . . engaging in activities. With women."

Tale, wrapped around me, up inside me. Song.

"What? No!" I cry, and the lie snakes hot and bitter in my gut.

She *tsk*s, peering at me hard, and then she says, "Yeeees, well. Come. Sit over here."

And then we pray. Mama loud, with waving hands over all the candles she can find, and me with my head bowed in silence, listening as she asks God to save me from temptation and to shield me from mistaken lies. She asks him to deliver me a nice, God-fearing man to prove the tongue-wagglers of the church wrong. Asks that he will find his way into my music, and again, *Save your daughter Neo from temptations of the woman flesh.*

Over and over until her voice goes hoarse and the candles have burned low, and then she prays some more in silence.

I'm actually glad of school the next day, glad for textbooks I can hide behind and problems I can try to solve.

I'm grateful for my bestbest friend taking my hand and standing right beside me.

Still. They say it takes a village to raise children, and in Khayelitsha, everybody's business is laid bare.

Everybody heard the show, or heard *of* it, or saw the comments, and everybody talks:

"Pastor Simphiwe says it's wrong. That all love is not equal in the eyes of God."

"She can't be. She seems so normal."

"What would they even *do*? Nothing fits together."

Every single time, Janet is there, cutting down the whispers with her sharp tongue and assurance—with an arm around my shoulder—that the talent has nothing to say, but all concerns are deeply unfounded, and would they kindly get a life?

"Here." Joseph Mthandeni does not whisper, he more accurately bellows. "Mahone. Let's talk." He cuts across the classroom surge far ahead of my best friend, and wraps a heavy arm around my shoulder, steering me outside. "You're not . . ." His tone is cheerful, but he's loud, and I don't believe the friendliness. ". . . *y'know*, are you?"

Every muscle tenses.

And Janet lands beside us. "Hey, guys."

"Hi," I breathe.

Joseph squints at both of us in turn, then leans in, low and mean. "You're not. Turning. My girlfriend."

Janet hears, and sucks the air in through her teeth as she steps closer, stands on tiptoes to lean on his other shoulder, and her bright, confident voice rings louder than anything else today. "I've known Neo my whole *life*, goon. She's my best friend." I wait. Which brand of defense is this? The *Neo's not like us; she's married to her music*? The *She couldn't possibly . . .* ?

But this time, Janet doesn't need her words. She rests back on her heels, takes his hand and kisses it. "Come on." And she leads him off behind a tree.

And I'm left catching laughter in my throat at the idea that *anything* or anyone could turn my friend from her own mind at all.

As grateful as I am for my best friend, I'm even more so for the school bell. Finally, I'm safe, and I can slip into the station, to the world of music, in my cupboard, where no one will care who I am or I'm not.

"Miss Mahone."

Mr. Sid bellows from his office as I reach my door.

I freeze. "Yes, sir?" He has never called me that before, and it feels different. Dangerous.

I should have known.

"Come." He gestures to the chair beside his desk. "We need a conversation."

I sit, and he continues, "I spoke to your father today."

And the brooding poison-leaded silence drops into my gut and *spreads*.

He what?

"Nice man. Most upstanding, very honest."

"Yes, sir."

It makes me nervous when they talk.

And I know that Baba hates me being here, but *sure*, he would not spread this whispering.

I scan the desk, looking for some clue about their conversation, or what Mr. Sid called me in here to say, but there is nothing save his rot-sweet tea and a half-empty plate of biltong squares beside the silver knife.

He leans forward over steepled, eager hands, and he smacks his lips together hungrily. "Don't you want to know *why* your father and I engaged in a conversation, Neo?"

Something's wrong. He's playing with me.

I nod my head as steady as I can, and it takes everything I have in me not to leap up from the chair and *run*. Because where would I go? Umzi is my house of dreams.

"He came to me," he says, watching like a hawk, "concerned. Concerned that music—music and *my show*, my *station*—is corrupting his innocent daughter. And that perhaps he should pull you out before it rubs off on your siblings. Imagine my surprise!" He pauses, breathes, and I *see him* relax, but somehow I don't trust it. He chuckles, and I'm sure it is a trap. A lure for unsuspecting prey. "Of course I told him that it isn't true. I told him Umzi is for families. For youngsters. That we would never poison *mice*, let alone the city's children."

I nod. But my world has dropped away.

Rub off on my siblings? Really?

How could Baba think like that?

Mr. Sid sighs, so heavy that I think his breath will sink right through the floor. "But then I got to thinking, why would any father think that? What on earth could lead him to that thought?"

Good question—Run, Neo—I do not want to know. All three answers crowd my head at once, and none of them quite make it. I just sit and wait.

"And . . . I found some things."

Get out—Where?—Get out.

"There are accusations."

*F****ng lesbian devil's maid.*

Dildo muncher.

Rub off on your siblings.

He leans forward and his top lip curls. "And, you know, I'm not entirely sure that they're unfounded."

"I—"

Tears burn sharp behind my eyes and my throat feels too small and I sit there not blinking, not breathing, gripping the arms of the chair because *I cannot let him see.*

He sits there for a while, watching for movement like a cat with prey.

Don't give it to him.

"Well?"

I swallow hard and wet my lips before I trust myself to speak. "I . . . saw those comments. And I'm surprised you didn't see it for the trolling that it is. It's probably some kids in Jo'burg having fun with us." And I try to laugh, I do, but it sounds hollow.

"Hm."

He reaches for the *biltong* with one hand, drops a fistful of the dry-meat chunks into his mouth and sucks upon them, leaving me in silence.

I feel *small*, like when you're five years old and sitting on a chair so tall your feet can't reach the floor, and the teacher turns on you.

"You're saying," he says, after a while, still chewing, "that these honest people's fears are all unfounded?"

And I know that Tale wants me to be quiet. I know.

And I know that Mr. Sid is bigger stronger faster, has the power.

But I cannot lie. Not now. Not about this. "I'm saying, sir, that those comments were unnecessary and abusive, and there was *nothing* in my show that should have prompted that."

"So you *weren't* promoting *homosexual ideals?*"

I can hear Tale in my head: *You stay quiet. This is not your song.* But then I see her curled in on herself, and I want justice.

I don't know what to say.

"I thought so." He nods gravely at my silence. "I do not like being used, child. I am not accustomed to it. I will not *grow* accustomed to it for this deviant agenda. I understand. I do. This Western lure is strong for youth today: fast food, fast cars, fast sex." He leans right back in his leather chair. Right back. It squeaks as he moves. And he reaches down to adjust the buckle of his belt, and shifts, and it is *very* obvious what he houses underneath his suit. I pull my gaze away, but I can feel him watching, feel him noting my discomfort. "I understand that their ideals are loose and free, but this . . . It is unseemly. And I will not have it in my house; I will not have it jeopardizing everything I've built, you hear?"

I swallow hard, but my voice cracks with anger anyway. "Yes, sir."

"Good. I'm glad we understand each other. You can go." He waves me away, reaching for the biltong with his other hand. That's it. I do not matter anymore. "But I'll be watching you."

The next day I hear the rumors everywhere; I see things in the shadows, at the edges of my vision, and behind me, as clear as the sky is blue until the second that I turn to look.

I hear them too. Footsteps. Mr. Sid's *I'll be watching* in my ears. Laughter, cruel and whispered. Fear.

It's *exhausting*, living in this world of careful steps and blood that runs dread-cold. And by Friday night I almost do not step out of the door.

I could stay home.

I could curl up in an armchair with my sisters and watch reruns of *SA's Got Talent*, or do homework and it not be rushed for once.

I could curl up in bed beneath the blankets and listen to the creak of wind against the walls.

I almost do not go. I almost listen to the voice of dread.

But in that little bar is something beautiful and mine, and after everything, I need that. It's like the crescendo right before the final verse—the rolling of the drums, the rising chords, the tension, all so powerful that you're swept up and powerless.

I could not stop it if I tried.

I do not anticipate the deadweight sound the band rings out tonight, as though the life has drained out through their feet.

And I do not anticipate Tale's reaction once we step into the night.

She wheels around to face me, and in the moonlight the whites of her eyes glow fear.

"What the *fuck*, Nee? What the fuck?"

"Shhhh."

"NO, I WILL NOT 'SHHHH.' You can't tell *me* to 'shh.' What is this? Don't you get it? Jesus."

"But—"

"No, Neo. You're fucking with your life here. My life. Do you think I want this?"

"What?"

"This isn't politics. It's not some rally, it's real life. And if you want to stick around you need to stay *quiet*." And she looks at me with so much contempt, so much anger, so much fear, all balled up into a verbal fist.

It winds me.

And Tale turns away. She's done.

She's walking away, so sure, and I *know* that if she slips into the shadows, then we're done for good.

I cannot let that happen.

"Wait! Wait! Tale!"

I catch her at her door, fumbling with the padlock. "Don't!" I grab at her hand, still on the lock. "Don't leave!"

"Go *home*, Neo."

"No! I—"

"I know. But I don't need your campaigns here. Not here. Not in my home." And she pulls away, pulls the padlock and chain free.

"Please. I wasn't—I don't *understand*."

"Uuuaaargh! No. You don't. You *don't* understand." And I think she's going to leave me there, but Tale pulls me after her, slams the door behind us. "You don't know what it's like to cry that line and *lose*."

I freeze, and I feel the space between us as though it were a thousand miles.

"What?" My voice sounds small. Not big and strong enough for subjects such as this.

And Tale sighs, sinks down onto the bed. And she looks so wrecked, I just want to comfort her, but there's too much between us.

"You spill this stuff, Neo, and people *hear*. And unless you've cried that line and lost it all, you have *no right* to force it on the rest of us. This isn't your fight, Neo, and this isn't how we fight it."

And suddenly I see the loss and fear and understand, more than I ever wanted to, and I'm beside her, wrapped around her, holding holding holding, because if I let go I'm scared she'll fall, or melt away, or run.

I hold her and we sit in silence and then somehow, sometime in the night, we move, slide up from the floor and into bed, and there is holding of a different sort, and I wrap Tale in the safety of my skin, and then she kisses me.

I never knew that kisses could contain such *sorrow*, and I almost want to pull away, but beside me, Tale's broken and all I want is to fix her, to make her whole, and so we kiss, and I swallow every scrap of sadness as she lets it go. And it's more than kissing, slow and sad and mourning for the world we're in. A two-hearts dance for everything that's lost. And then it's *angry*, fast and furious and hard until there's nothing left and we fall back to the earth, to sadness. And we kiss and kiss and kiss and I hold her tight until she falls asleep.

My voice shakes all the way through today's podcast, and each time I play out a song and find myself gulping for the air because I *cannot* breathe while I'm talking to them; there's no room in my tensed-up chest for air.

I wonder who is listening out there. Baba? Tale? Lovers? Haters?

I imagine Mr. Sid's ears pricked behind the door, waiting, waiting for the right moment to pounce.

Should I deny it loudly and on air? Claim there is a boy or I am saving myself for the one? Laugh, all light and free, and hope they do not catch the lie?

I can't. So silence takes its place and sits like deadweight on my chest, and I fill the air with chatter, tell them potted history of every track, but I don't hear the words. They're dust against the wind. They're nothing. Silent.

You can have whole swathes of conversation using song. Call and response. Musical association. Simply sharing something that you love. But I tried to start a conversation here. To welcome all. And people shut it down with words of hate.

Music transcends everything and welcomes all. But only when we are allowed to sing and do it freely.

And I try to understand. I do. But I just can't see how it *matters* who I am outside of music, how it matters who I choose to lie beside.

What difference does it make?

And the more I play for them, the more it worries at my brain, and by the time our hour is up, I barely know why I am here.

To: J

    Hey. Wanna meet today?

    From:)

Sure, at da station?

No. Not here. Not here. Someone will hear.
Not the BigTall tree either. Too open.

To: J

By the wall?

I hit send, shaking hot, and immediately I want to pull it back.
What if she—

What? It's an unspecific fear. Runs? Tells? Stays and makes my
fear of sharing foolish?

My best friend has all the power right now, and she does not
even know it.

But I hear *unless you've cried that line and lost,* and it's time to
sing my song.

Besides. We're sisters, almost, and I've shared her joys and
secrets since the dawn of time. We're sisters, almost—so different
that I don't think she'd have stayed this long if she didn't care.

I don't know if she'll stay. I don't know if she'll run. But I have
to trust her with it, have to know.

• • •

I crouch by the wall and wait, let my fingers run across the rubble, touching memories.

It all started here.

And there she is, my bestbest friend, as big and sure as always.

"Hey."

"Hey . . ." Sitting here, I'm so tempted to start with *Do you remember when we used to play house?*

Mansions, she would say.

And I would nod and we'd remember and the world would stay exactly as it was. But I can't put it off. I can't hide anymore.

I tell her.

Everything.

"No." she says, "No, no, no. You're just confused."

"I'm not." And because she is my best and longest friend, I tell her more. I tell her of the swell, the rise and fall. All my love laid bare.

And Janet *sneers*. Recoils.

And then she yells, reminds me of the dresses that we wore and the double weddings that we planned. Tells me that this isn't *right*. Isn't how her life's supposed to go.

And then she tells me, quiet, that she loves me and I should do what I want, but she *cannot*, with this, cannot watch me burn.

And as she turns her back and runs, I think I get it; I think I always knew. But our songs wove together from the start, and I don't get it at all.

This morning I scrub Mama's floors to the rhythm of Jed's safety list.

Always travel in a group.

And watch your back.

Do not answer back to the police.

You don't have to answer anyone.

Stay safe.

Mama maybe takes my silence for obedience, or maybe I am too preoccupied to notice any disapproval.

All I know is that today's the day.

And I'm excited.

Scared. Because *what if she knew?* Scared because the others are.

But mostly . . . mostly I just want to stand up proud.

I work Mama's floor polish hard, that word playing over in my head.

Proud.

Proud.

Stand up, proud.

And I imagine standing, right there in the salon, and speaking Tale's name. Watching Mama's face as I explain.

But on the door of Mama's shack there is a mural. A bald, smiling head: WE CAN MAKE YOU ANYTHING YOU WANT TO BE.

And as I see it, Tale curdles on my tongue.

I see that mural come to life and leer at me.

Anything but that. You can't be that. It's wrong.

I shrug Jeso off. He's fast, but his legs aren't so long as mine, and I dart quick between the houses, past a woman herding babies—three—and another scrubbing sheets and under-wear, through alleys just like Mama's, full of shirts and soaps and desperation. I round a corner, and see Jeso nearly pitch over a lazing dog, all rag and bone, and by the time he rights himself, I'm gone.

I feel bad. But today's the day, and I can't take him with me. Not if it's as dangerous as everybody says.

When I'm sure I've lost him, I slow down. Feel the sun upon my back, the ground beneath my feet. And *smile*. This is it. Me. In the world.

It's hot and I am happy and I stop to buy an orange—the happiest of fruits, perhaps, with its sharp sweetness wrapped inside a tiny sun—and only when I hand over the coin do I see Grandma Inkuleko striding fast toward me.

And I try to run, but Grandma's gaze is strong as Tale's and I'm pinned.

She waves me over.

"Hi," I say. "Good day!"

My thumb digs right into the orange peel and the whole street smells *grand*. Does it mask my fear?

"Young Neo! Where are you off to in such a rush?"

"Oh, nowhere."

"Nowhere, eh?"

"No, ma'am."

"Ehhh, you know . . . I used to have some of those records they scratched out, hidden in my house. They never got to them."

I stare. Hold out the orange, offer her a piece, because I don't know what to say.

She takes one, pops it in her nearly toothless mouth and speaks around it. "That's right, I listen. You are quite the star!"

"I—" Grandma Inkuleko heard my show? She—

Does she know? Will she tell Mama?

Anything but that. You can't be that. It's wrong.

"Listen. You do what you need, my girl. Love is precious, as precious as life itself. Indeed, maybe they're the same."

I nod. Not believing that I'm here, that she is saying this. She *knows*.

"You know . . . when they took Mandela and they took our homes and hearts and music, some of us stood firm. We kept house, and we stayed proud and we sang. Once, I hid a scared young man inside my house for three whole days. There was a policeman knew, but would I let him in my kitchen? No . . . You remember they're nobody's boss, my girl. That heart? That heart of yours, they cannot have that heart."

"I—Yes. I will."

And Grandma spits the skin of her orange segment to the ground, and grins before she turns away.

Grandma Inkuleko *knows*.

And she approves.

I wish that I could walk this street with Janet at my side. I do. She'd love it, all the color and the voice and circumstance. The *being here and being seen* of it.

I miss her.

But there's Grandma Inkuleko, and there's Jed and Zee and Cap, and even Tam from back behind the bar. And today, we celebrate. Today we show our pride.

Khayelitsha Pride is not the red carpet affair or wall of righteousness I had imagined, quite, but it is *real* and bigger than I really ever dreamed—a hundred people gathered at the starting point, with banners—*banners*, loud and permanent—and hand-painted shirts.

CAN YOU SEE?

EQUALITY!

GAYZ & LESBIANS ALSO HUMAN

I AM NOT INVISIBLE?

FREE GENDER: PROTECTING WOMEN

There's Zebra in his rainbow flag shorts, Jed beside him draped in a rainbow flag cape.

And Cap, smiling in the sunshine, hood down.

I wondered, suddenly, how anyone could ever see him any other way except for who he is. He's Cap.

Everywhere I turn, there's people, waving, hugging, looking for their crowd.

"Are they all—" I ask Zebra, quietly.

He nods. "Mostly. There's a few supporters, I would guess."

Wohhh, all of them. Everybody just like me. Tall and fat and short and thin and girls and boys and maybe neither, men in suits and men with nothing but bare chests, and one in a knee-length purple dress, proudly showing off his hairy knees and work boots. And the women, some in *kanga*s and thick head wraps, leaning in to kiss each other's cheeks, others in jean shorts and high-vis jackets. Several women have babies hung upon their backs and one girl about Jeso's age is prancing around us all, offering sugar cookies with one hand and rainbow badges with the other.

I take one of each and proudly pin the badge upon my shirt, *dare* anyone to see it. The strength of having numbers. I feel safe.

How can Tale not like this?

And then we're off, and I wish that she were here so we could march together hand in hand and marvel at this one moment of good.

We move, one loud-voiced woman at the front keeping us together, keeping us on the decided routes.

At first, I feel uneasy. "Do you feel that?" I ask.

"What?"

The hairs on my neck stand up. I shiver. And I feel them watching.

Who?

I look around, but all I see is crowds. No one that I know. No one menacing.

"I don't know. Like someone's watching. Are we being followed?"

"Of course we are. This is a *march*. We're everywhere."

He's right, of course. It's what we're here for, and I roll my shoulders, breathe, relax, and let the laughter and the marching of a hundred pairs of feet into my soul.

Somewhere behind us, there is singing. Songs of power and of praise.

And there's chanting and the waving of the banners and the signs.

We. Are. Heard.

And it doesn't matter that the people stare, or move their kids inside, because we're here together, and we are invincible.

It doesn't matter that the police line the major roads, set stern and ready, facing *us* instead of them as though we are the potential threat. Because we're here, together. And we're marching so that next year might be better. So that next year, maybe, Tale will be marching at my side.

And I wish that she could see just how good it is already. Just how many of us are here, marching proud and loud and safe, and not worried about who hears our song at all.

At our final point we gather, foot weary, and everybody huddles close.

"We are a great nation. One of the first to *care* about human rights and sexuality. And yet—

"People are not safe. We're not accepted. People see us in the street and laugh. They take our children. Break our legs. This *great rainbow nation* does not care for us.

"Because it doesn't know us. It doesn't know how.

"And so, today . . . today we show them. We say, 'Ho! We're here! And we want—no, *demand*—to walk the streets like this in *safety*. Without fear. Without persecution. It is written in our laws, and we demand it.'" The speaker steps down, and there's a moment's silence and a roll call. *Every year,* Jed whispers.

Remembering the fallen and forgotten. Every year a longer list.

There are speeches. Horror stories, tales of triumph, one after another. All of them proclaiming, *This must stop. We're equal.*

There's Eudy Simelane and Zoliswa Nkonyana and Gift Makau, all gone, and Precious—only Precious please, one name—who is very much still here, but has not seen her kids since they were born in case she infects them with her gay sickness.

There is anger and there's tears.

And there are stories of long and hard-won reconciliation, of voices people thought they'd never hear again. Of starting new and choosing family. Of jobs and children and acceptance.

I did not notice Cap leaving our group, but he's sidling up to the front of the crowd, and taking the microphone, and he speaks slow and sure, and with his hands—much faster, fluid—and I promise myself that I'll ask him how when we are done.

"There was a time," he says, "when I would have been drowned at birth"—he pauses—"for my broken ears. There was a time when black and white could not walk the same streets. And there will be a time"—he speaks louder, punctuating every word—"when all of us can laugh—a little bitterly—about these times, and say, *There was a time . . .*"

There's a smatter of applause.

"That day will come. And it will come because of you. And everyone who came before and everyone who follows. Marching. Living. Choosing not to hide whenever it is safe. It will come because we stand up and say, *Here I am,* and, *I deserve this. I am not a monster.*

"It might come at a price. But we keep shouting and eventually it will be loud enough that even I with broken ears will hear.

"That. Day. Will. Come."

. . .

I stand between my friends and listen to the stories of people just like me. And my world opens up.

It's scary. I'm not going to lie. I stood there wondering what all this was, whether we would ever, ever win.

Wondering how all this could happen right beneath my feet. Wondering how I did not even know.

. . . I didn't. I knew nothing.

But it was exhilarating. All these people with the faces just like mine, who felt the music, who knew that you could not stop it, and that this song was worth singing, and singing loud.

I stand between my friends, and see the world.

Gradually, the speeches get less rowdy and impassioned and the crowds disperse.

"I'm *dry*," Jed complains.

"Yeah. I marched my glitter rainbow socks off. Are we done now?"

"After party?"

"After party."

"Yesssss."

And so we go.

Tale's there already, biting on her nails as though she thought we'd never show, and I bounce up to her so full of love for everything that I almost knock her over.

"Heyyyy," she says. "How was it?"

"I wish you were there!" I babble, "I wish you could have seen—"

"I know." And then, "I'm sorry."

And she looks so sad and beautiful, and the stories—young girls cast out of their homes, beaten, bullied, the girl whose grandpa tried to boil the gay right out of her—and the heckling and fear sit sharp on my chest and I cannot be mad. I'm only glad that she is here with me right now. That I still get to share this day with her. That she invited me into this world.

"It's okay," I say, reaching up to kiss her. And I mean it.

Everything is different now. I understand. I've seen the scars. I've heard.

There is quite a crowd in here tonight, bubbling over from the march, I'd guess, judging from the rainbow stripes and the extra exuberance. But Tale and I do not dance, or join them pouring cold beers down their necks. We slip away into our corner, and we talk.

Slowly, after everyone is watered thoroughly, the bar empties and the music dwindles and the conversation dies. It's time to go. And as we step into the night, I try to hug the *warmth* of everybody to my chest. A shield against the dark.

Jed and Zebra lead each other off, and Cap tightens the hood of his sweatshirt and strides confident into the night.

But Tale stays, and pulls me close.

"You okay?"

"Mm." I nod. But as the people disappear, so does the happiness, the safety in the numbers, and I'm left with Eudy Simelane and Zoliswa Nkonyana, Gift Makau and Precious, and with them, all the hatred and the whispers in the shadows, and I feel like I am being watched. "I just . . . Ever get the feeling that you're being followed?"

I watch her face shift through shock and horror, anger, and then . . .

"Oh, shit."

And I see her face the other night, crumbling right before my eyes, and I can't see her go through that again. Not for me. Not ever. "Don't worry!" I say quickly. "It might not even be. I'm paranoid. It's been a long, strange day."

"No, wait. Oh shit, *today*?"

I nod.

"I think that might be my fault."

Tale?

"I just . . . want you to be safe."

"Eh?"

"I didn't want to go. I really hate those things; too many memories. But then I panicked, because what if something happened to you and I wasn't there? But I *still* didn't want to, and I knew I'd ruin it. So . . . I might have tailed you from a safe and grumpy distance."

It's so ridiculous that I can't help but laugh. And Tale's laughing too, warm breath in my hair. And we're leaning into one another, holding one another up and laughing, and suddenly the shadows recede and the night is friendly once again.

When we've stood still long enough for the air to scratch icy at our skin, Tale whispers, "Let me walk you home?"

And I'm off, giggling again, but Tale lifts a finger to my lips. "Shhh. I'm serious. No one needs to be alone today."

"Okay." And then, before we move, "Hey . . . I'm sorry too."

"Huh?"

"I should have listened, but I didn't get it. I'm sorry. I get it now."

And Tale leans into my hair and murmurs, "I love you, you know?"

It's different from the way I had imagined it, walking home with Tale in the dark. It's calmer, with no hopscotch over low-slung clotheslines, no chasing-catching-grabbing, or darting here and there.

It's different. But her hand's in mine, and my heart sings, and everything is right.

"Have you ever noticed that the air smells different at night?" I whisper it, so as not to break the spell.

She stops, looks at me with one raised eyebrow. "D'you go sniffing much at night?" But she inhales deep and exhales slow and smiles at me, surprised. "It does. Earthier and fresh."

I nod. "And sort of peppery . . . It sounds different too."

We stand there in the middle of the street and listen.

"Mm," she says. "It *murmurs*. Soft. Like it's too polite."

"I always thought it sounded drowsy-wide-awake. A two-tone energy, hummed across two frequencies."

She nods, and I add, even quieter, "Just the way you make me feel."

"I make you tired?"

"No. Content. And restless."

"Huh."

"Forget it. It's stupid."

"No, it's not. . . . I was thinking how the best music does that. It makes you feel at home, and pushes you to get out and explore."

Night. Music. Tale.

Three perfect echoes in my perfect, perfect world.

And it gets better.

Somehow, knowing there's a *world* of queers out there, it changes everything. I'm bolder.

Oh, I don't go *telling* anyone. I wouldn't dare. But inside? Inside, I am taller than I've ever been. And somehow the silence, when I sit with it at Mama's table, is easier to bear. It doesn't change me back to who I was or who she thinks I should become. I'm free.

And Tale's different too.

We picnicked. One Saturday, in a small field behind the bar. All of us, and with my microphone and recorder in case somebody questioned us.

Zebra sat their throwing peanuts at everyone's heads until a proper fight broke out and Cap landed in all the sandwiches.

And in the dark, at night, the space that's ours? It doesn't feel so full of secrets anymore.

"You know . . . I was your age, once." Tale spoke soft into my hair. "But I was not so brave."

"You're the bravest person that I know."

Her voice cracks. "I'm not. Not then, not now."

Tale, with her so-sure touch and guiding hand and voice that captures hearts, not brave? "I've seen you."

"Eh?"

"I've seen the way you move. The way you own the stage. That's brave."

She laughs, and it is weak and honest. "Did you know that any other stage, I sing and play, but I won't look out at the audience?"

That Wednesday bar? I murmur soothing noises, and she carries on.

"The only place I've ever felt safe is Tam's bar. Or here, with you."

"That—" What? I don't understand, and I so want to. I reach for her, but Tale pulls away. She is not ready. Not quite. Not yet. Not tonight.

So I let it go; what else could I do?

The next night we're together, she tells me how Tam rescued her once, from a partner who hated herself for being gay. Someone so messed up that she would take it out on both of them.

Repeatedly, and subtly, until Tale believed everything she said. And then she started on the ways that bruised where you could see.

And Tam? She offered her a bed under the bar until she got herself together.

"There's good people out there, Nee. But . . ." She leaves it hanging in the air.

"I'm not brave. I'm not. But this world doesn't let me be."

It's horrible. Horrible, horrible, and worse than that. But, "You're here. You're here, after everything. That's brave."

Braver than anything.

The bravest.

Mr. Sid lets up, as well. He smiles when I pass him in the corridor, and the suspicion's faded from his eyes. Ratings are still great, and besides the odd abusive *let me have you* comment, everyone seems happy.

This week is rock, and I am ready to go *wild*.

It seems you *can* have everything. Music, Tale, radio. Three perfect echoes in a perfect, perfect world.

H ow about that movie?"

"Eh?"

Okay, TV. It's not Bond, but the community center is showing the TV on the big projector screen all night.

I lean right into her and place a hand against her heart. "You sure?"

"Who wouldn't want to watch *SA's Got Talent* or the *Funniest TV*? Little dogs dancing for tricks? Come *on*."

I laugh. "Okay!"

And so we go, hand in hand. We take the quiet streets through town, stick to the shadows, but we go. And in the safety of the theater, we lean into one another as much as you can on plastic chairs, and Tale's fingers lace with mine every time we both reach for the popcorn. And she laughs and laughs and laughs and I don't know if it is at the guy who cannot sing, or me, or freedom, but it might just be the greatest sound that she has ever made. Better than the higher higher of that first night's song. Better than the noises I can pull from her in bed. This—this giggling with abandon—is the greatest music I have ever heard.

She walks me home, practically dancing through the shadows. Ghostlike. Fairylike. And the night sounds clean and bright, as though her perfect laugh escaped and now it's bouncing across rooftops.

She stops against a tree and pulls me close and whispers, "I feel safe with you." And then she's racing off two steps ahead and bouncing. I grin. Watch her move. Imagine, like I did that first night, song, painted right across the sky, in the walls, hanging in the trees. Only this time Tale's playing the night, all of it is hers. It's beautiful.

She grabs hold of another tree and spins around it, leans out as though she's flying.

She giggles.

And then they step out from nowhere and the laughter's gone.

I told you I'd be watching."

Mr. Sid. And he is not alone. They stand there, a silhouetted jury at a midnight trial.

"Run!" I bark at Tale, but it is too late, the ring has closed around us, and thick fists pull us apart and hold us where we stand.

She was right. *How* can she be right?

"Tale!" I try to wrench away. To bite and kick and punch or *anything* to get myself away. But they are many. Strong.

Across the circle, I can see that Tale does not even try. She stands there, quiet.

Stay quiet. This is not your song.

She doesn't even fight. Come *on*. I pull hard against fat fingers, twist hard one direction then another—

Mr. Sid steps forward. "Tale, hey?"

She says nothing, does not raise her gaze to meet him, and he reaches out and runs a finger down her chin.

I whimper. Or perhaps she does. Or we both do, in harmony.

"Come," Mr. Sid commands, and whoever stands behind me walks us both toward him in an awkward two-step.

What?

And where I fought and fought to get to her, now all I hear inside my head is *No no no no no no no. No. No.*

I freeze. But Iron Grip walks forward, and I do not have a choice.

And Tale's right in front of me again.

Right there. And I *long* to reach out, wrap my arms around

the girl, pull her into me, and climb right into her until we're safe. "Look, just let her go—"

Mr. Sid steps back half a step and smiles, and he stands there like a preacher with his open palms as if he's offering a gift.

"Kiss."

Someone in the ring around us jeers. And I can see the fear in Tale's eyes. So much of it. Balled with hate and loss and desperation. And we're back in Tale's room, all *Silence. Hold your tongue,* and shattered hope, and all the air tastes dead with fear and this time, "No" is all that I can do to keep her safe, to bring her back to me.

"No?" Mr. Sid announces to the night. "You won't kiss this *fine* specimen of womanhood?"

"No."

"But she's your . . . What is it you call yourselves? *Girlfriend? Soul mate? Sister Witch?*"

"Let. Her. Go," I say, and my voice cracks at the last word.

Was that a warning flash through Tale's eyes? I stare hard at her face, but there is nothing now.

"Oh, but it's simple. All you have to do is kiss the girl and you're both free." He steps back half a step again, gestures openly toward her. "Prove your love to her."

The whole circle—the whole night around us—holds its breath.

Fear prickles at my neck and down into my gut. And I *know* that it's a trap. It has to be. But there is no way out and Tale is right there in front of me and she's right there, right there, those big male hands upon her, and she won't even fight. What do I do?

One kiss.

Maybe, maybe if he *sees*?

"Nnnnnnnngh!" I scream, pulling hard against my bonds, pulling, wrenching, twisting, but his grip is *strong*. And I kick behind me, aiming for a groin, but I strike nothing but air.

I strain.

Tale.

She's *right there*. So close I can taste the salt tracks on her cheeks. And all I have to do is reach her, fall two inches forward and we're free.

"Let. Me. Go!"

I fight and fight and fight. My muscles scream, and his fingers wrench and tear my skin like rope. I fight.

And fight, and fight, and I get nowhere. As the hot-tired floods my limbs and I have nothing left to fight with, Mr. Sid steps in again. "I'm sorry. That was cruel. Of *course* you cannot kiss her like that. How awful of me. Kisses should be soft and tender. Where's the *mood*? Anyone have candles?"

And for one *awful* second I think he's going to play with fire and I imagine burning, blistering.

I swallow back a scream.

The circle tightens, watches eagerly.

"Where's the *intimacy*?" And he nods at my captor. "Closer." And he shoves me roughly in the back, pushes forward, mashing us together.

I can feel her. Breasts and breath and skin, *right there*. But this Tale is unyielding, broken, cannot even look at me. As if she's nothing but her parts.

Kiss her and you're free.

Eyes stare. I swear I can hear the wetting of lips and smack of tongues, the air hanging solid between us just waiting to shatter.

Maybe.

It's our only chance.

I steady myself against his pull, lift myself up on my toes, lean toward her. And the tears from her cheek rub off onto mine, cold against the heat of shame.

"I love you," I whisper, quiet, so no one else will hear.

And I wait for an answer. Movement. Anything.

"Kiss." He says it firmer this time. Nothing but bare threat. He delights in it.

Around us, the crowd shifts, impatient or eager or—And then I realize something I think Tale knew when they appeared.

It's over. There's no freedom after this. They'll never let us go.

You hear stories. Whispered hate. And then you never hear again.

"I love you." I say it again, right into her ear, and I hope the heat of it gets through the wall. I hope she hears.

And then I sink back to my heels, peel myself away, and shake my head.

"No?" Mock surprise. "No. Because you know it's wrong."

He waits. For a confession? Pleading? But I will not say it. Ever.

The rainbow badge is still in pride of place upon my shirt, and Umzi's leader sees it now and picks it off with deep disdain.

"What's this?"

"It's nothing," I say, hoping to appease him, somehow, hoping he will set us free.

"Nothing," he repeats. And in one stride he's over by Tale, pushing the pin right into her shoulder.

I feel it, searing pain, as though it were my own. But Tale's gone. She doesn't even flinch.

"Nothing. But it looks good on your witch, wouldn't you say?"

I spit, and miss him by a mile. And he just stands there and *smiles*.

And he nods. The circle shifts, opens, closes tighter, drags my Tale out of sight.

"This *temptress* lead you down a path no girl should walk," Mr. Sid says, leaning close. And I can smell the dead meat on his breath. The power seeping from his pores. "And we . . . your *family*, are here to draw you back into the fold. To teach you the true ways. What it means to be an African. A woman."

And then I'm on the ground surrounded by these looming eager men, and there are hands, pulling, pushing, tearing, and the cold night judging all the newly revealed parts of me.

Hands pulling me apart. And *flesh*. And I can smell the earth and fear and skin and sweat and I can smell the sex of them. It's *everywhere*, hanging in the air like rancid power.

One after another these men fall on me. I try to get away. To crawl back on my hands and get away. But they are everywhere. Inside me.

"You like it like that. Yessss, you like it."

"This is what it's meant to be, you see." Whispered nothings in my ears, which fall like stones.

And there's *blows*. I hear them first. Heavy. Solid. And someone screams and it rips through my heart.

Tale!

And I try to get to her but there are hands pulling me back, pulling me open, and there is hot and fast and clawing, and all the while I hear it, *thud*, *thud*, *thud*, *thwack*. I don't know *how* I hear it over everything, but there's this noise, strangled, wet, and loud. The worst sound I have ever heard.

And then there's *silence*.

And I know there's more. More pushing, pulling, bruises landing hard. More in and out. More breath upon my face and hands roving across my chest. More hunger, anger, more disgust. But there's that noise, slick and thick and wet. And it consumes my soul.

And then they fall away.

"We're done," a voice says. And it leans in and the smell of dry meat makes my stomach heave. "That station's *everything* to me, and you will not defile it."

He moves, and cold and silent air pours in, and then as I almost breathe he's there again, clear and bright as bullets. "I'll see you on Monday."

*S*ilence.

I wake in the still-dark with that sound lapping at my ears as if it were a rising tide, creeping closer, louder.

"Tale?" I try to cry out, but nausea swallows everything I have.

And the blackness falls again.

$\int$ ilence.

I awake again as the night starts to fade. And it *hurts*. It hurts deep and wide and empty, with that emptiness all filled with shame.

And worry. Quiet-slow at first, but as I blink open my eyes it whooshes in, faster, louder, harder until it overtakes the pain. Because at the back of everything is still that noise.

Tale.

I have to find her. And this time I crawl, to where I think I heard—

I swallow, cannot even think it—and I crawl, clawing at the inches with fingertips.

I have to find her.

Have to find her.

Have to . . .

Fuck.

No.

It can't be her.

It doesn't look like her, not even quiet-surly. This . . . it's . . .

Broken and impossible, all snapped bone and bruises spread across its skin.

But it wears Tale's shirt. Its dreadlocks fall about a face exactly like hers would when she's asleep.

Tale?

Tale?

I reach out. Can't help it. And the thing beneath my fingertips is cold.

I think I scream then. Terrified of this dead and gone thing beside me, terrified of what it means: that she is really *gone*. Of emptiness. Terrified of touching something that's not— But I don't let go. I can't; what if . . .

What if that's how I lose her? Letting go.

I'm sorry.

Sorry.

Sorry.

I try to pull her hands up into mine, cradle them against the panic of my heart, but there's more resistance than I've ever had from her before, and I can't break her further. Won't. I scoot down instead, lie close, kiss her fingers one by one and breathe onto her knuckles.

I thread my fingers through hers. Squeeze. Desperately hoping she'll wake up and smile, all apologies and sexiness and scorn.

She doesn't.

It's strange, lying in a silence that our heartbeats do not fill.

I kiss her hand again, press my lips right into the not-right skin of her, and whisper that I'm sorry, that I love her, that I'm here.

I should be scared. I *am*. But it's just Tale and me in the dirt and gentle air exactly like we were before. It's . . .

Peaceful. Right that we're together.

I sing to her, almost maybe expect that she'll lift her head and pull me into her, or lift her voice to mine, soft and low and laughing.

I never could sing. *Warped as a frog,* Mama said. *Kill a frog with that voice.* My best friend would laugh.

And I stop, then, in case my voice does harm instead of good, and instead I wrap my arms tighter around her, tell her everything that we'd have gone and done.

I don't think I ever told her about us and Sunday mornings and the beach, and so I tell her now. How we'd cook fried chicken every week, me tenderizing meat and her giving me rhythm, sitting there watching me work.

How I'd give her the world.

But meat and flesh mix in my mind and I feel sick.

I tell her that each thousand tears will grow a tree and, *fuck,* there will be forests springing up here. They'll have to log them just to find the road.

It's *right* that we're together here. Peaceful.

And it hits me that we're not, that this stiff cold thing beside me isn't her, not anymore. That there is blood smeared on my arms and face and shirt and not all of it is mine. That he—

That they—

That she will not sing to me again. And I don't know how to make her hear that I'm still here, I tried, I'm sorry.

What am I going to do?

I hear noises, then. Footsteps jolting through me as raw fear. Someone whistling, on the way to work. And what if they come back for me? Finish the job?

What if someone thinks—

Thinks I—

That I did this?

Whoever it is passes without glancing off the road, but my

heart is in my throat and I can't breathe and I can't stay, and suddenly the hand threaded in mine feels like a vise designed to keep me here for somebody to find.

I pull away and push up to my feet, and run before they have the chance.

I t's not real. It can't be. It's not.

Every pounding step against the earth is a denial.

It isn't real. It can't be.

But each heel to earth jolts fists right through me, a memory of blows and fresh new pain that blooms and blossoms every place they touched.

I feel them pressing in. In and out and back and forth and grabbing everywhere. And I run harder, try to shake them off.

Run.

Except I can't run hard or fast enough and Mr. Sid is in my ear, all *Kisssss*, and then she's there beside me cold and stiff and never letting go—

It isn't real.

The sun rises, all light touch and sparkle: *Look at me, a fresh new day.*

I run. Focus on the sun on skin instead of clammy fingers and slick blood. Blood that if I look down is—

I run.

And Khayelitsha yawns as it rises up to meet the day, a bucket-filling, tea-pouring, teeth-cleaning orchestra on this, a good day full of promise.

No day like this can exist alongside—

It isn't real.

It's real.

Every step is an abandonment. Me leaving her.

I don't know if she knew. And suddenly, my legs go leaden heavy, filled with fear and hurt and rage. They shake, and two more steps I've faltered, up against a wall and barely brave enough to gulp for air.

She's gone.

Khayelitsha whirls around me, dizzying and loud, and I want none of it. It's too close, too big, too empty of her.

I press back against the brick, but it is not enough. I cannot hide. And I can't stay here; anyone can see.

Somehow, somehow, I can't tell you how, I push forward, let go of the wall and stagger on, each step now a thousand needle pricks in limbs that do not work.

Was this what Tale felt? Is this how it stops? Drains from you in a rush of numb and pain all swirled together?

Is this—

Did she—

Somehow I stagger on, and one day soon the roads will be a forest sprung up from my tears.

I t's locked.

Tale's door. Of course it is—who'd ever leave their home unlocked in Khayelitsha?

I can't believe I didn't grab the key. I didn't think.

I know I should go back and get it, that being out here isn't good or safe or wise, but everything that's her is here. Everything except the deadened stare and nothingness and I cannot go back to that.

I slump to the ground and as I land I realize that I'm shaking. Limbs and breath and everything, and I don't know if it's fear or deep-bone-tired or rage, but I could not stand up again even if I tried.

"Neo?" a voice floats into my head from nowhere.

"Tale?"

And there are soft, warm hands on mine. "*Suuure*, what happened to you?" But it's *not* Tale, it's Cap. He's not the voice I need.

Oh God, he doesn't know.

I'm shaking all over again, faster now. I pull away.

"Neo? Where's Tale? What happened?"

But I cannot answer, can't even raise my head and look at him.

He waits. Just a moment. And then he steps away, and there is hammering, a rhythmic *bash, bash, bash* of rock on metal as Cap works on the lock. *Bash, bash, bash*, the whole hut shaking underneath his force, and I don't know what is shaking, it or me, or both. And I worry that the noise will summon Mr. Sid, that he will know I'm here and—

No one comes. In Khayelitsha, you don't answer when some-body screams and if you hear them breaking in then you are safer behind your own doors.

No one comes, only Mr. Sid, and the weight of every blow is up inside me, through me, all around. And in my head there is the push and pull of bodies against mine, and in the world the hut shakes, and the two things become one. *Bash (grunt), bash (take it), bash, bash, bash (you're mine)*, until finally the thing inside me breaks and Tale's padlock cracks and Cap is pulling me inside.

"Tale?" I manage to push the word out as he drops me awkwardly onto the mattress.

It smells like Tale. And I sink into it and the Tale mattress hugs my wounds.

Cap pulls first one and then another blanket up over my back. "Better?" he asks.

And it *is*. It's safe and warm and safe and—

Tale.

She was cold.

She was—

Here. In bed with me, all safe and warm.

"What *happened*, ya?"

But I don't know how to answer, and this bed is soft and safe and warm and it is all that I can do to pull the blankets up over my head and screw my eyes up tight and breathe her in.

I try to push my head out, look around, but the room swims and that sound, slick and wet and cold, laps at my ears, and rises, rises, rises, and I'm drowning in this bed alone.

And the mattress sinks beside me and she's *there*. Tale. Lying here beside me. She snuggles close, wraps her arms around me from behind, and pulls me into her until we're lying cheek to cheek as one.

We fall asleep like that, the two of us. And I'm safe beneath the weight of her. . . .

"Gooood morning, Cape Town."

She's up, busying herself with *something*, I don't know. I hear her moving just beyond my vision.

"I wish you could see young Maximillius's face right now. In fact, let me take a picture, and if you're online, I'm tweeting it on the Umzi account. . . ."

Except it isn't Tale. Tale sounds different when she moves.

It isn't her. It's Cap. Pouring water from a bottle under Tale's sink, scrubbing at my skin so hard it burns, wrapping it in strips of ice-hot cloth.

"Neo?" he tries. "This is bad. I . . ."

And I don't hear the rest. He isn't Tale. He is not the voice I need to hear.

"There.
"Looks *rough*, eh?"

"Shush."

And I remember. Full force.
Tale standing there in front of me, not fighting.

"I will not."

"Shush, you."

Stay quiet. This is not your song.

"What was it, Maxie? Late night with the ladies?"

"Yahhh, man. You know how it is."

Shadow figures close in at that. The way he says it. I can't help but wonder: *Was he there?*

I close my eyes against the sickness, try to swallow it back down, to pull myself under into slumber land, where everything's all right.

But it rises like a tide, unstoppable.

And there's the back and forth and in and out and bruising and the hands that aren't mine, in control. The whispers and the slick wet noise and Tale dragged away.

And I throw up. Every drop of last night's beer and joy and talk of pride spills onto Tale's sheets in ugly choking waves.

She isn't here. She's gone.

I t's morning, busybusy, and we're up and at the bus station, all of us—Tale, Cap and Jed and Zebra, me, and engine oil and sugary fried doughnuts and the smell of sun-baked roads all mingle as loud as the passengers haggling for seats.

"Where you head?" A young guy with a caterpillar moustache leans out of his bus and grins, all hustle.

"Not that way."

And as if a cloud rolled in there's *urgency*. We've got to go. Got to get onto a bus and go. And suddenly we're running, all of us, darting left and right, looking for something and looking not to be seen. We've got to get away. But nothing's right. All the buses here go off into Malawi. One, big and shiny blue with wings, to London and New York, and for a moment I think we will jump inside, but none of us has that kind of money, and it's not right anyway.

We've got to get away.

There! We race into the sweat-stank bus, cram ourselves in against bags and chickens and the always-there's-one leery guy and—

Tale isn't here.

Tale! Tale! No, we've got to go.

I wake as the motorbus pulls off out of the city, staring out of the back window, searching, but she isn't there.

She isn't there.

And I remember.

Every time I fall asleep she's there, and I try *so hard* to keep hold of her, to bring her with me back into the world of waking. But every time she's really gone, and I can't save her.

. . .

I wake to a full circle of heads, silent-tall, and panic floods through everything. I scream and scream and scream. The circle closes in, clambers into Tale's bed with me, tethering my broken soul to its bruised and open body:

Everyone is here, Cap and Zee and Jed. All but one.

I break. Tearless sobs and gulps of air.

"What happened?" Zebra whispers wet into my hair.

"She . . ."

But the words won't come, and so we sit there, all heavy tangled limbs and heavy hearts and silence.

Cap asks next, "Where is she?"

And still I cannot say. How can I break their worlds like that?

You can't.

You don't.

It's not your song; you hush.

They let me sit, and hold me, and we fall asleep like that, I think. But every time I wake it sinks in just a little more, that creeping awful truth. Every time I wake, it's harder to ignore, harder to sink back into the Tale mattress and imagine that it's her.

Finally, Cap stands, and you can see the nerves rippling off his shoulders, hear the firmness in his quiet voice. "Nee, I'm sorry, but . . . we really have to know."

Have you ever told someone anything like that, anything close? You can see it ricochet around the room. Bounce off the walls, right through them. See it hit, all numb and shock and pain and disbelief at once.

"She's dead."

It comes out cracked and blunt and numb, and I want to chase it with *I'm sorry, sorry, so so sorry*. But I don't have the words, and they wouldn't hear it anyway.

I ruined everything.

"No no no no no. No, no. What? No. Fuck." Cap backs into a corner, as though walls could stop his whole world crashing down.

And Jed and Zebra fall into each other, to the floor, hands to mouths. I think they scream, and cry, and scream again, but all I hear is my own voice, too loud and blunt and forming words that can't be true.

"She's dead."

I ruined everything.

I don't know what comes next, or what's supposed to. How do you move on from those two words?

But Cap—quiet, solid, wonderful—breaks through it first.

"Right. Okay." And he crosses the room and looks at me. "Let's get you to a doctor."

"Uh-uh." I pull my knees in close, roll up in a ball. I can't. The thought of people . . . no.

"Neo—"

"No!" I yell it harder than I'd meant, and then I realize, no, I meant it.

"The police."

"Uh-uh."

"Neo. You're a mess."

Of course I am! I—

I don't want to be here. With them. Anybody. I don't want them near me.

"No."

I swing my legs onto the floor and stand, barely, and my sore-stiff-shaking limbs would let me fall if Zebra didn't land beside me just in time.

"What are you *doing*?" he says.

But his hand on my arm burns. "Leaving."

He does not let go until I pull away with force.

"Nee."

"I have to—"

"Rest," says Cap. "At the least. And let us clean you up."

I shake my head, wrap my arms around my chest. "Don't touch me."

"Okay!" He holds his hands up, backs away until I breathe again, then, "Tell us?"

And it all comes out. Everything.

Almost. I can't tell them that it's *him*. That I brought him into Tale's life and everything's my fault. Can't tell them that maybe beef jerky should have been enough clue, that maybe koeksisters led him on. *Can't tell them I'll see you on Monday.* He's too big, too strong, and I can't. But everything else spills—the shadow circle and the mash of bodies and the way she stood—and it's enough.

It's strange how telling something—speaking it out loud— feels hot and hard and empty all at once, cements it.

Not one of them speaks, except a strangled sob when I say "I heard—I couldn't get to her."

And then I'm done; there's nothing left of either the tale or me.

Maybe they'll find her?"

But I don't want them to. I can't see her like that again. "Eish."

"Maybe they'll stop *him*. Stop all of them."

I pull myself in tighter. Can't think about it. Can't look at him.

"Neo." He sits on the bed, close enough that I can feel him but with inches between us. I'm not sure it's enough. "Remember Pride?"

And he must see me recoil in horror at the sudden, vivid-happy image, because he adds, quickly—

"Remember the stories? The survival?"

"Ugh."

"Exactly."

I look at him then, surprised.

"You shouldn't *have* to survive. No one should. You shouldn't have to fight, to fear, to lose." And I think his voice is going to crack, but somehow he keeps on. "But the only, only way we stop those bastards is by speaking out. You have to *tell*."

I don't want to do this. Walk into this big square building with its razor wire and its bureaucrats and bullies. Every inch of me screams *no* and *run* and *hold your tongue* and I don't want to speak. But Cap stood there so sure and sad and how could I say no when I have ruined everything?

We stand there for an age, the two of us, in silence, and I don't know how I'm ever going to move.

Bodies jostle past us, and I flinch at every one I see, every one who comes too close.

I can't.

I can't be out here with humanity. (*Humanity*, I think it with a spit.)

All I want is her.

And Cap decides that it is time—maybe sees me shaking, edging back, ready to run—and reaches out to squeeze my shoulder, so gently that it almost doesn't hurt. I nod. And together we walk into the police station and square up to the desk.

It smells like paperwork and coffee, too much like the corridors of Umzi, and my stomach turns before we even start.

"Yes?" A big, bored policeman barely looks up from his paperwork.

"I'd like to report a . . ." The first words come out as one long terror-rush, but I stall. A what? I cannot use that word, so full of blame.

"My friend and I, we were attacked."

"Mm-hmm." He raises an eyebrow, still not looking. "This your friend?"

"No. She—" *What?*

Cap flashes me a puzzled look and even though I *know*, it takes me a full second to remember that he's reading lips and we need to be slow and clear.

Only, he's more in control than me. Leans forward, right over the desk. "Sir. My friend was hurt."

And finally he stops what he is doing.

"Ehhh, what happened to you?"

I flinch. I don't know why—the memory of Mr. Sid's eyes sliding over me, or judgment now, this policeman looking at my body as though he has any right to.

But maybe he is just concerned. Right? That's his job.

"I . . ." I almost tell him everything. Tale deserves that. But who'd believe that Umzi's Mr. Sid, Khayelitsha's superstar, went after two young girls? *Murdered* one—my stomach lurches at the word—and raped the other?

Nobody.

And sure, I have the marks upon my skin, and inside too, from the way it pulls, but that only proves that something happened somewhere with someone, and nothing more.

Besides, I saw the looks on the constabulary's faces as they stood and watched us march, and I *cannot* tell that I didn't lead him on, that I didn't want this. And I will not get undressed and show them all my wounds.

I can't.

It will not bring her back.

"Someone jumped us. *Someones.* There were more than one."

He sighs. "Pretty things like you should not be out at night."

Cap *growls*.

"You'll need to see someone, to document your injuries."

I can't.

They'll see . . . everything. What if there's, I don't know, what if there's something wrong? Some sign? Not enough bruising? Something to make them see that it's my fault?

That I didn't try hard enough to get away, to save her?

What if they see whatever Mr. Sid saw? Would they have helped him, then?

I can't.

And anyway, I am not here for me. I'm here for her. "Look," I say, anger flaring right up through my chest, and nothing mattering except Tale and what those men did to her. "I ran. She didn't. She's still out there."

"So you don't want to make a complaint."

"Yes! She's still out there. You have to *do something*."

He sits back, and his eyes go up and down and take me in and I feel *sick*.

"Miss. What exactly happened?"

You shush. Hold your tongue.

But there is Pride and Tale cold and it *is* my song now.

And I would run, but Cap is there with a hand wrapped around mine, and whispers, "Tell him," so I do.

"This allegation, miss." He pauses, lets the gravity sink in. "It's serious."

"I know." I held her. He doesn't have to say.

"Right. Well. Then we need to talk."

He leads me—us. I insist. I won't be alone—into a tiny white-washed room without a single window, just a desk, three chairs barely crammed in. And he makes me tell it once, twice, three times, sitting in this tiny room where there's no air.

He makes me tell him everything: the time—late, but I don't know. Who and what and how it felt. And then he stops me.

"What about before?"

"Before . . ."

"Last night, what were you two doing?"

And there's laughter, coziness, and stupid, boring conversation where there should have been *I love you*s and *I'm sorry*s. There's her hand in mine, and her skin slathered in the moonlight, and there's beer and lips and kissing, and—

"Just hanging out. You know."

"Hmm, uh-huh, I do."

"She walked me home."

Beer and lips and kissing, and the streets all quiet and safe and ours.

"What was she like, this friend?" he asks.

I stare until he asks again, and still it makes no sense. Those words. How can someone not know Tale? How does anybody's world turn without—

I open my mouth, try to explain the big wonderfulness of her, how she's *everything*, but it's too much. I can't.

"Bubbly? Confident? A little happy with the menfolk?"

What?

I stare.

"Isit . . . Maybe *she* knew some of these men, do you think?"

No.

Yes, but no.

I shake my head. "It wasn't—"

"I know how it is. You girls. You were probably drinking, yes?"

"No! . . . Yes. But it wasn't—"

"And things get easily confused."

"No!"

"And you're *sure* she didn't, ah, choose not to follow you away?"

What is he suggesting?

Tale did not choose this. Can't he see her there, standing silent in the middle of that circle? There wasn't any choice.

And there's hands and pushing pulling, and there's blows and there's that *noise*.

"No. She didn't."

He sighs. "Okay. All I'm saying is . . . You're not prepared to be examined, can't remember anything about these men, and what, exactly, should my men investigate?"

UmziRadio is passion, Miss Mahone. And you might just fit in.

I should tell him.

I should.

He—

But I just sit there, saying nothing, and it's like my voice has gone with hers.

"All right, all right," he says, and he rifles through a drawer I had not noticed. Slaps the SAPD's missing persons form and a pen down in front of us. "You're not giving me much to work with, but you fill this out; we'll see what we can do. . . ."

"But she's not missing." I lurch to my feet, scraping the chair back, screaming, "She's *dead*. Dead. He killed her."

No one moves.

No one even breathes for a whole beat. And then he stands to leave, waving vaguely at the form. "Hand this in at the desk."

When he's gone, I breathe out slow and Cap curls a hand around mine, leans in. "I'm proud of you."

And I feel sick. There's nothing to be proud of. This is all my fault and Tale's gone.

I reach out for the form. Stare at the words. Age, height, weight, concerns or other discerning features.

There is nothing on here about finding . . . victims, nothing of attacks or injuries.

We fill it out anyway, and walk together to the desk.

When we do not leave immediately, he raises a high, cynical eyebrow. "Yes?"

"Will someone go out looking?" I ask. "Now? Come on!"

The bored man sighs, and answers in monotone. "We'll add her to the file, post a bulletin. The constables will keep a lookout."

"That's it?" I squeak.

He sighs again. "Look, miss. Whatever argument you and your friend had, I'm sure that she's fine. People go a bit too far on a Saturday night. It's sad. Never used to be like that in my day. But they do, and then they kiss and make up. You'll see."

ap wants to take me home. To Tale's, or to his, he doesn't care. Just home. But I can't. I can't I can't I can't. My head is full of scorn and hate, all loud whispers of *No one would believe you; I know what it's like; I'll see you on Monday.* And rancid meat and pounding and that noise. And Jed and Cap and Zebra, their faces frozen in that moment.

It's all my fault. Every single bit of it. And if I stay I have to live in it. If I stay, Mr. Sid might just come looking.

No. I can't.

I stand there for an age, my fingers resting on the latch.

But I have to go in. I'm home.

I push open the door. It creaks, the tiniest of noises, and at the kitchen table, Baba stirs.

He's sitting with the paper. Barely glances up. No *Where've you beens*, no yelling, not even a disappointed shuffling of the pages. Nothing.

And I should have known then that he knew, that Baba's never silent. But in the moment, as I shuffle quiet and tender back into the family life, I'm simply grateful.

Linda and Cherry do not even speak to me, just stare and stare and stare until they fall asleep, as though if they take their eyes off of me, I might have my way with them.

I turn my back to them and close my eyes and try to dream myself away.

And then there's Jeso—silent all through dinner, not daring to look at me—but now he's here, standing at the bed and poking nervous at my face.

"Nee?"

"Mmm?" I whisper.

"Are you all right?"

Does he know? Surely not. Surely no one told them this. Not this.

"I—" I don't have an answer; none that would not break his world. But he is *here*. He's here, and Tale's not and everything is so messed up and—I cannot stop the tears, and my baby brother does not even have to ask; he just climbs onto the bed and curls himself around me. And even though he's gentle, even though I know it's him, I stiffen at his touch. It *burns*.

He pulls away, and I force myself to breathe, relax, let myself melt into him because he's here and that is everything, and I don't ever want to let him go.

And we lie there together, and as I cry hot silent tears he buries his face into my neck and clings, and we stay like that till morning.

J eso babbles all the way to school, his protective-brother stance melting quickly into pure excitement—he doesn't know. He can't. He'd never be like this—and he's swinging so hard from my arm that every bruise beneath my shirt and skirt and tights can feel it, and I can only walk through gritted teeth and fear.

He worries, once. I see it pass across his face, and that's enough to make me paste a smile on mine. I nod and smile and try to make it look as though I hear his distant talk, but really I am dead inside, almost glad of the pain stabbing me down there with every step; I earned it. Tale's never going to feel again.

I don't notice much that day. I could not tell you how it passed, except that every tick of the clock hands is one vast moment further from her and one closer to the moment when *I'll see you on Monday*.

How do you walk back into a part of life that dies?

Autopilot? Fear?

I honestly don't know. Still don't. But somehow, somehow the glass door of UmziRadio swings inward and I'm stepping through that blast of air.

Baba stands behind the desk, all smart and serious today. And I can't meet his eyes.

I concentrate on moving, one foot in front of the other. Not on the thick paper-coffee smell, the way the air prickles against my skin. Not on the quiet. There's no music here today; nothing drifting through the speakers, and I wonder for a second whether Mr. Sid's done that on purpose: *Come in. Bring the music.*

He's sitting in his office with the door ajar.

Waiting?

Waiting. He looks up as I cross the corridor, and smiles, and I can't look at him I can't I can't I can't stand here with him looking at me. I duck into the cupboard and lean back against the door, heart racing.

What am I *doing here*?

I can't do this.

But—

I'll see you on Monday.

In this room, there is a box. A history of scratched-out truths and unheard voices. And I stand there up against the door, all fear and anger and disgust and stupid, shaking limbs, and it hits me: I understand.

Hush. We do not want your song. You hush.

"Gooood *day*, Khayelitsha! Welcome to your ABCs of music. The letter of the day is *O*, and we're going for the oldies. Classics. All the songs familiar enough that they define you. Songs that you forget, don't hear because they're part of you."

I want to stop. To pause midsentence and apologize and then tell the world exactly what kind of man lives behind the scenes. I want to share that this world's best and deepest voice is silenced. Want to play exactly that—an hour of silence just for her.

But Mr. Sid is just across the corridor, big and strong and in control.

I can't.

I stick to the script—old, inoffensive, everybody songs—barely even noting what I play. I just want to get through. And I upload, and no, I do not take him tea—I will not give him that—and I am gone. Until *P* and *Q* and *R*, at least. He's won.

What's *up* with you?" My best friend lands beside me with a *thud* that makes me wince. Too close, too loud.

"Nothing." How can I explain?

I can't.

elcome, friends, to this, your regular installment of musical alphabet."

Every show goes by in counting seconds. Fear.

I do not hear the music anymore, and my own voice sounds out of my control, as though it's not my script, not my language, and I do not know the words.

Sun streams bright and strong through curtained windows. Ours. And Tale leans into my neck and nuzzles at my ear. It's perfect. And we're walking, our feet sinking into soft-cold sand. Alone—the clouds are black and rolling, and no one else is wild enough, in love enough, to come out on a day like this—and as the thunder rolls and the first fat drops of rain land heavy on our skin, she wraps her arms around me. Warm. And thunder rolls and Tale's voice soars up to greet it and I don't know if it's animal or sweet or both, but it is beautiful. The two of us there on the beach lost swirling in the storm and in each other, only we're not lost at all. We're home.

And then I wake, and she is gone.

I try. I really do. I walk my body through the motions: get up, go to school, do homework. I hug my brother tight and mind my mother, and when Sunday comes I bow my head and pray.

I try.

I give Linda her double date, tell myself I'm normal now: the good girl, doing what she always should have done. And I sit around a blanket on the beach. But my fingers find the sand, wonder whether I could dig myself a hole. And I wonder whether the harsh lapping waves would carry me away.

I am not much of a conversationalist, and poor Khwezi sits there *desperate* for me to talk.

I do not think they will ask me again.

I try.

I walk through the old rhythms beat by beat. But beats alone are nothing more than desperate cries thrown out into the void.

My world is broken.

Quiet. And the silence presses down down down upon me, pulls me under, drags me from one beat to the next, not knowing where it ends. And when I try to fight, to breathe, the silence fills my lungs and everything else disappears. The rhythm and the push and pull and hands, the screaming and the tenderness and hope that we are getting out alive, all gone, and there is nothing but the silence. Cold. I'm *drowning* in the lack of her.

y brother might be only seven, but he has the *moves*. And in the kitchen, Jeso lets it rip, hips back and forth, and attitude beneath his baby grin.

"What about youuuu?" he croons, and when he grabs the strawberries from Mama's table and whirls around with them at the words *forbidden fruit*, even our mother laughs.

Linda's up and joining him, sucking on a strawberry like it was . . . not a strawberry, and Cherry, too. All of them, twisting twirling laughing.

"Love forbidden fruit! Love forbidden fruit!"

And the beat pounds in my ears and their joy stabs and—

"Nee!" He grabs my hand. "Come dance with me! Come on!"

And I can *never* say no to my brother, and the others, they would know, and for three whole steps I'm *there*, feet slapping on the floor in time, feeling Toya rock right through my core, but—

No one's told him what that song means. No one's told him *anything*. And I can't be here. I can't be part of this.

I pull away and run into my room and slam the door and cry.

Jes follows. Of course. All indignant rage I haven't seen him wear since his team captain burst their one and only ball.

"What IS IT?" he yells, as I fall onto the bed. "What is it?" He balls his little fists up tight, and *fumes*. "Whatever they did to you, I'll get them."

And the sight of him—my tiny-fierce defender—breaks my heart. "Jes—"

"I can do it. I'll get big. I'll . . . I don't need to be big. I'll join up with Mthandali's crew. They'll give me fighting lessons and then they'll give me a gun."

"No." I sit up fast and grab hold of his still-balled, shaking fists. "You never ever *ever*, Jeso. Don't you dare."

I pull him hard into my chest and wrap my arms around him, and I want to tell him why, tell him that his power isn't in his tiny fists and anger, that guns can't change me, bring her back, that they won't fix a thing.

But now I'm shaking too, too hard to speak. I squeeze him tight instead, as though our lives depend upon it. As though the words could get from skin to skin.

And somewhere in there, as I force the last breath from his lungs, Jeso's hot voice breaks. "I love you."

I'm *angry*.

The hot kind that sits behind your eyes and in your gut and spreads right to your toes and fingertips.

I barely feel the winter rain, which makes my brother run at double time. Barely notice anything except that she should be here and it isn't fucking fair.

Angry that she isn't here.

Angry that I am.

Angry that the world is spinning and that song still passes people's lips.

Song was supposed to save us. Elevate us. Keep us safe.

I'm angry.

At the man fixing his bicycle, the woman hanging washing in the rain so that mud will splatter up the cuffs—who does that?— angry at my brother's slapping footsteps and his innocence. An innocence I'll never have again.

And as we run past rain-wet ruined posters flapping in the breeze I am angry at those, too—all the buying-selling, all the lost things no one's ever found.

Still angry while I record the next show for Mr. Sid. I swear I hear him breathing from across the hall and *how dare he?* How dare he take her breath and keep his own? How dare he sit there smug and safe and so untouchable? How dare he? I sit there sick with rage, and every time I play a song I cry.

Each one saps some of it from me, leaves me cold and wet exactly like the notices all flapping in the rain and—

Oh.

Maybe I can't speak against him, but somebody must have seen us, right? A Saturday night as everyone went home?

Maybe all is not lost after all.

I print them in the office, heart up in my ears and foot against the door as if maybe that would stop anybody coming in. I slip them in between the sheets of math and grammar work, and walk right out with them.

HAVE YOU SEEN THIS WOMAN?
Missing since the early hours of
Saturday June 12.
Any information welcome.

I paste them everywhere. On every market table, every latrine, every tree between UmziRadio and home.

I paste her carefully beside the now faded and weather-torn

RUSZANI BHEMBE: MISSING. You can barely read her flyer, but I will not cover up her loved ones' only hope.

I paste one at the back of the MotoloCafe, careful no one sees me.

And I slip three rolled up in between the railings of the school, just waiting for curious minds.

Someone had to see.

Someone braver. Someone with a voice, or with nothing to lose.

Comments: 23

Sorry to say I losin interest. Dis ws gd to start but I afraid I jyst not feelin it.

What happened Neo grrrl?
>seriously. I tune in religiously but it feels like you checked out on us. What happened to the magic
>>Yuuup.
>>THS
>>YES!!!!*!!

OMGawd I can't belev u played that song but not—

"Really?" Mr. Sid turns his computer screen back around and sighs. "Neo, Neo, Neo. This is not the standard I expect. Come on."

How can he sit there like that, sly smile on his lips, all care and concern? How *dare* he?

It's all I can do to walk out of that office whole before I throw up and sink to the floor.

Maybe—and I hate admitting this—maybe Baba was right.

Maybe a girl like me can't have it all.

Maybe it's music or the girl. And even as I think it I don't know whether the price is Tale or it's me.

I should be working on the show, crafting perfect segues, but that box of broken vinyl keeps on staring. *You're like us now,* I hear them say, except obviously they don't say anything; they had their voices marked and rubbed away.

Maybe I could get out, somehow. Do what Baba always wanted. Join the adult world, that morning train where no one sings.

Maybe.

It would be nice to have some company.

I miss it.

Friday nights. The shadows and the warmth. All of it—the song and buzz and secret danger of it. But the safety, too, of knowing that she's there, someone who understands without me needing words. Someone whose voice matches mine.

The safety of Umzi before—

Before . . . you know.

And suddenly I need her. More than I have ever needed anything, I need her right beside me, with her fingers laced in mine, and her post-gig beer breath in my face. I need her on that first night, with that note so strong it breaks through everything.

I need her song to save me from this life.

Slowly, tentatively, I pick up my headphones and press play, and the slow-sad voice of an old man from Khayelitsha's masses sings "Bonny Mary of Argyle," alone, as though his life depended on it.

And maybe it does.

unday. Somehow. And we file into the pew, Baba, Linda, Cherry, Jeso, Mama, me. And everybody's voice rises in praise.

It's beautiful. It really is: so much faith and goodness lifted up as one.

But my voice does not join them. I can't.

Have you ever sat right in the middle of a message everybody shares without being a part of it?

It's lonely.

And if you'd asked me then, I would have told you that I sat alone, just me and a god who'd turned away.

Mama didn't like that.

"What?" she said all sharp afterward. "The Lord's music is too good for you now?"

"No!"

"Eh, right. Well, you'll just give your *other* music to me till you fix your attitude."

She bustles out of our room with my cassettes and my Walkman and she winds the cord around the radio and takes that, too.

And I should care. I know I should. But somehow silence is exactly right.

I reveled in the silence. Every single breath of it, and all it's loneliness. I'd brought it on myself.

If I'd only listened. If I'd stopped and thought or asked her *why* she was so scared, I would never have gone.

You hear stories, rumors hushed and whispered but never admitted, but you never think they're true. They can't happen to you. They're stories, fairy tales to make the children toe the line.

I ruined everything.

I ruined her.

She warned me, warned me I was messing with her life.

And I took it anyway.

Nobody's responded to the posters.

I keep checking my phone.

I keep looking, hoping that—if they cannot call—somebody might leave a message scrawled across the paper.

They're getting ratty now. Faded damp and wind-torn. I replaced them once, but we all know that nobody will speak.

Who would risk that for a dead girl?

I check the band's page, hoping, hoping that she's risen, returned from a lengthy holiday—a prank to catch us all—and that they'll play again.

But there's nothing. Not a word. No upcoming shows or dread announcements. As though she's frozen in time, not here but not yet gone.

And otherwise, I carry on. I can do nothing else. I have no choice. I carry on.

When Mr. Sid calls me into his office yet again, I want to run.

He sits there, leaning forward, a picture of concern and kindness. And he sighs. "These comments"—he waves a hand at his computer screen, not even showing me this time—"they aren't getting any better."

I don't let my eyes meet his. I can't. And he fills up the silence reaching for a piece of meat and chewing loud. "Nothing to say for yourself?"

Yes! I want to tell him. *You're a creep. An animal! None of this is my fault; it's all you!*

I want to tell him that I don't care what he does to me, at all—he's already taken everything.

I want to reach out and to shove that jerky down into his throat so hard he chokes.

But no. I don't. I shrug.

"I took a chance on you," he says, "but *clearly* something isn't working. It's a shame. I thought you had something. The spark, the magic. But perhaps, ah, perhaps you should leave. Unless you think that you can pull it back and become part of us again?"

Eh?

He's letting me go?

Or is it . . . discarding me?

But why?

I want to run so far and fast and hard that he'll never see me again, but—

What does he want? What does this mean?

"Think about it. And you let me know."

I t is with true regret that I play you this episode of Umzi's ABCs." Mr. Sid's voice booms out with a tinny menace through the speakers, and then mine, all dead and blunt and not my own:

"A lot of you have noticed the decline in content, and I'm *truly sorry*. But I cannot be the voice you need, and so I'm handing over the rest of this run to Mr. Sid and Umzi, and I'm going to devote my time to my studies for now. I want to express thanks to Mr. Sid and his whole team for *such* an opportunity, for teaching me so much and opening their doors to this high school kid. Y'know, that's the mark of a radio that values its home. It's people. And speaking of, I want to thank *you*. For everything. I hope you've enjoyed our time here as much as I have. Thank you."

And with that, I'm free.

Everyone at school knows. Whispers.

How? How could they know?

Their words are everywhere, so full of bitterness and scorn:

Gay.

Slut.

Learned her lesson, though.

Is she okay now?

Everybody knows.

Nobody will partner with me in the classroom, even if the teacher says.

Cebile refused, on grounds that it was against everything she stood for and her baba would refuse to let her home, and the boys all laughed and said there was no point—it would not get them anywhere. Anyone who was made to be my partner sat as far away from me as possible and shielded their work.

Janet will not even look at me.

Joseph Mthandeni pulls her close, arms wrapped round her waist protectively, and *glowers*. And I should be scared, I would be, but there's nothing he can do to me. Not now.

I learn to watch my step, look out for legs and tables and odd sticks that could be thrust into my path. I only needed to learn that once: landing on my chin on the way out of class, and everybody jeering, "Eh, look. Right where she belongs."

One lunchtime, boys from Linda's class, freed from matric

review and all stir-crazy, surround me, grab their crotches, and thrust in my direction with laughing calls of "Ever need a quick refresher, we're better than those dried-up men."

Behind them, I see Linda turn to flee.

A week after leaving Umzi, Mama gives the music back. Gently, almost, handing me the box with half a smile.

"Here," she says. "It's yours. Just . . . be careful."

And my heart breaks into tiny tiny pieces at the softness of her voice and the hard truth that it's too late for that.

It's all here; Brenda Fassie, Brothers of Peace, Blk Sonshine, all of them, every voice that ever sang for me, lined up in their plastic cases in their tidy cardboard boxes.

Perfectly recorded. Safe forever.

And it's still too late. I wasn't careful with the voice that mattered.

I have ruined everything.

I rifle through again, but I don't find her voice and I'm alone.

And it's not *fair*.

And all these voices of the greats, these pale, weak imitations, they sit in their boxes, smug and safe and not caring a bit that she is gone.

I hate them. Hate them with every part of me.

And music, and the gaping hole it's left inside me.

And I never, ever want to hear another song again.

I do not want it. Do not need it.

Not if it's not her.

And in a flash of pure and unadulterated rage, I punish them. For every song on every track. I drag the boxes to the fire pit and dump them in, and light a match and watch them burn in acrid flames. And Mama follows, stands and stares, her hand up at her mouth in frozen horror and something like sorry, but she doesn't stop me. And as they melt, curl up on themselves, the only thought I have is *Good, see, now you know exactly how it feels.*

Over dinner, Mama tells me that she's sorry that I had to learn that way. Tells me that she's sorry. Tells me that perhaps now I can get on with my life. Perhaps she could ask her friends for Saturday work, if I'd like? Something different from the salon. Or I could concentrate on school.

It's *good*.

And there is no Tale and there's nothing in that life for me, and I almost, almost nod and tell her that she's right, that I've learned my lesson and I'm home.

But, leaning over his plate of potatoes, Baba smiles.

I've seen that smile before. In an office, from a different pair of lips.

And my stomach turns; he knew.

He knew. He planned this, or okayed it, or—he knew.

And in that moment it is clear as the first note man ever heard that I do not belong here and I never will, that *home* is not always the place you think, that I can't stay.

He knew. And everything is over.

Jeso cries when he sees my bags. He wraps his arms around my waist and *begs* me not to go.

"I have to, Jes."

He sniffles, squeezes tighter. "Noooo. We're partners; you can't go!"

And my heart cracks, and . . . "I'm *so sorry* Jes. I'm sorry. But I can't stay here."

"But why? I'll be better. I'll be better!"

I kneel down and wrap my arms around in, breathe the boy scent in—earth and sleep and sweetness—and try to tuck it safe inside my memory. "I'm sorry."

"Is it the music?" No judgment, just Jeso curiosity. And for one crazy second I am going to take him with me.

"Sort of." I push my face into a smile. "Sometimes . . . sometimes people love something—someone—different. And yeah, this is about the music. But it's also about—"

And Baba steps into the room.

"Get off him."

"Eh?"

"Get. Your. Hands. Off of my son."

I pull Jeso's arms away from my neck, whisper in his ear that it's okay. That if he needs me, I am always here. I'm in the *walls*.

"How *dare* you?" Baba says. "How dare you fill his head with *this*."

"I bet there's chocolate in the tin," I say. "In Mama's stash. Why don't you go and look?"

"Nnnnnnnn." He clings tighter, and he's *shaking*, and I just want to pick him up and run.

But this isn't Jeso's fight.

"Jes."

He pauses at the door, looks back at me uncertain. I nod. *Go.*

"You know," my father says, so calm that the words slip like a hot buttered knife into my chest, "I did it for you. For the hope of a life."

And I see the shadow ring. Only now they have a face.

I scrawl Jeso a note, and I walk slow, give him time to slip away and follow me, and I stuff it awkwardly and visibly into the rubble of the message wall.

I love you.
Always.

And I know I should be scared, of shadows and the hands that hide in them and of the certainty of this—I can't come back, I won't—but I do not have a choice. I'm gone.

I don't *want* to stay at Tale's, but I see the padlock rusted on the door; it's empty, nobody quite knowing yet whether she has gone and they can claim it. And there is no Mr. Sid or Baba looming here, and so it's mine.

I break in, drop my bag, and breathe.

It still smells of her. Still feels like she could walk right in, all sweat and glow and happiness, stripping from one T-shirt and pulling on another, grabbing a CD or mic lead or keys, leaning in to me.

But no.

The only sound here is the sound of my own heart.

It's too quiet. Much too quiet. And I know that it will never be the same, but I have to find the music, and I have to find it now.

I step out into the darkness, and I run.

Tuesday night. Or Wednesday? It's hard to know when you've been living in the silent one-beat, when all there is is *now*, and you have no expectations for the *then*.

Tuesday night, I think, and the bar looks dark and sad. Or dim at least, the half-light of the doorway *flat*, unflickering without the bodies passing in and out like shadows. No Tale floating out across the stage.

I step across the threshold anyway, hoping, hoping that I'm wrong, that I'll cross into a different world, where music *lives*.

Nothing happens. Inside, away from the night air, you can

make out the tinny sounds of Brenda Fassie on a tiny speaker. But even she feels stale.

No Tale. No music. Not even a crowd, save one man propping up the bar and two more nursing drinks—the first alone, the second *teased* by a short-skirted red-lips.

The room smells of dust and disappointment and spilled beer. Too quiet. Too sad.

And as the bartender looks up, gestures, questioning, I run.

And run and run and run. To nowhere, really. I just need to find her. It. *It*, Neo. You won't find her.

The music strings are cut and I am lost and desperate, and so I run, listen to the beat beat beat of my out-of-breath heart, and even that is more than I have really heard since I don't know. And I don't want to lose it, so I run.

I *almost* run to UmziRadio, hammer on the door as if he'd be there. Scream into the night until it listens. Almost run right back to the police station, scream at them until they have to listen even though I washed away the traces long ago.

But every time I turn that way and take a step, I freeze. And I can't freeze. Not now. And so I turn the other way, and run and hope that somewhere in the shadows, Tale's waiting with her song.

There is nothing. And eventually my legs run out of power and I cannot go another step. I crash against the wall of someone's home, and for a moment all I hear is the whoosh of blood against my ears. The silence taking over, creeping lead- and dread-like back into my veins.

And then:

A lullaby.

Old and croaky. But it's there. And it is full of heart.

Thula thul, thula baba, thula sana
Tul'ubab 'uzobuya ekuseni.
Thula thul, thula baba, thula sana
Tul'ubab 'uzobuya ekuseni.
There's a star that will lead him home, my love
The star will brighten his way
The hills and stones are still the same, my love
Daddy will be home by dawn.
Soft and sweet and strong, even as it breaks.

And I stand there in the dark, and I breathe in that voice until it fills me.

It's not Tale, and it does not make me feel in the same way, but it is real. And it rips my heart out, and I don't want it to stop.

I find the band on Friday night. I slink into the bar, head down, trying to find words to open with—*I'm sorry. How are you?* Not that, no need for that, I know. *I'm sorry,* then. But it is not enough. How do you ever, ever bridge that gap?

I never find the words. Zebra's long, lithe arms are wrapped around me before I even know he's there. And they are *all* here, and there's tears and muttered words that do not even matter, and I think maybe we are okay.

chool—the guys insist; they'll support anything, but not if I leave school—is hard. I've taken to sitting back behind the classroom block alone, hidden where no one can see and no one bothers me.

Some of them still whisper things, wonder where I've gone, what happened, why I'd let a good thing go. And some have stopped. It's boring, and since the date with Khwezi, they figure maybe I am cured, have seen the error of my ways. But the whispers and the stares are there, full of anger and mistrust.

Today, I sneak Tale's radio into my bag with an old set of headphones, and I twist the dial past static to a local station.

An a cappella voice sings out, and stabs me in the heart.

It isn't her.

But there is a voice full of sorrow that sounds just a bit like mine, and even while it hurts it heals.

On the second day, I find a different beat. Angry, thrashing drums and loud guitar meet my weak apology and nervousness and turn it into fire.

And on the third day Janet, silent, joins me.

We say nothing for a while, and then she hesitantly takes an earbud.

"Sorry," she says. "I don't get it, but I'm sorry."

We sit, the four of us, on the floor in the shadows back behind the bar, an oil lamp and a crate of still-cold Greens between us. With a radio on low, because at first not one of us knew what to say.

We are not okay. Not really. And I don't know that we'll ever be.

Sometimes, for a moment, but then . . .

We are not okay. But we are here.

"Wohhhh. I can't believe she kissed you *here*." He glances around the muddy, beer-soaked corner.

I shrug, and Jed says, "Really? This is *Tale*." And we laugh, and mean it, even though it rubs things raw.

"It was more than kissing, if I remember right." Cap grins.

He *saw*?

"Hush, you." I hide my blush behind the beer. Swig.

"You know, she almost had *me* once?" Jed says, and Zee looks up quick-sharp.

"She what?"

"Almost." And his eyes dance, but his lips stay closed.

Zebra nestles into him. "Someday, I want to hear that story."

"'Kay."

"I want to hear that story *now*," says Cap.

We laugh and cry and share.

We tell of song spells and latrines, and the one time she ran through Cape Town wearing nothing but a pair of *takkies* and a feather boa: You don't make a bet with Zee and win. We *scream* at the injustice, at the police, the *But there is no body; there's no crime.* We tell of kindness, fierceness, love.

"Y'know, she taught me not to let anyone else say no for me when I wanted to say yes . . . even if she wouldn't always follow that advice," says Cap, raising a bottle to his lips.

"She taught *me* how to sass," says Zebra, and I'm not sure I believe him, but it makes us laugh.

"She taught me . . ." And I stop, and swallow hard. She taught me everything. She gave me music and community and the way two bodies move.

"Yeah," says Jed. "We know." And I'm as glad that it is out there as I am that I don't have to say it.

"You know, she never once regretted it," Jed says, and he's looking at me. "Stepping out of that bubble of hers. She said it made her free. *You* did."

"None of us could do that."

And when we're done with words and done with tears, we *sing*. Cap first. No lyrics, just a melody above a gentle, driving rhythm tapped out in the earth. I imagine the vibrations spreading, spreading right through Khayelitsha to wherever she is. And one by one we join her and we sing, and it doesn't matter that our voices waver, doesn't matter that I cannot hold a tune, and I don't even *care* about my frog voice; we all sing until we've used up all the words of every song we know. And I just hope she hears.

And then it's dawn, a new day without Tale forced upon us. And without the shadows to hide it, everything is raw and dull again. Too quiet.

Tale would have hated it, and I can't leave her memory like this, alone in the quiet. Not even a part of it.

"One sec," I say as we pick up our things. And I take the radio and place it by the wall. On low, barely loud enough to hear, but it is there. "To keep her company."

And then we head into the day.

R eady?" Cap appears, beside me. And they're all there. Cap, Zebra, Jed.

Janet. Who it turns out is not as freaked out as she first appeared, is *still* a bossy-as-hell manager, but gets things done and always remains fierce.

"No."

I'll never be ready.

It took months of organizing. Paperwork and over-beers proposals. Many, many favors and more promises, and enthusiasm and support from places that I never could have dreamed.

There's a small crowd in the bar street today. At least I imagine that there is. She *always* had a crowd.

Or perhaps it's empty, mourning. But we're there. A hundred thousand of us pouring through that speaker. There. Singing Tale's song.

"It started in a bar, and ended *here*. So there you have it. The whole story of the way one girl picked up her voice and sang.

"Music is for everyone. There's room for Ladysmith, AND Prophets of Da City, AND Sibongile Khumalo. All standing strong upon the stage.

"Tale, she was brilliant, but she was wrong.

"She once told me that to survive you have to hold your tongue, stay quiet, and for a moment I believed her. But she's wrong. Music's in the being there and being part of it, and the *only* way we make it through this life is if we hold our nerves and sing.

"This fight belongs to all of us. And I'm here today—and every day to come—*giving you a space to sing*. Welcome, welcome, *welcome* to Kaleidoscope: the truly rainbow station for a truly rainbow nation.

"I hope you'll stay.

"And now I've bored you all to tears, I'm opening the line to callers with *one question*. You've heard my song, and now I want to know, what's yours?"

AUTHOR'S NOTE

Kaleidoscope Song explores—among other things—what it's like to discover attraction, whether you're attracted to music, or the way a person looks or moves, to their kindness or confidence, or the sense of sameness and community you find with them. And a lot of Neo's queerness stems from mine.

I grew up welcomed in very adult queer spaces as though I were one of them—my family of boys and bears and queens. As a teen I found my own band of queer folks, those few of us at school who did not feel like everybody else. Nowadays, my queer community is largely based online, but we gravitate toward each other just the same. We share. We celebrate. And we survive.

For most of my life thus far I've identified (uncomfortably, and poorly, in retrospect) as a queer woman. Parts of Neo and the others, their community and their experience, are mine. But I am not black or South African. Here, our experiences radically differ, and you should not read this book without acknowledging that those differences exist.

My white Britishness affords me with countless privileges. Among them, living in a country where it's relatively, comparatively, safe for me to be myself and to express that publicly.

The reception and treatment of LGBTQIA+ folks in South Africa is complex and often contradictory, informed by—among other factors—traditional South African values and colonialism, apartheid, and the human rights movements that contributed to its end. Despite apartheid having ended more than twenty years ago, its effects linger; that segregation and oppression is still a sad reality, and oftentimes traditional and postcolonial beliefs and practices are at odds.

On paper, South Africa is a progressive, welcoming country. It was the first country in the world to outlaw discrimination based on sexual orientation and the fifth to legalize same-sex marriage. Same-sex couples can adopt, LGBTQIA+ individuals may serve openly in the military, and transgender individuals may apply to have their gender markers changed. Tourism makes the most of this, selling South Africa as the perfect vacation spot for queer folks. Cape Town is considered the "gay capital" of Africa, with queer nightlife, a large pride parade, and generally liberal attitudes.

At the same time, social attitudes do not necessarily reflect the constitutional and legal rights of LGBTQIA+ people. Nor is treatment of tourists the same as that of locals.

Neo lives in a world where she, as a young woman, is highly sexualized, and it's expected that men will be given what they want. She lives in a world where:

- One in four men admit to having nonconsensual sex, and nearly half of these admit to raping more than once.
- Sexual harassment or coercion is considered normal. Fifty percent of men do not believe that *no* means *no*.

- Neo is also expected to conform to a particular traditional lifestyle, to marry and have children. Homosexuality is still considered by many to be "un-African" and wrong. It's a dangerous place to be queer.

- There are ten reported cases of corrective rape (a practice steeped in homophobia, where queer individuals are raped under the guise of "teaching them" not to be queer and to behave in a manner which the assailants deem socially acceptable) in Cape Town every week. That's one city, and only the reported cases. Given the stigma and fear, you can imagine what accurate figures might look like.

- Physically violent and/or sexual attacks are frequent and brutal.

- Attacks are often instigated by people the victims *know*; neighbors, pastors, teachers, parents, uncles, husbands.

- Women who become pregnant as a result of these attacks are often denied access to their children (by family members or church communities) in case their "affliction" rubs off on the youngsters.

- Homophobic rape is not yet classified as a hate crime.

- Reported cases are often dismissed as victims "stirring trouble" and it is not uncommon for the death certificates of victims— even where mutilation and signs of rape are evident—to read "cause of death unknown."

This book explores some of that. But please don't take this story as the *one* story. It isn't. Far from it. It's one fictional exploration. There are others: fiction and memoir and academic texts. First-person accounts from black queer South Africans living that experience. And narratives that tell of countless *different* South Africas, concerned with lives and places nothing like Neo's at all. Seek out other voices—black voices, queer voices, South African voices, and all combinations thereof. Your world and bookshelves will be richer for it.

SUPPORT

We all need help and advice from time to time. If you're struggling with any of the subjects raised in this book, from figuring out your identity to experiencing abuse of any kind, seek that support. Talk to a friend, a parent, or a teacher that you trust. Report abuse if you're able. And if you need someone else to talk to, these are good (nationally accessible) places to start. You are not alone; your voice is important. Please use it.

USA

The Trevor Project
www.thetrevorproject.org
866-488-7386
or text "Trevor" to 1-202-304-1200

GLBT Hotline
http://www.glbthotline.org/
National Youth Hotline 1-800-246-PRIDE (7743)
National Hotline 1-800-843-4564

UK

Galop
www.galop.org.uk
help@galop.org.uk
0800-999-5428
Switchboard LGBT+
www.switchboard.lgbt
chris@switchboard.lgbt
0300-330-0630

SOUTH AFRICA

Triangle Project
www.triangle.org.za
Helpline 021-712-6699
Counseling 081-257-6693

OUT

www.out.org.za
0860-688-688 (Collect calls accepted)

THE DISCOGRAPHY

Welcome, music lovers and curious readers! Here, in one handy list, are the eclectic highlights of my playlist for this book. You'll find all the music that's explicitly mentioned in *Kaleidoscope Song*, and a few of the other songs that made up my writing soundtrack. The majority of this list is work from South African musicians, although it is supplemented with a few musicians from elsewhere in Africa, and the very occasional song from home.

This list is not exhaustive. Not every track by a musician or band is going to sound identical, and there's soooo much more great music out there. If you find an artist or a style you like, explore!

All of this (and more) should be easily findable (thank you, age of digital music), but please remember to support musicians, pay for your music, and spread the word if you find work you like. ☺

1st NIGHT AT TAM'S PLACE
Underneath that metal roof when UmziRadio plays live and Neo chases Tale's voice up to the stars. Here's your very first introduction to Neo's world.

Siya Makuzeni Sextet—"Moya Oyingcwele," live at Safaricom Jazz Festival

I imagine Tale to be a slightly more muscular Siya Makuzeni lookalike. The musician started gigging seriously while still in high school. Here, she's lead vocals and trombonist. The first **Storytellers** track that Neo hears is higher energy, but the opening vocals might sound similar (except that Tale's voice has more gravel to it).

Bombshelter Beast, feat. Siya Makuzeni—"My Boyfriend is a Hustla," live at the Orbit

Gasper Nali—"A Bale Ndikuwuzeni" (The second musician to take the stage that night was a nervous *ramkiekie* (a homemade oil-drum guitar) player. There's not much in the way of recorded music here. Gasper Nali is a Malawian musician and all-around lovely dude who plays a one-stringed *babatoni*. So there are obvious differences, but in my head, I heard a song with a similar vibe to Gasper's work, so I'm sharing it here.)

Brenda Fassie—"Vulindlela" (Sometimes listed as "Vul'indela" **or other phonetic spellings)**

Nkosi Sikelel' iAfrica (See section below.)

MADAME SERIOUS'S SALON

Working in her mother's salon is not Neo's idea of fun *at all*. But even under Mama's disapproving gaze, she can't help but find music in everything she does.

Thula Sizwe: The Group Zulu—"Shosholoza" (Traditional. A work song, sung by prisoners at Robben Island, used while building railroads, adopted as a song of strength and effort in many situations, including football stadiums. Neo's rendition here would be slow and heavy.)

NKOSI SIKELEL' IAFRICA

There are many phonetic spellings of this track. There are also many incredible renditions of the song, recorded in schools and churches and stadiums as often as studios. In particular, check out:

Miriam Makeba, Ladysmith Black Mambazo, and Paul Simon, Graceland Tour Live

Boom Shaka

Prophets of Da City

UMZIRADIO

When Neo walks past the reception desk and into UmziRadio for real, it's like she's stepping into all that history of music and togetherness.

Blk Sonshine—"Building" (Jazz duo featuring Malawian-born Masauko Chipembere and the South African Neo Muyanga. The music video for this one really fits both the track and Neo's corresponding feelings in the text.)

THE CUPBOARD

Here are artists (with music across genres) mentioned in Neo's sorting of the UmziRadio archives, and a track recommendation to get you going.

Abaqondisi Brothers—"Sweet Love"

Amampondo—"Salawena (Stay If You Want To)"

Mister Devious—"Raak Wys"

Errol Dyers—"Dindela"

Deborah Fraser—"Masimbonge"

Brenda Fassie—"Mama"

Freshlyground—"Working Class"

IppyFuze—"Amaxhentsa"
Izingane Zoma—"Obama"
Arthur Mafokate—"Kaffir"
Vusi Mahlesela—"When You Come Back"
Hugh Masekela—"Stimela"
Mango Groove—"Hellfire"

SCRATCHED RECORDS

During Apartheid, the South African Broadcasting Company was particularly stringent about the music it allowed to be played. Anything in the lyrics (or words and actions of musicians) deemed damaging to the state, the SABC, or the National Party would be banned. The list included sexual references, occult elements, drug use, blasphemy, and unfair promotion of political ideals or parties.

Offending tracks were "cut" from records, stickers placed on the record sleeves, titles scribbled out, and in many cases the tracks were heavily scratched out on the records themselves so that they were unplayable.

Many, many tracks and artists were banned. Neo finds the following in UmziRadio's collection:

Miriam Makeba

Stevie Wonder

Mzwake Mbuli

Diana Ross

Abdullah Ibrahim

Other banned musicians include the Beatles, Pink Floyd, Rodriguez, Fats Domino, and Ray Phiri.

THE ABCS

I can't bring you Neo's show, exactly, but I *can* bring you the tracks she plays within it. . . .

SHOW 3: MR X/LOCAL MUSIC

Warongx—"Uhambo"

Khayelitsha United Mambazo Choir—"Manqoma"

Freshlyground—"Doo Be Do"

Abdullah Ibrahim—"Water From an Ancient Well"

Sathima Benjamin and the Cape Town Goema Orchestra— "Music"

Jean Grae—"My Story"

SHOW 6: FOOTBALL

Ladysmith Black Mambazo—"Shosholoza (Nkosi Sikelel'i Afrika)"

Shakira—"Waka Waka" (2010 FIFA song)

K'Naan—"Wavin' Flag" (SA 2010 FIFA song)

SHOW 9: ISICATHAMIYA

Miriam Makeba—"Mbube"

Ladysmith Black Mambazo—"The Star and the Wiseman"

Soweto Gospel Choir—"Amazing Grace"

SHOW 12: LOOOOVE

Watershed—"Letters"

Mango Groove—"New World (Beneath Our Feet)"

Malaika ft. Jabu Khanyile—"Kiss Kiss"

The Flames—"For Your Precious Love"

Freshlyground—"Pot Belly"

Stealing Love Jones—"Kicks"

SHOW 13: MANDELA

The Specials—"Nelson Mandela"

Peter Gabriel—"Biko"

Soweto Gospel Choir—"Asimbonanga"

Sathima Benjamin—"Winnie Mandela"

Hugh Masekela—"Home"

Nakhane Touré—"Christopher" (Nakhane is one of SA's first openly gay singers. His work is painful and honest and he doesn't shy away from his identity, good or bad.)

Nakhane Touré—"In the Dark Room"

Roger Kellaway—"9000 Days"

HANGING WITH THE BAND

Smooth, smooth jazz as Neo kicks back with Z and Jed? Here:

Abdullah Ibrahim—"Cape Town Flower"

THE ATTACK

I played the next eight tracks listed as I wrote the corresponding scenes. They invoked emotions anyway, and I can no longer listen to them without being transported back into those anxious, scared, hurt, and angry feelings.

Ke$ha—"Blow" (Deconstructed Mix) (One of the anomalous non-SA tracks. Sets me on edge from the opening chord, and the moment I first heard it I saw this scene play out in my head.)

Endurance OST—"Gigi's Lament"

Theme from the movie *District 9*

The Aftermath

Pentatonix—"Run to You" (Another anomaly. Makes me cry every time.)

Kenyan Boys Choir—"Kothbiro"

Sibongile Khumalo—"Thula Mama" (The traditional lullaby Neo hears, allowing her to begin healing. [Although she hears Baba. It's interchangeable.])

Freshlyground—"Baby in Silence" (Not part of my while-writing soundtrack for this scene, but it's relevant and brave, and it deserves to be on this list.)

Cry Freedom OST, George Fenton—"The Funeral"

Toya Delazy—"Forbidden Fruit" (When Jeso dances to this in the kitchen he's unaware of its meaning. Toya Delazy is an openly queer artist. The song explores taboos, differences, and forbidden relationships, and supports the idea that it's *okay* to be different. Both the song and video sparked controversy and discussion.)

FINALE/ THE FIRST SHOW OF KALEIDOSCOPE

Sara Bareilles—"Brave"

Toya Delazy—"Are You Gonna Stay?" (Neo plays this on the first Kaleidoscope show, but I think it's also something of a personal anthem for her and her journey up to the point we leave her at the end of the book.)

MISC

These are all tracks that have made it extensively into my playlist while I wrote, that would be around in Neo's life, and the kinds of music she'd be listening to. (With the exception of Macklemore, which speaks for itself.)

Miriam Makeba—"The Click Song"

The Fugees—"Killing Me Softly" (Technically, this should be up with the "first night" tracks, because it's how Tale makes Neo feel, but since it isn't local music/something she'd be hearing, I'm sticking it here.)

Zola—"Where I'm From"

Zola—"Mdlwembe"

Macklemore and Ryan Lewis—"Same Love"

Hip Hop Pantsula—"Music N Lights"

Simphiwe Dana—"Tribe"

Shwi NoMtekhala—"Shwele Baba"

The Mahotella Queens—"Nyalo Ea Tshwenya (Marriage Is a Problem)"

Sarafina! OST/ Mbongeni—"Lord's Prayer"

Hugh Masekela—"Sarafina!"

ACKNOWLEDGMENTS

As a writer (or musician, or artist of any kind), you let pieces of yourself out into the world with everything you do. It goes with the job. But sometimes it works the other way and the story (song, whatever) gets inside you, and it changes you. This is one of those books. While writing it (and honing it and getting it out there), I've questioned who I am and who I claim to be. I've questioned how I want to use my voice, and why.

It's not always been comfortable or easy, and I'm endlessly grateful not to have faced it alone. "It takes a village" is cliché, but true. Although in this book's case, it's more a band. A fierce, loud, wonderful band who push me to be better, always:

Marieke Nijkamp and Kayla Whaley are the best friends and critique partners a guy could hope for, and if you listen carefully you can hear their voices embedded between the lines, strong and safe and sure beside my own. Lucinda Murray's too; Thank you, lovely, for living with not only a distracted housemate, but also the Rage Wall.

Bek Stradwick, who made me cry with gratitude on the subway

in New York when she threw my own words back at me and asked for more (*"Tonight I found people like me": Let us see that*). It's one thing to be seen, and quite another to be wanted. Thank you.

Thank you to friends and readers: Lucy Christopher (and the forgotten takeaway—the surest sign that *just maybe* this thing might be a book), Rae Knowler (there's an ending now), and Ella Muers, the first teen to lay eyes on this book.

Massive thanks to Branden Grant for thoughtful feedback. And the biggest respect and gratitude to M and the others who not only read, but graciously answered my questions and set me straight when I was wrong. You may wish to remain anonymous, but your mark is there, and I'm forever grateful. This book is a thousand times better because of each of you, and all its failings are my own, not yours. ♥ ♥ ♥

Gill McLay, for belief and bravery. I cannot thank you enough for either.

David Gale, for really, truly getting it. For not balking at either this story or my own personal revelations. In the words of Charlotte, that is a tremendous thing.

Liz Kossnar and Amanda Ramirez for expert author-wrangling, Yau Hoong Tang and Krista Vossen for the gloriously kaleidoscopic rainbow cover, and Justin Chanda, Katrina Groover, Martha Hanson, Katy Hershberger, Chrissy Noh, Audrey Gibbons, Michelle Leo, and the rest of the S&S team: These voices behind the scenes—the literary arrangers, artists, managers, promoters, tech guys, cleanup crew, and oh so many things you never think of as a reader—are the ones that make it happen. Without this crew, there would not be a book at all.

And you, dear reader, for listening all the way to the end. I hope you like this thing of mine. But more than that, I hope that it inspires you in some way to seek out more voices, and to sing whatever song rises in you.

The hilarious tales of the trials and triumphs of Beckett, a gay teen in a conservative southern town, and Jaxon, the jock who turns his world upside down.

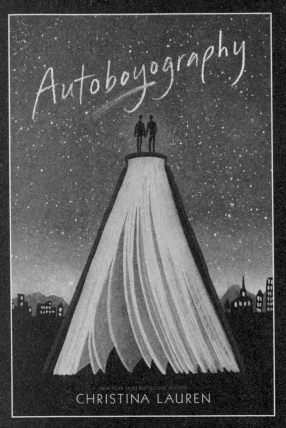

Autoboyography

NEW YORK TIMES BESTSELLING AUTHOR

CHRISTINA LAUREN

"As sweet and devastating as first love,
Autoboyography is a masterpiece. . . .
I love this book."
—KIERSTEN WHITE, *New York Times*
bestselling author of *And I Darken*

"A hopeful and moving love story."
—*Publishers Weekly*

Writing a book
in four months
sounds simple
to Tanner Scott.
Four months is
an *eternity*.
After all, it
only takes
Tanner one
second to notice
Sebastian, his
Mormon writing-
prodigy class
mentor.
And less than
a month for
Tanner to fall in
love with him.

How much can you
really tell about a person
just by looking at them?

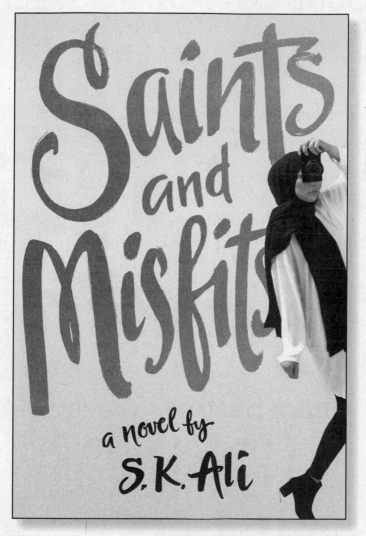